I0647670

Journey
To
Skye

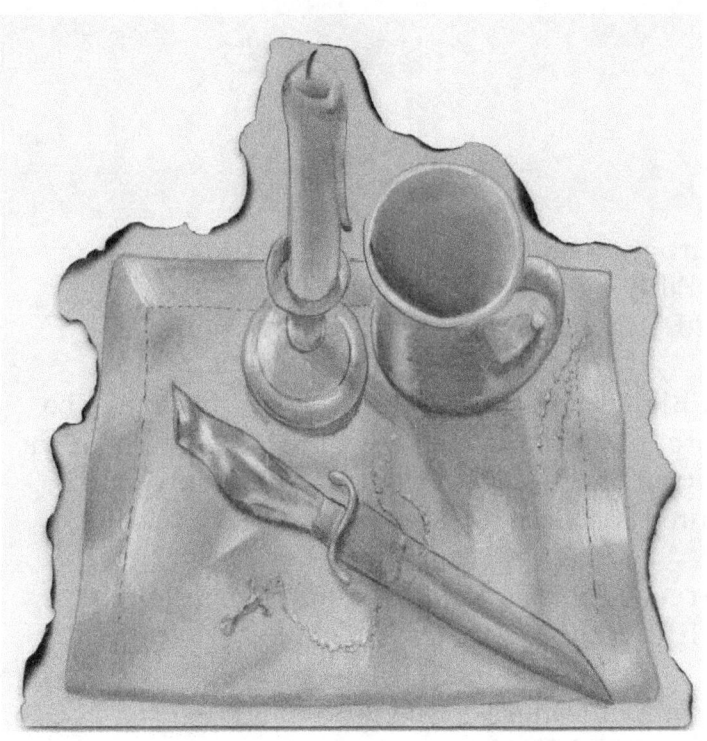

By Maureen Arcuri
And Matt White

This is a work of fiction. Names, characters, businesses, places, events and incidents are either the product of the authors' imagination or used in a fictitious manner. Any resemblance to actual persons, living or dead, or actual events is purely coincidental.

Journey to Skye
1st Edition, 1st Printing – October 8, 2016
© 2016 by Maureen Arcuri & Matt White

All Rights Reserved. No part of this book may be reproduced in any manner whatsoever without the written permission of the authors. Printed in the United States of America.

I Street Press – 828 I Street, Sacramento, California 95814

Library of Congress No.: 2014953729
ISBN: 978-1-941125-81-6

Many Thanks

Editing by Kim O'Donnell

Cover Design by Karen Phillips
Phillips Covers
phillipscovers.com

Cover Photograph by Tomasz Szatewicz
Land of Light Photography
landoflight.co.uk

Original Illustrations by Jesse Prewitt

Back Cover Photograph by David Higgins

Special Thanks

To the actors of St. Andrews Guild
The Court of Mary Queen of Scots

Apart we are many clans.
Together we are one family.

For Christopher

Maureen Arcuri

To my co-author – thank you for your patience with me
and for pushing me beyond my self-imposed
boundaries. This was fun...for the most part.

To Himself for reminding me that forgiveness is
greater than revenge and that in the end, love wins.

Matt White

Foreword

While this story takes place in Scotland during the reign of Mary Stuart in the year 1562, the theme is universal and timeless: In the end, love wins.

This is the sequel to *Tales of the Wycked Aye Tavern*. The reader is invited to continue with Maureen MacLeod on her journey of adventure and self-discovery. Share with her the fear and anxiety of knowing your loved ones are in danger and the joy of being reunited with those you love.

This journey takes place in 16th Century Scotland. A time of political disorder and religious turmoil. We also journey to the Isle of Skye, so expect a bit of magic along the way.

Agus go n-éiri bothar leat
(And may the road rise to meet you)

Matt White

Chapter One

The Sacred Circle

Except for a few glowing embers in the fire, the cottage was in complete darkness. It would be at least another hour before the break of dawn. Before the rising sun cast a burnt orange glow upon the horizon, and sent its first morning rays of light across the Scottish Highlands. It was a peaceful time, when the creatures of the night had returned to their dens to sleep and those that inhabited the day had not yet awakened. The whole world seemed at rest.

Maureen lay awake in her bed, warm and secure. She thought back on how her decision to return to her home in the lowlands had started a sequence of events that had touched the lives of everyone at the Wycked Aye Tavern.

She rolled over on her side and looked into the embers in the fire. She would need to get up soon to stoke the fire and put on the kettle before her chores began for the day.

The morning sky began to turn from the darkness of night to the grey sky of dawn. She thought of her cousin Katie, where Katie was this day and if she was safe on their home Isle of Skye.

She wrapped her quilt around her and rose from her bed dragging it behind her as she shuffled over to the hearth to place more peat on the embers. She stirred the smoldering embers and they quickly jumped into flame. As she poked at the fire, her mind raced over the events of late. So much had happened in the last year.

Katie had left the shire in early spring to return to Skye and care for her cousin Andrew. Andrew's health was failing, an affliction of the blood the surgeons said.

1

They could not help him; he was now in Katie's care and the hands of God.

A missive from Katie had reached the tavern that a clan war was brewing between Clan MacLeod and Clan MacDonald. Katie had tried to take Andrew and leave Skye, but the Lairds would not let them go. They had been forced to leave Andrew's home and travel to Dunvegan Castle for protection. Now caught in the middle of a clan war, both Katie and Andrew were in great danger.

It was now approaching the fall equinox. Soon Maureen too would be leaving the shire to travel with Heber and Meg MacPherson to Heber's home, Badenoch on the River Spey. He had taken Maureen as his charge and heir, and she was bound to do as he wished.

Although she wanted desperately to travel to Skye, she knew that Heber's decision to take her to Badenoch was for her own protection. He was taking her away from the vengeance and threats of Clan Armstrong; vengeance for the death of old Ian Armstrong and the disappearance of a large amount of gold, for which they held Maureen responsible. They would not rest until her debt was paid, with the gold and her life.

Heber felt she would be safe under the protection of Clan Chattan. And so the decision was made for her to leave the Wycked Aye.

Phillip MacAlasdair, Katie's husband, and Maitiú MacRobaird de Faoite and his son Dónal were sailing to Skye to try and find Katie and Andrew and bring them home. Maureen wanted desperately to sail with them to Skye and to Katie, but Heber had forbidden it. To challenge his decision or question his authority would be an act of dishonor and disrespect for the kindness he had shown her. This is the last thing she would ever do. So, she would take leave of the Wycked Aye Tavern and travel to Badenoch. There she would stay for as long as Heber desired.

The kettle was beginning to steam and the sun would be rising very soon. Maureen had much to do in addition to all of her regular daily obligations. She poured herself a cup of tea, filled a small basin with warm water to bathe in and then readied herself for the day.

As she closed her front door behind her and turned to leave her cottage, there waiting at the end of her walk was William Macaulay.

"Good Lord, William. What ya be doin' here at this time of the mornin'? 'Tis barely daybreak," Maureen asked.

It had been only a few days since old Ian Armstrong's son, Logan, and his two henchmen had tried to take her. Had it not been for Father Bryan Desmond, they would have succeeded and Maureen would now be in the hands of Clan Armstrong. A place where she had suffered before and vowed to never see again. Since that day, William had not let her out of his sight.

As she reached the end of the walk, he stepped up to meet her.

"I have news lass. I can nay keep me promise to ya. I will nay be able to help ya get to Skye. Me Da can nay spare me from the blacksmith and the courier's office for so long."

"'Tis alright William, truly, do nay worry over it." She slipped her arm around his waist, "Come, 'tis a beautiful mornin'. I do nay want to worry this day over Skye, or the bloody Armstrongs, or what can or can nay happen. Just walk with me now." He put his arm around her shoulders and together they walked the short distance to the stables.

"So, yer da will nay approve a trip to Skye, eh?" She asked. "He does nay like me, does he William? He be thinkin' I be nothin' more than a worthless tavern wench; not a suitable match fer his eldest son. Has he found another match fer ya?"

She should not have asked such a question, but she could not help herself. She could not bear it if she came back from Badenoch to find William pledged to another.

William stopped and turned her to face him, "Nay me girl, he has not. He will nay be makin' that choice fer me. I be makin' it meself." She nodded her head in understanding, then they turned and continued up the hill in silence.

When they reached the stables, William asked, "Will ya be alright now, here by yerself? I worry for ya lass, I do nay like leavin' ya alone. The Armstrongs be nothin' but a bunch of heartless border reivers and they will nay stop until they have what they want."

Maureen looked up at him. She knew he truly cared for her. William had become a very important part of her life, and she did not want to leave the shire and leave him behind. She was falling in love with William Macaulay, and was counting on him traveling with her to Badenoch and on to Skye. But it now appeared her grand plans were falling apart and she must simply continue down the road ahead, wherever it led. She had neither the power nor position to change any of it, and neither did William.

"Ya can nay follow me around all day long William. Ya have work to do, as do I. Besides, Heber will be up at the stables early this day. He be helpin' me get the horses and the carriage ready to leave for Badenoch. So I will nay be alone fer long."

When she mentioned leaving the shire, William closed his eyes and tilted his head back, drawing in a deep breath in frustration. He slipped his hand behind her head, weaving his fingers into her hair and pulling her to him. She loved being wrapped in the strength of his arms. It felt like the safest place in the world.

"Ya best be goin' now William. 'Twould nay be proper for Heber to find us up here at this time of the mornin'. Come by the tavern after yer day's work, I'll have an ale waitin' fer ya." She said as she smiled up at him.

"Yer sure ya'll be alright?" He said as he put her at arm's length.

"Aye, I will fer certain, now off ya go man before yer Da comes lookin' fer ya." Maureen gave him a playful nudge to send him on his way. William reached back catching her by the arm and pulled her back into his embrace. Before letting her go, he gave her a kiss, a quick slap on her arse, and then turned and headed back down the road.

"I be seein' ya at the tavern," he said.

"I be waitin'," she returned. She watched him walk down the road. At that point in time, she had no idea how she would be able to leave him. But for now she had other urgent matters to deal with.

She looked back to the sunrise. She had at least three hours before Heber would arrive at the stables to help her with the harnesses and carriage. Maureen needed to get to work. She needed to have most of her chores done at the stables before Heber arrived to leave herself enough time to ride to the forest and back to the Wycked Aye before anyone missed her. She had an errand to take care of before leaving for Badenoch, an errand that no one else could help her with, and this time she would have to go alone.

She flew through her chores in record time. The horses looked at her as if she was a woman possessed. By the time Heber arrived, she had already cleaned all the stalls, and fed, watered and brushed down all of the horses. When Heber walked into the tack room, she was working on the harnesses for the carriage. She was a sweaty, dirty mess. She was working so frantically she had not noticed him.

Heber stood quietly and watched her in puzzled amazement as she quickly oiled the leather strapping and checked the harnesses. He thought she had lost her mind. When he finally spoke, Maureen screamed out, dropping the harness on the floor.

"What the bloody hell are you doin'?" Heber asked as he entered the tack room. "How long have ya been here?"

"Maureen put her hands on her heart, "Christ almighty M'lord, ya scared the shite out of me!" She quickly pulled up her apron, wiping the leather oil from her hands and then picked up the harness from the floor. Heber took the harness from her and placed it on the table.

"When did ya start this day lass? 'Tis only ten of the mornin' and ya be done with all the horses already?" He asked.

"Aye, I...um...I thought it best to have the daily work all done fer ya M'lord, that way we could get through the tack and have the carriage all ready to go...so, so we would nay be delayed in any manner...or...," she was stammering.

Heber did not speak. He just looked at her with that expression on his face that clearly said he did not believe a word she was saying. Heber knew his little green-eyed wildcat well. He also knew there was one thing that Maureen could not do, and that was lie.

6

She saw the look on his face and knew it was no use to try and deceive him. But she had not shared her gift of sight with Heber yet. She knew he would not allow her to ride into the forest alone without good reason, and probably not even then. As she looked at him, she could see he was patiently waiting for her to tell him the truth and to trust him.

"I be truly sorry M'lord," Maureen said as she lowered her eyes. "I did nay mean to try and deceive ya."

Heber continued his silence. He could see that she had something she needed to tell him, something of consequence. So he waited, allowing the girl to find her courage. Finally, she continued.

"Many things happened while ya were away in Morocco. If ya please M'lord, can we sit for a bit and talk? There be somethin' I need ya to know."

As they seated themselves at the tack room table, Maureen began her story of the night Dónal returned to the Wycked Aye with Heber's sword in hand. How she fled in sorrow from the tavern, riding Olaf blindly into the forest and falling asleep in sorrow on the forest floor, and awakening in the Sacred Circle of Rowan. She told Heber of the Fey mound and the vision of her mother, and how she saw the vision of him alive and well when everyone else thought him dead. Lastly, she told him of the visions of Katie on Skye, and of the death and destruction from the clan war with the MacDonalds.

"That night, a gift was awakened within me. I've the sight M'lord, I be a seer." She looked at him with uncertainty. Would he believe her? How could he not? How could anyone make up a story like that, she thought.

Heber leaned back against his chair with a look of astonishment on his face.

"Well, that be quite a story lass. I can nay say I truly believe it meself. Yet, there be legends about the MacLeod women of Skye. I always thought they be nothin' but old wives' tales."

"I fear this one be true M'lord," Maureen whispered. "And so far, 'thas brought me nothin' but pain. That be why I asked to go to Skye with Philip and Maitiú. They need me to find Katie."

"That does nay explain yer urgency with yer chores this day. What be the big rush? We nay be leavin' fer four more days."

Maureen hesitated, "I need to ride into the forest M'lord, to gather the leaves of the great rowan tree before we leave. I must have the leaves to see. It be a clear day and I wanted to be done with me chores so I could ride to the forest and be back in time fer me shift at the tavern."

Heber looked at her shaking his head, his voice stern. "After what just happened with Father Desmond and the Armstrong boy, ya'd be takin' a chance like that over a bunch of tree leaves?" Maureen lowered her eyes. He was right, it was a foolish thought. Yet, she must have the rowan leaves and she was running out of time to gather them.

He saw the disappointment in her reaction. He would not, however, allow her to ride into the forest alone. Not now, not for any reason. But he was also curious about the story she had just told him and if, in fact, she had the gift she claimed. He wanted very much to believe her. But, he was afraid that if he told her no, she would find another way. There was only one answer.

"Enough story tellin', we be gettin' these chores done," Heber directed. "And then lass, we be ridin' together into the forest and ya can show me this great rowan tree of yers."

8

Séan Macaulay had arrived early at the courier's office. He had heard William wake early and knew he had slipped out to meet the MacLeod girl again. Séan worried for his eldest son, for he knew he was falling in love with the girl. He had tried many times to warn his son about the MacLeod women, but William did not seem to care. It appeared he had his heart set on this little tavern wench and there was not much Séan could do about it.

He knew full well the complications of being involved with the women of clan MacLeod. His mother was a MacLeod. She too was a special woman, with special gifts; gifts that were perceived by many as curses and had caused their family to be cast out. Some had even called her a witch. They lived on Skye on the outskirts of Portree. They raised sheep and horses.

When they went to the village, they were shunned. But when night fell, and the people of the village had a need for help, special kinds of help, it was Séan's mother they came to see. Under the cover of darkness, it was Morríghan MacLeod Macaulay who gave out the potions, who healed the sick, who could see what was in store for those who asked.

It was a lonely life, a life Séan did not want for his own son. When Séan's father passed away, he wanted to take his mother away from Skye, away from the threats of witchcraft. Threats that were becoming dangerous for them both. He tried to convince his mother to come with him to the Highlands, but she refused to leave the Isle. And so he left her behind and sailed from Portree to Cork City in Ireland and then on to Dumbartonshire.

He wondered what William saw in that MacLeod girl. His son was a handsome, strapping young lad who could have any lass in the shire. Why he had to get involved with a poor tavern wench Séan would never know.

When William had asked his permission to leave the shire to take the girl to Skye he was shocked. Everyone in the shire was aware of Clan MacDonald's assault on Clan MacLeod, and the clan war brewing on Skye. He had no intention of allowing William to travel to Skye and get involved in the middle of that war.

Séan heard the latch to the back door quietly slide and the door slowly open. William slipped through the door, gently closing it behind him.

"So, ya been up to the tavern stables already this day have ya?" Séan asked as William turned to face his father, startled by his voice.

"William, ya best be forgettin' about that little wench. She be nothin' but trouble boy. The girl has no blood family, no connections and no dowry. She does nay have a bloody thing to offer."

William did not respond. He had no desire to debate his feelings for Maureen. He resented the way his father spoke of her and thought if he only knew the truth, he would not speak so harshly. But that truth was not William's to tell.

William knew his father had hopes that he would find a woman of higher station; a merchant's daughter maybe, one that would bring an advantageous marriage to both families. But William had always hoped his father would consider his feelings over financial circumstances when it came time for a match to be made.

He walked quietly past his father and went to the hearth at the back of the office to warm himself.

"She be an orphan son, a homeless wretch. She be nothin' but a burden to ya." Séan said as he glanced back at his son.

William sat down in a chair in front of the fire with his back to his father. Eventually, he could hold his tongue no longer.

"Well Da," William began. "'Twas how it was before, it nay be that way now." William glanced back to see if he had his father's attention.

"Heber MacPherson has taken her as his charge and heir. She be a ward of Clan MacPherson and the Chatton Confederacy now." William paused for a moment and then got up to face his father. "Would ya nay be callin' that somethin' to offer?"

William walked to the door that led out to the family stables and blacksmith. "I be gettin' to me chores now, Da." He left the office before his father could respond.

Séan Macaulay stood staring at the door, speechless. This changed everything. An alliance with Clan MacPherson and Clan Chatton could prove quite beneficial. But the fact remained that the girl was still a MacLeod, and she was trouble for certain.

Both of the horses were saddled and ready to ride. Although Maureen had not planned on Heber riding with her to the circle of rowan, she was actually looking forward to it. She had been uneasy with the thought of going into the forest alone. Now she could relax and enjoy the ride. And besides, it would give them some time to talk.

The horses were getting restless. Olaf and Gunnarr had never been out riding together before, and they were both ready to run. Both were handsome, black stallions. Gunnarr stood a bit taller than Olaf, but Olaf

11

was stronger and heavier. It almost seemed as if they had something going on between them—a challenge of sorts.

Heber noticed their anticipation of the coming excursion. "Looks like we best be gettin' these two on their way lass," he said with a chuckle. "I hope ya be ready to ride," he taunted.

"Oh, I be ready M'lord," Maureen returned. She jumped up into the saddle as Olaf danced back a few paces. She leaned forward and whispered in his ear, "Come now me beauty, let's be showin' 'em how we fly." Olaf raised his head and neighed, giving his head a shake.

Heber was mounted up and yelled over to her, "I'll even give ya a bit of a head start!"

"That M'lord," she said with a laugh, "be a grave mistake indeed!" She gave Olaf a kick, he reared up and then took off like a shot. Maureen yelled back, "Come M'lord! Catch us if ya can!"

Heber could no longer hold Gunnarr back. As the horse jumped forward, he laughed to himself. He could see Maureen's long hair flying in the wind and was relieved to see his young ward happy and safe. He had every intention of keeping her that way.

It did not take long for Heber to catch up with her. When he rode up beside her, she turned to look at him with a smile on her face that reached from ear-to-ear. She tossed her hair in the wind, threw her head back and let out a hoot. She and Heber then pulled back the reins and brought their mounts down to a walk. It was not too far now to the edge of the forest. They had another twenty minutes of riding through the beautiful rolling hills before they reached the its edge.

When the horses had slowed and they both had a chance to catch their breath, Maureen asked, "Tell me

M'lord, what it be like in Badenoch? Tell me of the River Spey and Loch Ness."

"Ah, 'tis a beautiful place indeed. The valley along the River Spey be long and lush. Flocks of sheep graze along the river. The MacPhersons raise horses, which should please ya lass."

That made Maureen smile, she loved horses more than anything. It was one of the things that she and William shared as well. That was something she could look forward to.

"And what of the loch, M'lord? I heard tell of it ya know." She looked at him with curiosity.

"Well, lass, what I know of Loch Ness be that it be vast, and deep, and cold. Ya will nay be swimmin' there too often. As for the stories, well I think they be just that, stories," he said.

"It sounds most lovely and peaceful," she replied.

"Aye lass, most of the time it be just that. But all the clans be havin' their own set of disagreements with other clans, 'tis just the way it be in Scotland these days. One thing be for certain, no Armstrong would dare challenge the Chatton Confederacy. Ya be safe there, lass, that I know.

Maureen smiled at him, but did not respond. She was truly grateful to Heber for taking her with him and away from the threat of Clan Armstrong. Yet her own aspirations to find her way to Skye and to Katie pulled at her heart. Phillip and Maitiú needed her help and she feared for their safety as well.

Her heart was heavy being forced to leave William and the tavern behind, and having no ability to reach Katie on Skye. The things that matter to her most were on opposite ends of Scotland and she would be stuck right in the middle of them.

"And what of Fionnula?" Maureen asked. "She knows not of yer return M'lord. Ya must send word before we leave for Badenoch."

Heber knew she was right. He had thought every day of his wife and the torment she must be bearing, not knowing if he was dead or alive. He must send word. Now that their path was set, he would find Fionnula and bring her to Badenoch.

They rode along and were approaching the edge of the forest when Maureen turned her horse and headed north.

"Where ya goin' lass? I thought we be goin' into the forest?" Heber asked.

"Aye M'lord, that we are, but the entrance to the sacred circle be this way. Follow me now, quietly," she warned.

"Quietly?" Heber questioned. "What? Would ya be afraid of wakin' the dead?" he mocked.

"Nay M'lord," she whispered back. "Not the dead."

They rode a bit further when Maureen turned Olaf toward what appeared to Heber as the base of a tall mound with no passage through it. But as they got closer, he could see that what seemed to be a single mound was, in fact, two mounds, one slightly in front of the other with an opening between them. Strange, how many times he had passed by this way and never noticed it before.

Maureen held Olaf at the entrance and waited for Heber to ride up beside her.

"Only Philip and Maitiú have come with me to the circle M'lord. I do nay believe anyone else knows of this place. I do nay know how far they be lettin' you go or what they be lettin' ya see."

They? Who was she talking about? There was no one in sight, Heber thought to himself.

"Give me yer reins now, Olaf will lead us in," Maureen whispered as she extended her hand to take Gunnarr's reins.

Heber hesitated and looked at her with apprehension. After a few moments, he reluctantly handed her the reins. He then reached with his other hand for the broadsword sheathed on his saddle.

"No M'lord," Maureen warned. "Ya have nothin' to fear in this place. Please, I beg ya, ya must trust me now. I told ya everythin' so far. This, this be the last secret I have to share. Please M'lord, put it away now."

"Very well, lass, very well," he said as he returned the blade to its scabbard.

Maureen lashed Gunnarr's reins to Olaf's saddle horn, and then she dropped Olaf's reins as well. She leaned forward and whispered to the great, black stallion, "Now me beauty, ya know the way, take us in."

The path was narrow and Olaf walked slowly as the walls of the mounds rose on each side of them.

"Why have ya dropped yer reins lass?" Heber asked.

"We must approach the circle with nothin' but complete trust in our hearts. If they be feelin' any anger or fear, they will nay allow us to pass," Maureen quietly replied. "The forest be their world, they be part of it, and they protect it."

Heber could sense that the path was going downward now and the walls of the mounds had closed above them. They were now in a tunnel or cave of sorts. Suddenly a cold wind blew past them. Heber's horse began to spook. Olaf immediately stopped, turned his head toward Gunnarr and stomped his front foot. The horse understood and began to settle down.

Maureen knew they were being watched. She saw the small flickers of light as the wind blew past them. Heber too was becoming restless and subconsciously began to reach for his sword.

15

"No. Please M'lord, please; leave it be now." She sternly whispered.

The horses continued forward and downward. "Who be these people lass? Where the hell are we and..."

He stopped speaking, for now the tunnel began to shimmer with sunlight and Heber could smell the sweet fragrance of lavender. The walls of the tunnel were covered in deep green moss, delicate ferns and bright, colorful flowers. He was astonished at the peacefulness and beauty that surrounded them.

As they came to the end of the tunnel and exited into the sacred circle, Maureen looked back to see Heber staring in wonder at the beauty of the land that lay before him. She turned to him and said, "Welcome M'lord. Welcome to the land of the Fey."

He slowly dismounted and looked around taking in the world before him. *What is this place? Where is this place?* he thought to himself. He had traveled and explored most of the forests and moors near the tavern but had never seen any sign of this place before.

As he looked around he could see that they were standing on the edge of a great circle created by an enormous, dense forest. Toward the inside lay another circle made of stone pillars, and there, at the center grew the great rowan tree. It was the largest rowan tree Heber had ever seen. But, where were they? All he could see were trees and stone. He and Maureen were the only ones in the circle.

She released Gunnarr's reins and got down from her horse. She gave Olaf a kiss on his nose and let him wander free.

"Where are they lass?" Heber asked. Maureen could tell that the big man was uncomfortable in this place.

"They be in the trees," Maureen said as she cast her glance upward. "Wait here M'lord, I will nay be but a moment. Do nay wonder about, stay with the horses."

She turned and walked quickly toward the circle of stone. Heber watched as she moved toward the stone pillars. The circle was enormous. It was easily a league from the forest perimeter to the circle of stone, and another league to the rowan tree. The entire forest floor was covered with ferns, deep green moss and flowers. There was life everywhere: birds, butterflies, ground squirrels, rabbits. Everywhere you looked, the forest was alive.

Olaf walked along side Maureen until she reached the boundary of stone. She knew he would not cross into the inner circle. She gave him a pat on his flank and sent him back to Heber. She then passed into the inner circle of stone.

When Heber saw her pass through the stones his heart skipped a beat, for as she crossed to the inner circle she vanished right before his eyes. She was nowhere in sight! Heber's first instinct was to go for his sword, but as he rushed toward his horse, Gunnarr moved away and would not let Heber near him. Olaf stomped his foot and shook his head at Heber. A rustling began in the trees above him that stopped him dead in his tracks. He could hear the murmur of voices and could see the faint flicker of lights. He remembered Maureen's words. He must trust her now and trust in the forest. His only choice was to wait.

Maureen rushed toward the great rowan to gather the leaves and berries as quickly as possible. She was unsure what would happen with Heber in the circle.

She was almost done filling her pouch when she heard a familiar voice.

"I see you prepare for your journey child." It was Shalynn. Maureen had not seen her since that night in the cottage when together they watched a terrible vision of death and destruction from the coming clan war on Skye.

"Shalynn, a chara. 'Tis always good to see ya. Many thanks for not scarin' me to death as ya usually do." Maureen smiled at her, but she did not smile back.

"Why do you bring the MacPherson to the circle? He should not be here." She warned.

"I be truly sorry Shalynn, but he would nay allow me to come alone." Maureen glanced back and realized she could not see Heber. "Where did he go Shalynn? Would he be alright?"

"He waits outside the circle. He cannot see past the circle of stone. I need you to know child, the Fey are leaving for the Isle of Skye. Clan MacDonald is gathering and preparing to move against Dunvegan. We go the pools to wait and prepare." She looked toward Heber's general direction, "Darkness approaches child, you must convince the MacPherson to allow you passage to Skye. Make your way to the pools, you will find us there. Here, take this."

She handed Maureen a silver medallion on a fine silver chain. "Wear this child from now on. If you find yourself in need of help or shelter, let it be seen, and help will find you."

Maureen did not question her. She put the medallion around her neck and slipped it under her chemise.

"Go now child, your master awaits, and good journey to you."

"Many thanks to ya Shalynn; I wish ya safe passage and a safe return," Maureen offered. They quickly embraced and then Maureen grabbed her pouch and ran back out of the circle.

Heber came to her immediately. "Where did ya go lass?! I watched ya walk into the circle, and then ya were gone!" His expression was one of complete

18

astonishment. Maureen could see by the look on his face that he was confused and bewildered by what had happened. Shalynn was right, she should not have brought him here.

"I did na mean to make ya worry so M'lord. I did nay know they would nay let ya see. I should na have brought ya here. I should 'a come alone. Come M'lord, we must go." She placed her hand against the medallion beneath her chemise. "I have all I be needin' now."

They mounted up and rode out of the circle in silence. As they made their way back up through the passage way, Heber looked back to see the tunnel closing behind them.

They rode for a while in silence until finally Maureen asked, "Are ya alright, M'lord?" Heber simply nodded back. "That be all of me truths M'lord, you know all there be to know now." Heber again simply nodded and did not speak.

They rode on for a bit longer then Heber brought Gunnarr to a halt. Maureen was up ahead when she realized he had stopped. She too brought Olaf to a stop.

"M'lord, what be wrong?" She asked.

"I need to know one thing lass, how did ya find them?"

Maureen looked at him and said, "I did nay find them M'lord, they found me."

The ride back to the stables was very quiet. When they arrived, Heber turned Gunnarr over to Maureen and began to walk to the Tavern without saying a word.

"M'lord," Maureen called to him. "Ya must nay speak of them. I pray I have nay disappointed ya."

Heber paused a moment before he turned to face her, "I have seen nothin' more than a new part of the forest. Not much to talk about." He gave her a slight smile,

"Get these horses tended to lass, and do nay be late for the tavern.

Maureen let out a great sigh of relief. Heber understood. She nodded back, "Aye M'lord, as ya wish."

Lady Isabella and Master Thomas sat together at one of the small pantry tables in the back of the tavern sharing a bowl of stew and bread. It was just past midday and the tavern would soon be getting busy as the evening crowd began to arrive.

"Ya seem a bit quiet husband, what vexes ya this day?" Isabella asked.

Thomas looked at his wife. She knew him well and could sense when something was on his mind.

"Are ya worryin' over Heber leavin'?" She glanced over her shoulder and looked toward the front of the tavern to make sure they were alone.

"I do nay think Argyll be havin' any further interest in takin' the tavern, Thomas. Yer missives ta him were clear the tavern nay be Heber's to barter. We've done what we were sent ta do, have we not?" she whispered.

"Aye, we have indeed." He replied. "We need nay worry over betrayin' those that we love in this tavern any longer. I believe Argyll's interests be in a different direction. The tavern be safe in the hands of Chieftain Sara now."

He tore a piece of bread and dunked it into the stew. "I be a bit melancholy 'tis all. I be missin' the MacPhersons when they go, and the lass as well." He said.

"Aye, I be missin' her too. She be a good worker, 'twill be hard to replace her," Isabella added. "But I do nay believe she be gone fer very long. I can nay imagine young Mr. Macaulay nay goin' after her. He fancies her somethin' fierce ya know."

"That he does, wife. That he does." Thomas said as he scooted his chair closer to Isabella's and pulled her on to his lap. "And a man will go to all ends when he wants a woman."

"Thomas?" Isabella said with a flirting smile on her face.

"Ya know woman, our favorite hay cart be just out behind the tavern, full of fresh hay." He whispered in her ear.

She took his face in her hands and kissed him with all the love she had in her heart. They smiled at each other, and then hurried out the back door of the tavern.

Maureen flew through the door of her cottage in a mad rush to clean up and get to the tavern on time. She was running late, as usual, and was a filthy mess from head to toe. She quickly pulled off her dirty stable clothes and poured a basin of cold water. There was no time to warm it and it would just have to do.

She was bathed and dressed in no time. She braided her hair, donned her kerchief and hurried out the door to the tavern.

As she pulled the door to her cottage closed behind her, she suddenly realized that in only three days she would be leaving her little home behind. It saddened her, but she knew in her heart that she would return to this little shire and to the Wycked Aye Tavern. But for now, they must go on to Badenoch and, God willing, to Skye.

As she approached the tavern, she spotted Detta walking down the lane away from the tavern. *Ah shite*, she thought to herself. It was Detta's shift that

Maureen picked up in the afternoon. She was late and she knew both Chieftain Sara and Tánaiste would have words for her.

She found Sara behind the bar and immediately began apologizing for her tardiness. Sara raised her hand to stop her and said, "Enough girl, enough, 'tis alright. Heber said he gave ya an extra chore or two, and that ya may be delayed a bit."

Maureen looked at her with great surprise, "He said that now did he?"

"Aye, he did. Now go get yer apron and get to it," she said.

She headed back to the pantry and was getting her apron and tray when Master Thomas and Isabella came in the back door, playfully chasing each other into the pantry. It was always such a delight to see them together. They were the best of friends and madly in love with each other. They were still chasing each other around the pantry when they realized Maureen was there.

"Oh, Mistress MacLeod," Isabella exclaimed. Master Thomas came up behind her wrapping his arms around her from behind and kissing her on her neck, playing as if he could eat her alive.

"Thomas," Isabella giggled. "Enough now man!" She turned back to Maureen, "Well, girl, ya best be getting' ta yer shift. Off ya go, there be work ta do."

She was doing her best to compose herself and behave as a Tánaiste should, but Thomas would not leave her alone. She turned to face him, slapping him on the chest and giving him a gentle shove. As she turned away, Maureen saw that her kerchief was a mess and there was straw sticking out from under her bodice. She just smiled and went on about her chores – there was no need to ask.

The tavern was getting busy. Fine, warm days would always bring folks out and about the shire, and most of them would end up at The Wycked Aye. Fiona, Maggie and Maureen were busy serving patrons, cleaning tables and pulling meat off the fires. Everyone seemed to be in good humor; everyone except for Heber. It was Fiona who first noticed him sitting alone. She tapped Maureen on the shoulder, "'Twould appear the MacPherson be a bit troubled this day."

Maureen looked over at him, she knew what troubled him and she knew he was struggling with the task before him.

Heber sat quietly at the great table. With parchment before him and quill in hand, as he pondered the words he needed to write.

He had returned to the shire almost two weeks before and had yet to send word to his wife, Fionnula, that he was alive and well, and back at the Wycked Aye.

When Heber disappeared, Fionnula left the Wycked Aye and returned to her family in Ireland. She did not know if her husband was dead or alive.

Now Heber sat staring at the blank parchment, searching for the words that would let the woman he loved know he was alive and home, and longing for her return. He would ask her to join him in Badenoch on Spey as Mistress of House MacPherson, and send an escort to Ireland with the funds she needed to sail to Invernlochy. There he would fetch her and bring her home.

Isabella had been watching Heber from the bar. She too could see that he was struggling with the missive. She pulled the bottle of good whisky from under the bar, took two glasses and went to join him.

"Ya've been starin' at that parchment for a while now Heber," she said as she placed the whisky and glasses on the table. Heber smiled at her and motioned her to sit. She opened the bottle and poured a wee dram for each of them.

"There be so much to say, so much to tell, and yet the words will nay come," he said softly.

Isabella reached across the table and placed her hand upon his. "Just speak simply and from yer heart, Heber. Save the long story for when Fionnula returns. Fer now, ya just need her home." She tightened her grip on his hand. "Now take that quill, put it to that parchment and bring yer woman home."

She raised her glass, clinked it against his and downed her shot of whisky. "I be leaving ya to yer task now."

Heber gave her a grateful nod as she walked away. He downed his shot of whisky, readjusted the quill in his hand and began.

My beloved Fionnula....

Chapter Two

Aberdeen

As the ship pulled out of Dumbartonshire and left the channel for open sea, Dónal smiled and said "Now for an adventure with the heroes of me childhood stories!"

Philip gave Dónal a look that would put fear in any man and walked to the fore of the ship where the wind and crashing waves made conversation impossible.

Dónal's cavalier attitude toward their journey did not settle well with Philip. He did not appreciate Dónal taking this quest so lightly. Philip's need was urgent and he did not understand why the Irishmen were not taking the journey seriously.

"What did I say that be wrong?" asked Dónal of his father.

"The man be vexed about his wife, Katie." Maitiú replied. "He be mad as a hornet at Maureen for nay tellin' her vision to him. He be angry at the world and he nay be much company for a while," his father explained.

"Well then Da, this be a long trip indeed. What more can we do but what we be doin? What profit does it give to worry about tomorrow or regret yesterday? All we have be today, aye?"

Maitiú gave him an agreeing nod and then turned his gaze out to sea. They stood in silence for a while leaning against the port rails as the merchant ship made its way down the west coast of Scotland.

In an effort to change the mood Dónal asked, "Would you be tryin' your luck at dice, old-timer?"

"Old-timer be it? Be that anyway to address yer old dear father? A Dónal, a mhic, what will we be playin' for?"

"Tis the bag of smooth stones I took from the river near Sterling. They be shiny like polished marble. May even be marble, aye? I have a feelin' they might come in handy somehow on our trip. We will play for them."

Up at the front of the boat Philip looked out over the bow across the open sea. His mind drifted from Maureen's troubling vision to a vision of Katie from a much earlier time.

In his youth, he tried his hand as a gallowglass. He was a competent warrior to be sure and he had many an adventure. One time he went as far as Spain. But fighting other people's battles left him unfulfilled. There was a calling deep inside to nature and to creation, not destruction. He began to compose poems and discovered he was actually quite good at them, at least that was what he heard from friends and family. He abandoned the gallowglass trade to become a wandering poet.

The Gaels were great patrons of the arts, especially singing, poetry and storytelling. A person could travel from one lord's house to another and remain for days and even weeks. He was given room and board for his talents. Thus it was that Philip first came to Skye as a traveling poet. He remembered being struck with awe at the beauty of the place with its mountain peaks and ridges running down to the sea. He remembered the peculiar feeling about the place, a feeling that stirred deep inside him. Even when he was alone he never felt alone. Skye was an ancient place, a mystical place.

After his visit to Sleat and the stronghold of Clan MacDonald, kin to his MacAlasdairs, he traveled up to Dunvegan, the seat of the MacLeods. He arrived at a Clan gathering. His recitals of poetry were well received and combined with his tales of his gallowglass past, the MacLeods began to refer to him as the "Warrior-poet," a prestigious title and position amongst nobility and royal courts.

It was one night at a recital he saw Katie. To him she was a prize; the prettiest girl with the loveliest eyes. How did he dare approach her? Sly as a fox, he befriended her father and offered to visit the Macleod homestead on the Staffin side. So his courtship with Katie began by meeting all of her family, including her eccentric uncle, Sandy MacLeod, who had claimed to have ridden the legendary Soft Horse of Skye.

Skye had magic, but the greatest magic was the love he and Katie shared. After they were married, she followed him throughout Scotland supporting and comforting him until they settled near the Wycked Aye Tavern.

"Katie, my dear Katie" he said aloud to no one and his mind drifted back to Maureen's vision. "Why did she nay tell me?" he said silently to himself. "Why did she nay trust me? She, above all others, should have known I would have believed her!"

The sea was rough and the water that sprayed on board was freezing, the kind of cold that gives a raw feeling to a man's insides.

The ship's company was soaked to the bone. If it was better below deck they might have remained there but it reeked of the wretched smell of vomit from the sailors who were seasick, and shit and piss from all the livestock on board. Thankfully, when they did go below to sleep, they slept in hammocks and thus avoided a soaking in the vile bilge.

Philip said nothing when they were called to mess for a meal of hard, moldy, nearly indigestible bread and salty fish that could only be stomached with a swallow of weak ale that itself was sour and vinegary. Trying to strike up a conversation with most of the crew was difficult. Either their Gaelic was nearly unintelligible to the Irishmen or they spoke a heathen tongue called Norn, the language of northern seafarers. Some of the crew gave hostile sideways glances at the Irishmen when they knelt to pray. Clearly these sailors were well versed on the evils of the Romish church.

Dónal, a loyal trooper of the Papal Army asked, "Da, are these wretches enveloped by Luther's leprosy or by Calvinist cant?"

Dónal had been raised to be a devout Catholic, despite the stigma attached to allegiance to the Roman Church. His allegiance to the Church became a badge of identity. He was Irish and he was Catholic.

He could have followed his father into the brewery trade or followed his grandfather as a grey merchant, traveling all over Gaeldom facilitating trade. Yet, he was called to something else.

As a lad he was a fierce boxer and wrestler. He was a de Faoite after all. He could wield a mean hurling stick and was well known for his athletic skill as well as his fearless tenacity and toughness.

Once a sword was placed in his hands he showed an aptitude for combat and was recommended to the House Guard of the Earl of Desmond. It was there he received training from James Fitzmaurice. Under his tutelage, Dónal embraced the Faith and Fatherland philosophy of Fitzmaurice and, along with a small company of like-minded men, he went to Rome to offer his sword to the Pope and fight in the Papal Army.

After two years of devoted service, James Fitzmaurice petitioned the Pope to allow him to take a contingent of soldiers back to Ireland to fight the English heretics. As they passed through Lisbon they were pressed into the service of the Portuguese King to fight a disastrous campaign against the Moors.

It was there he came under the command of his father's old friend Heber MacPhearson, who Dónal had met many years ago in Ireland. At the low point of the last battle it was Heber who, on what he thought was his deathbed, ordered Dónal to carry his sword back to his father.

Dónal had served the Earl, the Pope, and the Sebastian of Portugal. But now he was honored to serve his Da. He never told his Da he loved him nor did his father say it to him. They did not need to say it, their actions reaffirmed their love for each other every day.

The ship was to pull into Aberdeen and Dónal was anxious to see this city he had heard so much about. Dónal was hoping he might meet someone whose Gaelic he could understand and talk with them about Aberdeen. Through all of his travels Dónal had always taken great joy in discovering new lands and new people. Every new port was a new adventure.

Maitiú, however, was gripped with anxiety. Aberdeen was a place that gave him a restlessness and dread he could not overcome. The entire north of Scotland was foreboding. His experiences in this place had come at great risk and hardship.

Aberdeen was near the lands of Clan Gunn and Clan Sinclair, enemies of his family and two clans he had dealt with on his journeys selling ale for the Earl of Desmond; journeys that had nearly got him killed, but it was more than that. The danger here was deeper and very different. The fear was not physical; it was spiritual. He had heard the term "godforsaken," but it meant nothing to him until he visited Aberdeen and beyond.

He had not the gift of vision as Maureen MacLeod, but he dreamed the most horrible dreams about this place. Dreams that caused him to tremble more than a splash from the icy waters of this relentless sea.

Neither the Irish nor Catholics were welcome in this part of the Highlands and he and Dónal would never have ventured to these lands had it not been for their pledge to Philip's quest. And now, Philip's hastiness and impatience had put them on a poorly supplied merchant vessel bound for Aberdeen by way of England. They would pass through the Channel and into the North Sea, and then out into the Atlantic. It would easily be a week or more at sea, depending on the winds, before they reached Aberdeen.

Maitiú and Philip had shared a friendship that spanned many years and endured through many adventures. When Philip asked them to come on this quest, Maitiú and Dónal agreed without hesitation. But the beginning of their journey was not what Maitiú had planned on. They would be at sea for many days on this shit hole of a ship and Philip's temperament was not helping.

Philip quietly approached Maitiú and gently laid a hand upon his shoulder. The unexpected touch startled him. When he turned and saw it was Philip he relaxed and let out a sigh of relief.

"de Faoite, were you having a vision too?"

"Ah, a chara, I have not the gift of vision, at least not as you or Maureen seem to have. But me dreams haunt me wakin' thoughts to be sure."

Philip gave him a curious look and said, "Tell me, de Faoite, do you see Katie in your dreams?"

"I see nothin'," Maitiú turned, looking Philip straight in the eyes, "but if I did, I would nay hesitate to tell ya for fear of yer ire! But I be prayin' fer her in me way as ya are in yers, and we be makin' haste to Skye. What else can we do?"

"Master MacAlasdair, ya been to Aberdeen before, Aye?" Donal asked. "Will I be able to understand their speech? I can nay understand any of the men aboard this ship."

"People in Aberdeen? I understand their Gaelic better than their Scots." Philip replied. "Alas, the noble tongue of Gaelic be fadin' away in the area of Aberdeenshire and the sailors on this ship speak Norn, an old Norseman's tongue. Alas, it be fadin' too. I fear the only ones we be talkin' to on this voyage be each other."

As everyone returned to their hammocks to sleep, Maitiú was uneasy at the thought of what they might encounter in Aberdeen. He thought of the wisdom of his own son, about living in the present and prayed for an increase in his trust in God to counter his fear. He prayed, "O God, I do believe! Forgive my unbelief!"

Chapter Three

Katie

Katie sat next to her cousin Andrew as he lay before the fire, weak and dying. The people of the many shires cared for by the Lairds of Clan Macleod had been brought to a secluded village just south of Dunvegan Castle. The Lairds had told them it was for their protection from Clan MacDonald. Had they been left on their own land without the protection of the Lairds, the reivers of Clan MacDonald would have slaughter them like cattle. But that was not the only reason they were brought there. They were to fight for Clan MacLeod. The men would be taking up arms, and the women and children would work and care for the wounded.

Andrew stirred a bit and uttered a slight whimper. Katie knew he was in great pain and that his time was short. Her heart ached for him. To think he would die in this wretched place away from his own home and his own land. All of her family had lived out their days on their own land, and had gone to meet God before the warmth of their own hearth. Poor Andrew would not know such peace.

She closed her eyes and prayed that the missive she had slipped to the captain of a merchant vessel had found its way to Phillip and the Wycked Aye Tavern. She knew Phillip would come for her and she knew he would bring the Irishman with him. But how he would ever find her in this godforsaken place she did not know.

They had been taken to a place hidden away from the main passageways to Dunvegan. It appeared to Katie to be some kind of a servant's village on the outskirts of the castle, tucked away in a valley that led down to the loch. They were living in thatched hovels with dirt floors and small hearths for warmth. They were all cold and hungry. But she knew she must endure. Andrew's passing was near and what would happen to her after that she feared with all her heart. For women without their own men to protect them soon fell prey to men who cared only to satisfy their own needs.

So far, the other village men had protected her from the Laird's guardsmen, so she could tend to Andrew and not leave him alone to die without his kin by his side. But that would not be the case when Andrew was gone. She must find a way out, and soon.

When Katie woke the next morning, Andrew was gone. She sat on the freezing ground next to him, cradling him in her arms. She felt the touch of a strong yet gentle hand on her shoulder. It was Oren.

"He be gone now mistress," he whispered to Katie.

Oren was a crofter and looked as most hard working crofters do. He was broad shouldered and barrel chested, with strong, sturdy legs. He worn a full beard, closely cropped and his shoulder length hair was always tied neatly back with leather. He reminded Katie of her beloved Philip. Oren was a man of the earth, and held to old ways and the old beliefs as Philip did.

Oren had left behind a fine piece of land that had proven to be fertile and productive, even for Skye. He also had a small herd of sheep and a few cattle. He was just beginning to see a profit from his land when the threat of the Clan war began and he was forced to leave it behind.

He had befriended Katie and Andrew during the trek to Dunvegan Castle. Oren had helped watch over

Katie as Andrew's health had failed him. When the Lairds had forced them to continue on, even as Andrew's strength left him, Oren had helped carry him.

"We must take him out Katie, we can nay keep him in here."

Katie looked up at him with tears in her eyes. "No please Oren, I beg of ya. They'll throw him in the pile with the rest and burn him as if he be nothin' but rubbish. I could nay bear it." She rested her head on Andrew's brow and began to sob.

Once word of Andrew's passing spread, others came to Katie's side. Everyone staying in their small shelter now knew that Andrew was dead. It would not be long before the guardsmen knew it as well. They would come for him for certain.

"Oren, can we nay take him out and lay him to rest in a proper cairn?" Katie asked.

"There be no where to dig mistress. We be on the edge of the sea; the land here be nothin' but rock." Oren explained. "'Tis either the pyre or the sea, and besides, 'twould take too long to gather the stones for a cairn. The MacDonalds may be about ya know, 'twould be far too dangerous."

He was right of course. It was too dangerous to be out for so long with the threat of MacDonald clansmen about. Although their own situation was dreadful, it was far better than being taken by Clan MacDonald.

"Oren, was there not an old curragh down by the loch?" Katie asked.

Oren thought for a moment and then replied, "Aye, I believe there was. But I would nay trust it to get ya too far, if that be yer plan."

Still holding Andrew, she looked at him and then to Oren, "But 'twould last long enough to carry Andrew to sea, would it not?"

He nodded his head in agreement, "Aye, I believe it would mistress."

Katie looked up to the others in the hovel and begged them not to say anything to the guardsmen just yet. They wrapped Andrew in cloth and tied it around him. They placed him outside, behind the hovel and covered him up. It was cold outside, very cold. His body would be safe until dark.

The day was one of nothing but grey mist. The sun would not find its way out of the clouds this day. It was bitter cold, and dampness filled the air. The guards had told them that they would be moving on soon to the safety of the castle. That was good news, for word had reached them that Clan MacDonald was gathering and heading their way. The castle had food, warmth, and the people would be safe there.

They spent their day as most villagers would. Tending animals, gathering wood and peat for fires and cooking what food they had. The men spent much of their time down by the loch fishing and foraging for food. The Lairds had greatly underestimated the needs of so many of their clansmen, and many had not survived the journey. The old ones and some of the children had died along the away from exhaustion, starvation and the bitter cold.

While he was down at the loch, Oren made his way over to the old Curragh as he fished. As he looked it over, he could see it was barely seaworthy and the sail in the bow of the boat was torn and tattered, but it looked to Oren as if it would still hold wind. The westerly winds were blowing straight out into the loch this day and would take the curragh out to sea. Tonight after dark, he would carry Andrew down to the loch and send him off to the Gods of the sea.

Oren walked slowly, working his way back down the bank as he fished. He cast out his line into the sea and said, "Oh mighty God o' the sea, give us a fine fish to put on the fire this night, so we might have a proper wake for a good man." Again and again he threw out his line, but to no avail.

He continued fishing for another hour or so with no luck. It was drawing near time to return to the village when finally, his line gave a mighty tug. He yanked back on the line to set his hook, and hand-over-hand pulled in a fine cod fish; one big enough to stay the hunger of many. As he pulled it upon the shore, he placed his hand upon the great fish and thanked it for its sacrifice. He then drew the wooden mallet he carried and put the fish to death. He pulled his knife and gutted the fish, then threw it over his shoulder and began to make his way back up to the village. Much to his surprise, two of the other men had landed big fish as well. Oren looked back out to sea, bowed his head and quietly whispered, "Many thanks."

Katie and Oren slipped out of the hovel into the vast darkness of the night. With only a single lantern to light their way, Oren lifted Andrew on to his back and began to walk toward the path that led down to the loch. But before they reached the path, they were stopped by one of the guardsmen.

"Stop there, just where do ya think ya two be goin'?" Luckily for them it was Cameron. Both Katie and Oren had become friends with Cameron, and he too had come to know Andrew along their way to Dunvegan. "Be that you Oren, Mistress Katie? I can nay allow ya to be movin' around at night and..." It was then that he saw the body slung over Oren's shoulder. "Would that be Andrew ya be carryin' Oren? Ya'll need ta be bringin' him to the pyre."

It was Katie who answered, "Please Cameron, I beg of ya, do nay tell the others. I could nay bear for Andrew to be thrown on the pyre." Soon they would light it before they moved on to the Castle and before anyone from Clan MacDonald could see it and be drawn to the village.

"Just what do ya plan on doin' with him?" Cameron whispered. "They be lighting the pyre tonight."

Oren stepped up still holding Andrew on his shoulder, "There be an old curragh down at the Loch, sir. Can we nay send him off to the sea?"

Cameron looked around, nervously searching for any other guardsmen. "Ya know, it be me arse on the line if anyone finds ya. I can nay give ya much time, ya must be quick Oren. And if ya try to be leavin' in that curragh, I'll come after ya meself. Ya understand what I be sayin' to ya Oren?"

"Aye, I do. Many thanks to ya Cameron. We will nay be long," Oren replied.

Katie placed her hand gently on Cameron's arm, "Thank ya." Then they turned and headed down the path to the loch.

Cameron walked back up to the edge of the village. He could see the guardsmen setting torches to the funeral pyre. He was taking a terrible risk, but he too had come to know Andrew MacLeod. He was a good man and if his kin wanted him sent to the sea, it was the least he could.

Katie led the way, holding the lantern as they hurried down the path. It did not take them long to reach the curragh. Oren place Andrew in the bottom of the boat; he set the mast and raised the sail. He waded out pushing the boat before him, waiting for the wind to catch the sail. But the sail lay limp and the curragh floated aimlessly on the edge of the loch.

Katie looked back up the path toward the village. She could see the flames of the funeral pyre rising. They had to hurry.

"Oren, what shall we do? We can nay leave the curragh floating here." She asked.

Oren walked back in from the freezing water. He began to remove his doublet and shirt.

"Oren, what are ya doin? It be freezing out there." Katie asked.

"There be a single oar in the boat Katie. I'll take it out a bit so the wind can catch the sail and swim back. It be only a short distance." Oren replied.

He waded back out to the curragh and began to row it out into the loch. He could feel the wind picking up as he moved farther out on the water, but the sail still lay limp. It was pitch dark and he was freezing cold. His only reference back to shore was the flames from the funeral pyre up in the village.

The old curragh was slowly taking on water. Oren rowed out a little further. Finally, the old tatter sailed caught the westerly winds and snapped tight. The curragh jumped forward and Andrew was on his way out to sea.

Katie paced nervously on the shore. She could no longer see the mast of curragh in the moonlight. Then she heard a splash and knew Oren was on his way back to shore.

Oren gasped for breath when he hit the freezing cold water of the loch. He headed toward the shore using the funeral pyre as his guide. It was farther than he expected. Oren could swim, but he was not a strong swimmer. The icy water was quickly taking his strength.

He swam on, the shore was in sight now. He could see Katie standing on the edge of the loch, but his muscles were cramping and his breath was leaving him. He tried to call out to her, but his breath was too precious and he could not utter a sound.

Katie finally caught sight of Oren and could see he was struggling in the water. She called out to him, but he did not respond. She wanted desperately to go out and help him, but she could not. She could not swim. She called out to Oren, reaching her arms toward the sea as the funeral pyre burned behind her.

Suddenly, she heard running on the rocks behind her. Someone ran past her into the loch and dove into the water. Within minutes, Cameron had found Oren and pulled him out of the water.

Both of the men were freezing cold. Oren was alive, but shivering uncontrollably from exposure to the cold water. Katie wrapped her wool shawl around him to help warm him.

"Thanks be to God for sendin' ya Cameron. I could nay have helped him," she said.

He simply nodded to her and said, "Come Mistress, we need to get near the fire. We need to be dry and warm."

Together they carried Oren up the path to the village. Katie owed a great debt to both Oren and Cameron. Now that Andrew was gone, she did not know what lay ahead.

As they sat near the fire, Katie thought back on the days at the Wycked Aye. She wanted to be back at the tavern more than anything and prayed that God would show her a way. Home to Philip, home to the Wycked Aye. She had been away far too long and her heart ached with a need to be safe in her own cottage, in front of her own hearth.

In the morning they would begin their final journey to Dunvegan Castle, the stronghold of Clan MacLeod. Surely she could secure passage out of the Loch and sail home. She had money enough to pay passage and then some. She and Andrew had brought every crown they had with them. Even if she had to bribe her way, she had enough.

She would speak with Oren on the road to Dunvegan.

Chapter Four

The Match

It was their last day at the Wycked Aye. Tomorrow morning, they would begin their journey north to Badenoch.

Maureen looked around her cottage. What belongings she had were now packed into a single small trunk, and her three swords lay on top. Two were hers and the other was her father's Claymore. It was the only thing she kept after he was killed.

It was a magnificent weapon. The center of the hilt was a beautifully carved stag whose antlers rose up into intricate knots. The blade was adorned with ancient runes and Celtic symbols from days long past. She had seen many finely crafted weapons during her days at the Wycked Aye, but none could rival her father's Claymore. It was truly unique. It was sad to think that something so beautifully crafted had been used to kill so many.

She was anxious to get to the tavern. It would be a busy night as many of the folks of the shire would be coming to say farewell to Heber MacPherson. But there was only one person she wanted to see this night and that was William Macaulay.

She had saved her best skirt and bodice. All of her other clothes were packed away. It was mid-afternoon when she entered the tavern. Detta still had an hour or so left on her shift so Maureen had some time to enjoy. Chieftain Sara was behind the bar. As Maureen walked through the great hall, she looked around the tavern, but William was not there.

Sara looked up as she came to the edge of the bar. "Well, well, are ya not lookin' fine this night lass. And who might ya be all fixed up fer?" Sara asked, teasing her a bit. She knew who Maureen was looking for. She leaned over the bar and whispered, "He nay be here yet lass. I have nay seen hide nor hair of him since yesterday."

Maureen looked at her with great disappointment, "What do ya mean he nay be here? He has to be here Sara. This be our last night and…"

"Now, now, settle yerself girl. He be here soon enough."

Maureen forced a smile as her eyes wandered through the tavern. Her mind was wandering as well. Come to think of it, she had not seen William since the morning at the stables. Where could he be, she thought to herself. He knew they would be leaving on the marrow. It was their last chance to be together, so why was he not here?

Sara could see the worry on her face. She reached over and took the girl's hand. Maureen jumped at her touch.

"Lass, I would nay worry about losin' young Mr. Macaulay." Maureen looked curiously at Sara.

With a devious little smile, she said, "Ya see lass, Tánaiste and I, we had a bit of a talk with Heber. After all, he did put me in charge of yer interests did he not?" Sara turned her attention towards the back of the tavern, encouraging Maureen to follow her gaze. There, sitting with Heber at the chieftain's table was William's father, Séan Macaulay.

Maureen's eyes grew wide, "Dear God Sara, what have ya done?" she whispered.

"Ya love William, do ya not lass?" she blatantly asked. Maureen hesitated for a moment, stunned by Sara's directness and, for the first time, being put in the position to affirm her true feelings for William.

"Well?" Sara pushed.

"Aye Sara, I believe I do indeed. But Master Macaulay does nay care for me one bit. He finds me unworthy and troublesome. He would never approve such a match." Maureen put her hand to her mouth and said, "Dear God, I think I'm goin' to retch."

Sara laughed and put her hands on Maureen's shoulders, "I'd say that means ya love him fer certain."

Together they watched as Séan and Heber finished their discussion. As the meeting broke up, Sara sent Maureen back to the pantry so she would not be seen. The men shook hands and their meeting ended. Séan left the tavern straight away.

As Heber walked past the bar, Sara looked at him questioningly.

"He said no, Sara."

Maureen waited and watched anxiously in the pantry while the meeting ended and Séan Macaulay left the tavern. As Heber passed by Sara, she could see Sara close her eyes and lower her head in disappointment. Maureen knew the outcome of the meeting; she did not need to hear the words.

At first, she too felt her heart sink in disappointment, but that disappointment quickly escalated into anger. She loved and trusted William. He would not have abandoned her unless something else prevented him from being with her – namely, his father.

The more she thought about Séan Macaulay the angrier she got. He sent William away, sent him on an errand for the courier's office so they could not be together. Sent him away so that when William returned, she would be gone and he would forget all about her. Bloody gobshite.

Most of her life, she had been forced to accept the circumstances that were handed to her, but no more. William would find her before she left the shire, she knew he would.

She was pacing back and forth in the pantry when Sara and the Tánaiste came in. They were expecting a complete emotional breakdown. Instead, they walked in on a mad hornet. Before either of them could speak, Maureen erupted.

"This nay be the end of it, I promise ya that! Thinks he can force us apart does he, well it nay be happenin' I tell ya. I love William and I nay be allowin' some gobshite ta keep us apart."

Sara and Isabella simply watched as Maureen's tirade continued. Their heads moved together, back and forth, as they watched her pace and rant. Chieftain Sara nudged Isabella and motioned for her to get a glass and some whisky. Isabella poured Maureen a double shot and handed her the glass.

Maureen took the glass and tossed back half of the whisky before she continued, "He be here, ya'll see. He be here, I know he will." She downed the rest of the whisky and drew a deep breath. She paced around with her hands on her hips. Finally, the Chieftain managed to get a word in edgewise, "Are ya alright now lass?" she asked with a bit of a grin on her face.

"Nay Sara. I be about as angry as I can possibly be. I believe I just be startin' me shift now and take me

44

mind off this whole bloody mess." She spun around looking for her apron and the whisky hit home. She stumbled back a couple of steps catching her balance.

Isabella pulled out a chair and sat her down at the pantry table. She put a small plate of meat and bread in front of her and said, "Eat. Ya not be going out on the floor until yer head be clear. Ya have nay eaten again today have ya lass?" Isabella asked.

The Tánaiste worried about the girl sometimes. Maureen always seemed too thin. She worked long hours between the stable and the tavern, and Isabella knew she did not take care of herself as she should.

"Now ya finish up all that food girl, ya hear me." Isabella ordered. "Ya need ta put some meat on yer bones or young Mr. Macaulay will nay be wantin' ya at all."

Maureen slouched back on the chair and rolled her eyes at the Tánaiste. Isabella pointed to the plate and said, "Eat!"

It was a fine night at the tavern. Fiona presented Maureen with a new kerchief that she had embroidered herself. It was a lovely gift. Fiona was Maureen's best friend. The two of them had worked many hours together at the tavern and Maureen would cherish it.

The girls were busy as always. There were so many well-wishers coming by to say farewell to Heber, the tavern was packed to the brim.

Hour-by-hour passed and still no William. Maureen was losing hope. It was close to eleven o'clock when she approached Sara and Isabella.

"Chieftain, Tánaiste," she said respectfully, bowing her head to them both. "I wish to be takin' me leave of the tavern for this night if it be alright with ya? I can nay stay here any longer; I can nay wait any longer and..."

Sara reached out and pulled the girl to her, embracing her as if she was her own. "Do nay lose hope lass, he be comin'."

Maureen nodded to Sara, "I pray ya be right Sara, I truly do."

Isabella cupped Maureen's face in her hands and kissed her on her forehead, "Oh, I be missin' ya somethin' fierce, girl. Ya come back to us now."

There were no tearful goodbyes. The women both knew that when the threat of Logan Armstrong had passed, Maureen would return to the Wycked Aye. It was just a matter of time.

When she walked back to the pantry to gather her things, Master Thomas was there waiting for her with his flask and two glasses in his hands. A smile crossed Maureen's face. Thomas could always make her smile.

"If ya think ya be walkin' out of here without saying a proper goodbye to old Master Thomas then ya better think again girl," he said.

"Thomas me friend, I would nay do such a thing," she said as he handed her a glass. Thomas sat himself down on top of the pantry table and patted on the tabletop next to him for Maureen to join him. She hopped up and scooted over next to him. She held up her glass and Thomas poured her a shot and one for himself. They sat for a moment in silence dangling their feet off the edge of the table like children.

Thomas put his arm around her shoulders and said, "Ya know lass, ya worry too much. Young Macaulay, he

46

wants ya fer his own." Maureen did not interrupt him. She had come to know and respect Thomas. He may be a bit of jokester at times, but he was also an honest and wise man. If Thomas pulled you aside to speak to you, it did you well to listen.

"I can tell ya this, if me Isabella was leavin' fer parts unknown in the mornin' there would nay be a damn thing anyone could do to keep me away from bein' with her. I'd ride 'til me horse dropped if need be." They took a sip of their whisky as Maureen leaned back against him.

"Ya think so Thomas. Ya think he will come?" She asked quietly.

"Nay lass, I know he will. Now here be what ya do. Take yerself home ta yer cottage, set a nice fire in yer hearth so he can see the light, and whatever ya do, do nay latch yer door this night," he said as he smiled and teasingly raised his eyebrows once or twice.

He raised his glass, she raised hers as well and they tossed back the rest of their whisky. Maureen kissed Thomas on the cheek and hopped off the table.

With hope renewed, she picked up her things to leave. When she got to the pantry door she turned to back to him, "Thank ya Thomas, thank ya."

Thomas did not speak, he just bowed his head and raised his glass to her. Then she turned and hurried out of the tavern.

Thomas poured himself another shot, he raised his glass to the empty doorway and said, "Bed him well, girl, bed him well."

It was just past midnight when she heard the door to her cottage creak open. She raised herself up on her bed. She knew the figure of the man standing in her doorway. He stepped through and latched the door behind him. He took only a few paces toward her, "'Tis not safe to be leavin' yer door open ta strangers girl, ya never know who might be about," he whispered.

"I was expectin' a visitor," she whispered as she sat up on her bed. She reached out her hand, beckoning him to come sit with her. "Does yer Da know yer here?" she asked. William seemed surprised at her question. He just shook his head - no. "Good," she added. "There be only a few hours till dawn. Stay with me William, stay with me till mornin' comes."

He walked over and took her hand as he sat down on the edge of her bed. William had been with other women, but they were simply to fill a need after having too much ale. He had never been with a woman he truly cared for. He had no feelings for the ones that had come before. This woman was different, he knew it from the first moment he met her.

They sat quietly for a few moments until Maureen asked, "He sent ya away did he not William? Yer Da, he sent ya away to keep us apart."

As William nodded his head he said, "He sent me on to Sterling. I tried to find ya before I left. I rode all night to make it back and..." She put her fingers to his lips, "Sssh, rest now William."

He turned his back to her and pulled his shirt over his head. Maureen placed her hand upon him, sliding her fingers down the middle of his back. When she reached the edge of his kilt, her breath left her as she wrapped her fingers into the cloth. She wanted it gone, she wanted to see him, all of him. She wanted to touch him, hold him, to lay with him.

The fire in the hearth was burning low. She slid away from him off the other side of the bed and walked toward the hearth. Through the sheer fabric of her chemise, William could see the silhouette of her naked body in the firelight. He could feel his body respond to the sight of her. He watched her as she placed more peat on the embers. The light from the fire danced around the walls of the cottage. As she walked back to bed, he rose, letting his kilt fall to the floor. They slipped beneath the quilt and William pulled her close against him.

Suddenly she felt her body tense in fear as it had done so many times before with the men who had forced themselves on her.

William felt it too. He knew she had been hurt by the men of the Armstrong clan. She was afraid, he could feel it. He wanted her, he wanted her with every fiber of his being. But this was not the time, it would not be right. He ran his hand across her brow, brushing back her long hair and whispered in her ear, "It be alright lass. I will nay hurt ya, I'll never hurt ya. I swear it."

He felt her relax as they lay together. Soon they drifted off to sleep, wrapped in each other's arms.

It was just past midnight as Heber left the Wycked Aye and walked toward his cottage. When he glanced up the hill, he could see the firelight still coming from Maureen's cottage. He watched as her door opened and the firelight spilled from inside. In the light of doorway, he could see the shadow of a man slip inside and close the door.

He shook his head and thought to himself, *Heber old boy, ya got yerself a problem.*

Chapter Five

The Road to St. Johnstown

William watched her as she slept peacefully in his arms. Daybreak was not far off. He did not want to wake her, but he had to go. He must leave her before anyone knew he was here.

He ran his fingers through her hair, pushing it away and placing a kiss on the back of her neck. As he drew away from her, he noticed a mark on her neck, just beneath her hairline. He moved her hair a bit more to get a better look. It appeared to be some kind of a burn and it looked strangely like a rose, a black rose.

But what he saw next pained him deeply. On her back were the scars of whip lashes that had cut deep and scarred her forever.

She stirred from her sleep, opening her eyes to see him smiling down on her.

"I be sorry to wake ya lass, I have to go," he whispered.

"No," she said as she rolled toward him and buried her face in his chest. He wrapped his arms tightly around her. Maureen ran her hands around his waist and down his back. "No," she repeated. William pulled her up to face him and kissed her, "Do nay be startin' somethin' ya can nay finish girl."

He was right, they had no time. Her fears from the night before were gone and now their time together was gone as well. Being together, truly together, would just have to wait until it was right and proper.

William rolled out from under the quilt. She watched him as he pulled his shirt over his head and began to fold the kilt he let fall to the floor the night before.

As she watched him, she wondered how God could have blessed her with such a beautiful man. If this was God's will, then so shall it be done. She had no problem with that.

Maureen knelt on her knees on top of the bed while William belted his kilt around him. He stepped up to the edge of the bed, sliding his hand around her neck he whispered, "I have to go, lass."

She raised up on the bed and threw her arms around him. William reached down putting his hands on her thighs. He slid his hands slowly up over her hips, pushing her chemise up around her waist. He kissed her long and hard. She could barely breathe.

When he released her, he cupped her face in his hands and said, "I be comin' fer ya girl. I swear to God, I be comin' fer ya." Then he turned and left the cottage.

Everything was ready. Maureen's trunk was packed and her cottage was in order. She truly hoped that it would not be long before she returned to this little shire and the Wycked Aye.

There was one thing she needed to do before she took her leave of the Wycked Aye, and that was to celebrate Mass with Father Desmond. She did not know when she would be able to attend Mass again, if at all. She remembered Maitiú's words of the destruction and desecration of the Catholic churches by the Calvinists. Catholic Queen or not, the Church of Rome was not welcome in Scotland anymore.

It was a clear and very cold morning. The change of seasons was near and one could sense the onset of winter in the air. She donned her cloak, pulling her hood tightly around her face, and began her walk to the little chapel.

The sun was just coming up as she entered. She went to the commoner's side and took her usual place. She loved to watch the morning sun come through the stained glass; a beautiful kaleidoscope of color that beamed in ethereal beauty across the altar and down the center of the chapel. It was almost magical.

As she knelt for her prayers, she thought of Maitiú, Philip and Dónal. She thought of Katie and Andrew and prayed for their safety. It was almost time for Mass to begin when she was joined by Lady Isabella and Master Thomas. Only Maitiú was missing from their prayer bench, and suddenly Maureen realized that she missed him very much. She found herself reaching for the medallion around her neck, clenching it tightly she whispered to herself, "Oh Shalynn, please watch over him, please."

"Good marrow lass, peace be with ya," Master Thomas said as he and Isabella took their places next to her. Thomas leaned over and gave Maureen a little kiss on her forehead.

"Good marrow Thomas, Tánaiste. I be so happy ya've joined me fer Mass," Maureen replied.

"Ya be lookin' quite rested there, lass," Thomas said with a smile. "Much to be thankful fer this day, eh?"

Isabella turned and gave him a slap on the leg. "Thomas, ya be in church fer God's sake," she said as she shook her head and rolled her eyes at him.

Thomas gave Maureen a nudge with his elbow. She just smiled at him, lowered her head and tried not to laugh.

When Mass ended, they all walked out to greet Father Desmond. He was getting along quite well considering the wound he had suffered at the hands of Logan Armstrong. He still walked with his quarter staff to lean on, but his leg was healing and it appeared he would not suffer any lifelong affliction from the injury.

Isabella and Thomas began to walk back toward the tavern, but Maureen held back.

"Are ya nay comin' lass?" Thomas asked.

"If ya do nay mind Thomas, I wish to speak with Father before I go. I be catchin' up with ya shortly."

Maureen waited for the rest of the parishioners to speak with Father Desmond and then, be on their way. When the others were gone, Father Desmond saw Maureen waiting for him.

"And what would ya be doin' waiting here all alone, Maureen? A bit early fer confession," he said with a smile.

"May I have a wee bit of yer time Father?" she asked.

"Of course child, come with me now." He led her back into the chapel and they sat down two or three rows back from the front of the altar.

"All ready fer yer journey, Maureen?" he asked.

She just nodded, but did not speak.

"What be wrong, lass? Ya seem troubled?" he asked.

"I wanted ta thank ya properly for what ya did fer me Father. I would nay be here if ya had nay come back fer me."

"I would never have left ya behind Maureen." He said as he placed his hand on her shoulder. He waited, as it was clear the girl had more on her mind. Finally, she continued.

"Ya be careful now, Father? I worry fer ya now. If Logan Armstrong be alive, he be comin' fer us both. Ya know that as well as I."

He took her hands and with a peaceful smile said, "I do nay fear him lass. God will watch out fer you and me, that I know." He reached next to him and picked up his walking stick, "And if that Armstrong boy should show up when God's nay watchin', I still have me quarter staff at me side."

Maureen gave him a guarded smile.

"Do nay take him lightly, Father. Logan Armstrong be an ugly and hateful man. His heart be nothin' but stone. He be slittin' yer throat without thinkin' twice and enjoy doin' it. No rosary or priest's robes will stop him. He be the devil himself, Father, this I know. So please, I pray ya, be careful."

Father Desmond now saw sitting before him a strong and caring woman where a young, frightened girl used to be. There was something different about her today, a touch of wisdom and caution that he had never seen before. He somehow felt he had a hand in that path for he had heard her confessions and counseled her through some very difficult times. A feeling of pride washed over him and he leaned forward and embraced her.

"I'll be careful lass, now off ya go. May Christ be with ya on yer journey, and I pray you and yer Irishman will return to me little chapel very soon."

They rode out at mid-morning. Maureen on Olaf, Heber on Gunnarr and Meg had the cart with Maitiú's ponies harnessed together.

They would not be able to reach St. Johnston in Perthshire in one day's travel. Heber had planned for them to take shelter just south of Menteith near the River Teith.

They had already said their goodbyes to their dear friends at the Wycked Aye. As they started their little caravan moving, Maureen turned to look back down the path to her cottage. She closed her eyes and thought back on the night before. She could still feel William's touch upon her and the warmth of his body lying next to her. He said he would come for her. It would be the memory of his touch and her trust in his promise that would keep her strong until they could be together once more.

Heber saw her face as she turned back. "It will nay be forever lass," he said as he tried to comfort her. "Yer only threat left be young Logan Armstrong. Can ya tell me, was he dead when ya left him on the road from Dumbarton quay?" Heber asked.

"I do nay know, M'lord." Maureen replied. "Father Bryan hit him square in the head and he was nay movin' at all. But we did nay wait ta see if he be dead or alive. Father be badly wounded as ya know, and we rode away with all haste."

"Well, it will nay be long before we find out." Heber replied. "If he be alive, he be mad as a hornet and he will nay let ya get too far away."

"I just want this to be over M'lord." Maureen lamented.

"It will nay be over until that little shite of a lowlander be dead." He warned.

As they approached the edge of the forest, they turned north and headed for the stone bridge to cross the River Teith. Maureen felt uneasy as they rode along the edge of the forest. They were being watched. She could only hope that the eyes that were watching them were the friendly eyes of the Fey and not the deadly eyes of Clan Armstrong.

It was a quiet, yet beautiful ride up the River Teith. All of the trees were dressed in their fall colors. Meg talked of House MacPherson and who Maureen would be meeting and her duties in the household. She spoke of the leaders of the clans and magnificent gatherings in the Halls of Clan Chattan at the manor house of Lachlan Mackintosh. It was clear that Meg was happy to be going home.

Maureen did not share her enthusiasm. She only wanted two things: to get Katie out of Skye and to go home to William and the Wycked Aye.

It was just before dusk when they arrived at an old abandoned croft near the edge of the River Teith. It was a place Heber had taken shelter in before on the road to Badenoch. They were all tired and saddle sore. Heber rode up ahead to make sure the place was empty and safe.

Maureen and Meg waited at the end of the road that led up to the small farm house while Heber inspected the two small stone shelters that sat on the croft.

Maureen was uncomfortable waiting out in the open. There was something about this place that did not feel right. They were being watched – just like before, she could feel it. Olaf sensed it too. He would not stand still, he paced in circles around Meg's cart as if guarding Meg and the ponies.

Finally, they could see Heber turn and begin to ride back. He stopped midway and signaled them to come ahead.

The abandoned croft was actually a beautiful piece of land. It was surrounded by a variety of trees and bushes with all of their leaves turning to the warm colors of fall. It looked as if they were surrounded by a golden forest.

Two weathered shelters stood close together. One a family shelter and the other a keep for roots and grain. Both were made of stone with thatched roofs.

They pulled the cart up to the stone keep and unhitched the ponies. Olaf and Gunnar both seemed happy to be rid of their saddles and blankets.

They set up sleeping arrangements in the old stone house. Part of the stone chimney had fallen and the hearth was not safe for burning. They built a campfire just outside the door and would bring the coals in to keep them warm through the night.

As Heber tended the horses, the women prepared some food over the fire.

Maureen pulled her swords from the cart and laid them up next to the door of the house. Heber had placed his sword there as well.

Meg commented as Maureen pulled her father's Claymore from the cart, "God's teeth girl, that sword be bigger than you are. 'Tis a most beautiful weapon indeed. Where did yer Da get it?"

"I do nay know." Maureen replied. "The few times he did return to me mum and me, 'twas the sword he always had with him. And he would never let it out of his sight."

Meg walked over and pulled the blade partway out of its scabbard, "Strange markings. Beautiful, but strange. I do nay know any of these symbols, do you?" she asked.

Maureen just shook her head. She had never seen them before either. Her reading skills were limited to the English taught to her by the sisters of the Church. She could speak Scottish and Irish Gaelic, but could not write either one. These markings did not belong to either of those languages. The sword was indeed unique and a bit mysterious.

When their meal was ended, they sat close to the fire visiting and sharing stories. The sun had long set and the mists from the river began to creep across the land.

Heber was in the middle of a story when his attention suddenly snapped away from the campfire and out into the darkness.

Meg came immediately to her feet and quietly asked, "What be wrong Heber, what do ya hear?"

Maureen turned to the darkness, trying to see into the night. She saw nothing – heard nothing. "M'lord?" she asked nervously. "What be..."

"Riders," he whispered. "Listen."

She looked back out into the darkness. Meg slowly came up next to them. Together they watched and listened.

The few seconds of silence seemed like forever. And then, together they heard the faint sounds of hooves slowly approaching.

Both women quickly looked to Heber for direction, "Both of ya, inta the cart—quickly now. Pull the canvas over yer heads and do nay make a sound. Go!"

Maureen protested, "But M'lord, I can help if they..."

"Sssh. No lass. Did ya nay stop to think ya may be the one they be after? Go now."

She argued no more and quickly followed Meg to the cart and climbed inside pulling the canvas over them.

It was completely dark under the canvas. The two women could barely see each other. Maureen reached down and pulled her doe-hoofed dagger from her boot. If anyone found them, there would be nowhere to run. All they could do was wait and listen.

Heber moved quickly, retrieving his sword and picking up Maureen's short sword as well. He positioned himself on the far side of the fire. He leaned up against a large rock with his sword in front of him and Maureen's blade beside him. And now, he too had to wait.

The sounds of horses grew louder and louder until finally the two riders emerged from the darkness. Heber began sizing up the two men from the moment they road into view. He did not know who they were, but he knew instantly what they were and who sent them.

Both men wore red, white and black kilts. They both had long swords sheathed on their horses. One carried a longbow, the other carried a small crossbow, known as a latch. Two hounds ran with their horses.

These men were border reivers from Clan Moffat. They were allies to Clan Armstrong and they were dangerous.

"Good marrow sir. We mean ya no harm," spoke the larger of the two men.

"Ya be a bit off yer regular path are ya not lads?" Heber remarked. "What brings two border gallowglass up into the Highlands?"

The two men looked at each other and then began to climb down from their mounts. Heber tensed and tightened his grip on the hilt of his sword. If these two came at him at once, there would be no way he could fend them off alone.

The larger man turned to Heber raising both his hands in a gesture of surrender. "Truly sir, we mean no harm. We just be passin' through on our way to Perth. We thought ya might let us warm ourselves a bit by yer fire. We heard conversation, where be the others?" he asked.

Heber did not answer. He just extended his hand toward the fire so they might warm themselves for a moment. He offered them a few pieces of dried meat and a draft of ale.

They sat uncomfortably around the fire as the two men asked more questions to which Heber gave only vague answers.

The hounds were wandering around the campfire foraging for food when one of them caught the scent of the women and began to follow the trail to cart.

The larger man noticed the dog and looked back to Heber, "Where be the others?" he asked again. "We thought we heard others. Be it just you sir?"

The gallowglass got up and began to walk toward the stone house. It was then that he noticed the Claymore leaning up against the doorway.

He glanced back to Heber, "Now that be one fine blade indeed. I knew a man once who owned a Claymore like that. Be that your sword, sir?" he asked mockingly.

Under the canvas Maureen cringed when she heard the man's words. *Damn it to hell, foolish woman*, she thought. She should never had taken it from the cart.

Heber answered, "Spoils of war, boyo. I be fairly certain ya be familiar with that. The others ya speak of have moved on and 'twould be best fer you two to do the same."

"Now call those slew dogs away from me cart," Heber ordered. "I do nay want 'em eatin' me food or pissin' on me canvas."

The men chuckled and whistled the hounds back to their horses. They mounted up, thanked Heber for his hospitality and then rode out. There was no need for them to stay. They had found out what they needed to know – the girl was there. All they needed to do was bide their time and take her when the opportunity was right.

Heber waited until the men were out of sight and he could no longer hear the sounds of their horses. He walked over and tapped on the side of the cart for the women to come out.

Maureen climbed out first, giving Meg a hand up. As they climbed down, Maureen looked to Heber, "Who be they M'lord?"

"Border reivers, lass," Heber replied. "They must have followed us from the shire. Well, we know one thing for certain, Logan Armstrong be alive and well."

They all walked back over to the fire and sat down to warm themselves. They sat in silence until Heber finally spoke.

"They be lookin' fer ya lass. They recognized yer father's Claymore. Me only question be who's payin' these gallowglass?"

"What do ya mean?" Meg questioned.

"These blaggards from Clan Moffett are nay yer everyday border reivers. These men be skilled, well paid gallowglass. Warriors hired by noblemen.

Maureen watched Heber's face carefully. She could almost see his thoughts. It was then that things became very clear to her. She turned to Heber and whispered, "Ya know, do ya not M'lord? The gold, ya know who it belongs to; ya've known all along." She looked straight into his eyes, waiting for him to explain.

Heber sat up straight, drawing in a deep breath. "I can nay say for certain lass, but I have a damn good idea. When ya brought that satchel of gold to me table at the tavern, I did nay know from where it came. I did nay recognize the Coat of Arms on the wooden chest. It vexed me for certain."

As Heber spoke, Meg became increasingly concerned. She rose from her place and walked closer to Heber and Maureen. "Gold? What be this ya speak of Heber, what gold?" she asked.

Heber looked questioningly at Maureen as if to ask her permission to tell Meg the whole story. Maureen nodded her head in agreement. It was only right that Meg should know.

Heber turned to Meg and bid her to sit. He told her of the gold hidden at the tavern, and the jewels that had been sent with Lord Cullen and hidden in Hermitage Castle.

"But where did it come from Heber?" Meg asked. "I be not wise to the ways of the wealthy or the noble. But I have learned enough from ya to know that no border reiver or gallowglass could ever muster such wealth on their own. It be stolen, be it not?"

Heber nodded his head confirming her words and then he continued. "'Twas not until me trip to the lowlands that landed me in the company of James Hepburn did I begin to put the pieces together. When Faolan rode up to that pub on Maitiú's sleigh, 'twas plain to see that the good Earl be a bit bothered by it."

Suddenly, Maureen remembered the conversation between the two country gentlemen that night in the tavern.

"The Norwegian noble woman?" she asked. "M'lord, surely ya jest."

"Aye lass, the Norwegian noble woman. Anna Tronds be her name. They say Bothwell met her on a visit to Copenhagen. Her father be an Admiral to the Danish Royal Consul and bloody arse rich. Whether the good Earl fell in love with her or her money 'tis hard to say. Meg, ya know what a scoundrel Bothwell can be."

"Aye, that I do. One cocky blaggard he be, and ruthless to boot," Meg replied.

"Well," Heber continued, "the story goes that he hand-fasted the woman and brought her to Scotland. He convinced her that he was in desperate need of funds and forced her to sell all her possessions. She even went to her family for more money on his behalf."

"When the bastard got her to Scotland, he abandoned the poor woman and left her with child."

"But M'lord, how did the gold and jewels end up with me Da?" Maureen questioned.

"I can nay say for certain lass. 'Tis me belief that the good Earl commissioned old Armstrong to do his biddin' fer him, and forced the woman to give up her gold and jewels for safe passage back to Copenhagen. I be willin' to bet yer Da was in on that as well. I be thinkin' greed got the better of him as it does most men. When he saw such wealth before him, he decided not to share it. 'Twould be hard to say which one betrayed the other."

Meg sat down on a rock next to Heber. She was completely gobsmacked. Maureen got up and began to pace around the fire.

"God's teeth! Heber. No wonder ya been so fearful for the girl," Meg said solemnly shaking her head. "The Armstrongs be no trouble at all compared to what that filthy Bothwell can do. He be Lord High Sheriff fer Christ's sake, not even Clan Chattan can stop him."

At that, Maureen stopped her pacing and looked to Heber and Meg. "M'lord, be this true?" she asked.

"Aye, it be true," he replied. "But he will nay make such a move lass. 'Twould be foolish on his part." Heber rose from his place and walked over to Maureen putting his strong hands on her shoulders.

"If the truth be known lass, I'd say ya done the man a favor. Ya have the gold that could get him hanged, and ya killed the man who stole it for him. It be safe to say that the bounty yer Da stole so long ago be yers for the keepin'. Now, let's get some sleep."

The two women looked at each other and then back to Heber. He understood without them speaking a word, "Do nay worry, they already got what they wanted. They will nay come back this night."

Meg put her arm around Maureen's shoulders and together the women walked to the stone house. As Maureen lay beneath her blankets, she pulled her Rosary from the pocket of her skirt and began to pray. When her prayers were done, she looked over to Heber. He appeared to be asleep, but in the faint light of the coals from the hearth she caught sight of a glint of steel beneath the blankets and she could see that his hand was resting on the hilt of his sword.

Chapter Six

Logan

It had been ten days since Logan Armstrong had made his way to Dumbartonshire. He had managed to find a barber-surgeon on the outskirts of town who tended to his injuries and closed the open wound on his head. He had paid him well for his services and for his silence.

He had taken a room at the Inn near the Blacksmith to rest and heal until he was well enough to find that little bitch of a MacLeod and her staff-wielding priest. He swore they would pay with their lives.

As he sat in the main hall of the Inn, he learned from the conversation that MacPherson and the girl had left for Badenoch.

He sat stewing on the fact that he would not be able to take the girl himself. His wounds had prevented him from getting to her sooner and now they were gone.

He had paid the barber-surgeon to get a missive to the Lord High Sheriff asking him to send his gallowglass to fetch her back. He wanted her back alive. And when he had her, he would ride her until she could not walk, whip her until she could not breathe and then he would hang her.

And the priest, he thought to himself, he would be meeting his God very soon. Damn papists, if he could he would burn him alive.

After being cooped up in his room for days, Logan was beginning to feel like a caged animal.

He needed a change of scenery, a decent meal and a good ale, and there was only one place for that.

He gathered his sword and placed a cap on his head to cover his wounds. With MacPherson gone, he was confident that no one would recognize him at the Wycked Aye.

He slipped in quietly and racked his sword. He walked warily up to the bar as the blow to his head had left him with some weakness in his step.

He took a stool at the bar and asked for an ale. Fiona drew him a pint and placed a basket of bread before him.

"Welcome good sir," she said cautiously as she looked at his face, for although the wound on his head was closed and healing, his face still showed some bruising and swelling around his eyes and mouth.

"Would ya be new to our shire?" she questioned. "I have nay seen ya before."

"A guest at the inn lass, just passin' through," he answered as he nervously looked around the room.

As she wiped her hands on her apron she asked, "Can I bring ya some warm stew, sir? Best lamb stew in the Highlands."

Logan accepted and she went off to bring the man his food. As he waited for Fiona to return, a large man came up behind him, pulled the stool next to him and sat down. Sitting on the stool next to Logan Armstrong sat William Macaulay.

William sat silently at the bar. It was not the same without Maureen to greet him with a cold ale and a loving smile. He turned to acknowledge the man sitting next to him. When he saw his battered face and the bandages under his cap he realized who was sitting next to him. Out of the corner of his eye he watched as the man drank his ale and nervously looked from side-to-side throughout the tavern. William's rage was escalating by the minute.

Fiona came back up to the bar and placed the bowl of stew in front of Armstrong. "Good evenin' to ya William, I be right with ya," she said as she quickly turned and headed to the back of the tavern. She sensed the anger in William's demeanor and knew something was very wrong.

Fiona knew her place well, as did all of Chieftain Sara's girls. It was their job to keep an eye on the patrons of the tavern and report anyone who might be trouble. She knew there was something not right about the stranger at the bar and she went straight to the Chieftain.

"Sara, Sara!" she called as she entered the pantry. Both Sara and Thomas turned to her immediately as they sensed the urgency in her voice.

"What be wrong lass?" Thomas responded first.

"There be a stranger at the bar, Thomas. I do nay feel right about him. His eyes be blackened and his face be swollen. I have nay seen him here before," she explained.

Thomas moved to the pantry doorway to get a look at the man sitting at the bar. "Be that William sittin' next to him?" Thomas asked.

"Aye," Fiona replied. "And he be riled fer certain Thomas. I think he be knowin' this man."

"Aye, and I think I know who he be as well." Thomas turned to Sara, "Chieftain, we got trouble brewin' here. I believe that to be the gobshite Father Bryan put in his place."

Sara came to the door to look for herself. She turned to the Tánaiste, "Isabella, go quickly for Father Bryan. Tell him what be happenin' here and to come quickly."

Without question Isabella turned and slipped out the back door and headed straight for the Chapel. Chieftain then said to Fiona, "Go back out to the bar lass and tell William he be needed in back. Tell him Master Thomas wants to see him and get him away from the bar."

Fiona nodded her head in nervous agreement, took

a deep breath and then went to speak with William.

"William, Master Thomas be in need of yer help. Could ya come with me to the back pantry?" she asked.

William looked at her puzzled. Master Thomas had never asked for his help before. Fiona leaned over the bar to make eye contact with William. She quickly shifted her eyes over to the man sitting next to him.

But William would not leave. "I think I be stayin' right here lass. Bring me an ale won't ya."

She hesitated. Looking at him with pleading eyes she mouthed the words, "Please, William."

He put his hand on hers and said, "Fiona girl, bring me an ale."

Fiona turned around to look at Master Thomas standing in the doorway and shook her head from side-to-side. She drew a Desmond ale from the keg. When she got back to the bar, William was already engaged with Logan.

"Cad é an scéal, a chara?" William asked.

Armstrong looked at Macaulay with a knitted brow and the corner of his swollen mouth turned down. "I do nay understand that cant man, what did ya say?"

"Pray pardon good sir. I asked, 'what be the news?' Be up from the lowlands ya are, I can tell from yer words. How fair things down on the border? Perhaps not to yer likin' by the looks of ya—or did that beatin' ya took happen up here?"

It took every ounce of restraint for William to contain himself. He knew full well who this blaggard was and wanted nothing more than to reach over and break his neck.

"I be here for a quiet pint and bit of food. Now, if ya do nay mind?" Armstrong replied as he tried to dismiss William.

"Oh, I do nay mind at all," William countered, doing his best to provoke Logan. "It just seems that yer swollen, misshapen head seems to be on a bit of a swivel. Lookin' fer someone be ya? Perhaps an old friend? Perhaps the ones who did this to yer..." William paused, "fair face?"

Through gritted teeth Armstrong seethed, "I do nay know ya good sir and I prefer to keep it that way. I just be passin' through. Now please, let me be!"

But William would not let it rest. "But sir," he continued, "It be the ancient Gaelic custom of hospitality that prevails here. I want ya to feel welcome. This be the famous Wycked Aye Tavern owned by one Heber MacPherson."

Armstrong gave a fleeting wince with his swollen eyes. William beamed.

William kept pushing. "Heber MacPherson I say! Do ya know the man? By God, I think ya do, and a friend of MacPherson's be a friend of mine. Yer name friend, what be yer name?"

Fiona leaned over the bar, "William, please, do nay do this," she pleaded.

Sara could see the confrontation escalating and hurried to the bar to get Fiona out of the way. Thomas had come out on the floor, as well as Braden and Connor, and was making his way toward the two men.

Some of the patrons nearby turned and began to glare at Armstrong and Macaulay, and it was not the attention Armstrong desired; he made a move to stand up and leave. William stood up to stop him.

William placed a hand on Armstrong's shoulder. "Leavin are ya? Ya've not had yer pint and yer stew! No, sit down man! Enjoy! Fáilte! Oh, pray pardon, 'welcome'."

Armstrong lost his temper, "Hands off gobshite!"

"Gobshite? Now that nay be a friendly thing to say ta me. Just tryin' ta be hospitable," William mocked.

With that, Armstrong snapped his right fist straight

into William's nose, sending him reeling back and off balance as a spray of blood and snot flew into the air.

Patrons began to scatter from their tables as Braden and Connor began to move in. Armstrong had hoped this first blow would take the Highlander off his feet, but the hard-headed bastard just stood there swaying. Armstrong made a quick left jab, which William just barely blocked. Armstrong came back with a second right.

William had taken up sparing with Father Bryan and the Irish Brew Master de Faoite, and knew exactly what to do.

He ducked his head and Armstrong's fist hit powerfully home right on the top of William's thick Highland skull. That took the big man to the floor. The crunch everyone heard was not William's head but Armstrong's fist.

A shock of lightening bolted up Armstrong's right arm. He knew his hand was broken and if it came to weapons he would have no use of his sword hand. Yet, he took satisfaction in seeing William on his arse.

He stood triumphantly over William and gloated, "Now ya be in yer proper place, ya Highland eejit!"

William smiled and quickly scissor kicked his strong legs together. One leg caught Armstrong in the back of his right heel, while the other leg struck the front of Armstrong's right knee. Another sickening crack was heard and another lightning bolt shot up Logan's right leg. His leg buckled and he fell in a heap.

Tánaiste and Father Bryan got to the tavern just as Armstrong landed on the floor.

William rose up quickly as Father Bryan made his way through the crowd that had gathered around the combatants.

"This be the fooker you clobbered, Father? Sorry Father, I meant fellow," William asked.

Father Bryan responded, "Nay William, ya be right the first time. That be the fooker!"

Logan sat crumbled on the tavern floor. Father Bryan looked at him and said, "I'll pray fer ya man," and then turned to walk away.

Logan grumbled to himself, "Keep yer prayers ya papist piece of shite." He clumsily reached to his boot and drew a dagger. He was ready to send it flying at Father Bryan when Fiona saw him and screamed out, "Father, look out!"

But she was not the only one who saw him reach for the blade. Before he could let the blade fly Connor and Braden each sent their swords clean through Logan Armstrong. The blade dropped from his hand, clattering on the floor. Connor and Braden yanked their swords free from his body and he fell dead on the tavern floor.

Chieftain Sara walked up to Braden and Connor. She gave Logan's dead body a push with her boot and said, "Get this lowland piece of shite out of me tavern."

They dragged Logan out of the tavern and threw his body on a flat cart. Father Bryan made the sign of the cross on Logan's forehead and said, "May God forgive ya fer yer sins my son." Then he nodded to the lads to take him away.

They walked the cart down through the shire to the undertaker, who also happened to be a barber-surgeon. When he came out of his humble establishment to meet with Connor and Braden and saw who was in the cart, he was gobsmacked.

Connor noticed his reaction and asked, "'Would ya know this man, sir?"

"Aye, that I do." He replied as he scratched at his

ragged beard. "Looks like those stitches I placed be a bit of a waste of time, eh?"

"Ya tended this man did ya?" Braden questioned.

"Aye, I did. But not to me likin'. An angry and hateful man this one."

"Well, he will nay be causin' any more trouble now," Braden remarked as he tossed the undertaker a full crown. "Take care of this mess won't ya man."

The undertaker nodded his head in agreement and watched as the two men turned toward the Wycked Aye. He thought of the missive Armstrong sent to the Lord High Sheriff. Out of caution and curiosity, he had read the letter before it was delivered. He knew about the two gallowglass to be sent after the MacLeod girl.

He looked at the coin in his hand and then at the two lads walking away and called out, "Lads!" Connor and Braden both turned back to him.

"I fear the evil this one can do be not quite finished," the undertaker said. "He sent two gallowglass after the MacPherson. He wanted the girl back. Thought ya should know."

Braden and Connor's anger grew with every step they took back to the Wycked Aye.

Connor went straight to William who was sitting at the Chieftain's table with a cold cloth to his jaw and a whisky in his hand.

"William!" Connor called out as he approached the table. "That blaggard we just dragged out of here sent two gallowglass after Heber and yer girl. The undertaker delivered a missive fer him to one of Bothwell's boys."

William's eyes narrowed as he raised his gaze to Connor. "How long ago?" he asked.

"We can nay be certain," Connor replied.

William took the cold rag and threw it across the room. He tossed back the whisky and slammed the glass on the table. Without further conversation he got up and headed for the door.

"Where do ya think yer goin', boyo?" Braden yelled.

William stopped half-way through the great hall and turned to face them, "I be going after 'em and I be bringin' me girl home."

"Not alone yer not!" Braden warned.

"No, William, ya nay be goin' alone!" It was the first time since Chieftain Sara had taken command of the tavern that anyone had heard her voice resonate with authority across the great hall.

She was Chieftain of the Wycked Aye and it was her place to issue a call to arms, no one else's.

"Hear me now man and hear me well," she said as she walked directly to William. "I will nay have ya running off half-cocked. Ya be angry, William, and ya nay be thinkin' clearly."

She turned to Connor and Braden, "Lads, I call ye to arms. I bid ya to find Heber, Meg and Maureen and see them safely to Badenoch. Be ya willin' to take the call?"

The two men stood shoulder-to-shoulder before their Chieftain and together they spoke, "We be willin', Chieftain."

Connor to turned to William, "We leave at daybreak Macaulay, be ready boyo."

William came busting through the door to the courier's office like a mad bull. When his father got a look at his son's face, he grabbed William by the shirt pulling him around to face him.

"What the bloody hell happened to ya boy?" Séan

asked. William had been involved in many a skirmish. But being as big as he was, no one had ever managed to hit him in the face.

"I got into a bit of a tiff at the tavern," William replied.

His father took William's jaw in his hand saying, "Well, that be a pretty solid pop in the jaw son. What happened ta the other fella?" Séan asked jokingly.

"He be dead Da," William said flatly as he pulled his face from his father's hand and brushed his hand from his sleeve.

Séan Macaulay stood silent, staring at his eldest son. William began to walk away when his father spoke, "William, tell me son, tell me ya did nay kill a man."

William turned back to his father, "Nay Da, 'twas nay me who killed him, but I sure as hell wanted to. 'Twas Braden and Connor who ran him through, he tried to put a blade in Father Bryan's back."

William could see the relief in his father's eyes as he waited for further explanation from his son.

"I can nay explain it all now Da. Chieftain Sara has called us to arms and I be leavin' on the marrow for Badenoch with Connor and Braden. We be goin' after Heber MacPherson and..."

"And that little MacLeod wench," Séan's tone changed abruptly as he finished William's sentence for him.

"I be goin' after her Da, and bringin' her home. Do nay try and stop me." William stormed out of the room. He had enough for one day and needed to be ready to leave in the morning.

Séan watched as William slammed the door behind him. He knew now that there was no point in trying to reason with his son. It was apparent to Séan that very soon, he too would be traveling to Badenoch and having another discussion with Heber MacPherson.

Chapter Seven

Sorley Boy

The sea remained rough and unforgiving, as did the ship's company, to the point that Maitiú was almost relieved to pull into port in Aberdeen. As they approached the docks, Dónal curled his nose at the awful stench coming from the city. Raw excrement ran down the middle of the street and its odor mixed with the smell of burning turf and peat used for fuel. Adding to that was the stench of hundreds of people crowded together. People from all over Europe filled the streets as it was a major port and trade center.

Word had gone out to all the MacDonalds throughout Scotland and the Isles, and even down to the Glens of Antrim in Ireland to rally to the cause of their kinsmen on Skye. Some heeded the call in Aberdeen and Philip found a ship leaving the very next day for Skye – a ship full of MacDonalds.

"How will this work Master MacAlasdair? We be headin' to Skye to save your wife, a MacLeod, in a company of MacDonalds?" asked Dónal.

"Say nothing, mind you!" Philip responded.

Upon boarding the MacDonald ship, Maitiú looked about for any familiar faces among the crew when he recognized the face of an old adversary, one Sorley Boy MacDonald.

Sorley Boy was the chief of the MacDonalds of Antrim, a region in the north of Ireland. They had long ago displaced the Irish MacQuillans centuries ago, back when the MacDonalds were at the pinnacle of their power as the Lords of the Isles. The MacDonalds of the

Glens, as it was known, held all Irish in disdain. It was Sorley Boy who accused Maitiú of being an English spy. Maitiú hoped he would not remember him. To Sorley Boy "all Irish look alike," but seeing him put Maitiú on edge.

However, Sorley Boy remembered Philip. He boasted to the rest of the MacDonalds of the poetic talent of Philip MacAlasdair and how he once sponsored Philip in his stronghold for two fortnights. A quick glance between Philip and Maitiú assured Maitiú that Philip would also "say nothing." There was no need of a glance between Dónal and Maitiú, as Dónal knew well the story of what happened in the Glens and for his Da's sake he would also say nothing. Philip introduced Maitiú and Dónal as servants in his employ and they were quickly dismissed.

Once the ship set sail, the sea's roughness was beginning to take a greater toll on Maitiú. Rather than becoming used to the rhythms of the sea, Maitiú grew more and more nauseated, and he began to ignore calls to the mess. Dónal took it upon himself to ensure his Da was not neglected as Maitiú remained below decks most of the journey.

As Philip sat in the lower deck of the merchant vessel, his thoughts drifted. He looked at his loyal friend Maitiú, laying in his hammock, violently ill from the reeling and tossing of the ship.

When Philip asked Maitiú to come with him on his quest to find Katie, he knew his Irish companion would accept without question. He had been blessed with Maitiú's friendship, one that had held fast for many years and through many campaigns despite the differences in their beliefs.

77

Maitiú and Dónal were devout Catholics, an institution to which Philip gave no credence. He was of the old ways, the way of the forest and the many Gods that watched over the Earth. He lived in balance and harmony with the land, the seas and all their creatures. His beliefs followed the greater powers of the Earth herself that have existed for longer than any Christian God ever had. He believed in the magic of the forest because he had seen it many times, especially on the Isle of Skye. He knew first-hand of the ancient beings that inhabited the Isle. Beings that were as old as the Isle itself: The Fey, the soft horse of Skye, the banshees. While many believed they were myth, Philip knew they were real. He had walked with the Fey, he had heard the painful cries of the banshees, and the soft horse had come to him once before on Skye. He had been in great need of help and the soft horse took him to safety.

He chuckled to himself as he recalled the event. He had tried to share this miraculous encounter with Maitiú around a campfire one night while on their own journey to Skye. Maitiú had told him that his brain must have been addled, for surely no such thing could have happened.

Maitiú groaned and turned restlessly in his hammock. Philip put his head in his hands and searched his heart. Had he brought these two good men on a journey that may end up being the end of them all? This quest had just begun and already his friend was suffering greatly as the result of his hasty decisions. Philip had no clear plan, no clear path. His decisions thus far had been impulsive and reckless. But he knew he must press on regardless of the obstacles ahead. And there would be many, for there were always problems when MacLeods and MacAlasdairs came together. It had been that way since the first day he and Katie had fallen in love.

He must get to Katie and he would do whatever it took to find her and bring her home, even if it meant leaving his companions behind. His mind was made up, he would waste no time and take whatever road necessary to get to Katie. And should the soft horse of Skye come to him again, he would ride it. For surely it would take him to Katie.

Maitiú suddenly sat up and leaned over the edge of his hammock and added what little contents his stomach held to the sludge that already covered the bottom of the ship.

Philip worried for his friend. He was growing weak and Dónal was having trouble getting him to take any food or water. He would be no good to Philip in this condition. He needed both of them strong, for the journey ahead would be rugged and exhausting.

Philip suddenly felt as if the sides of the ship were closing in on him, he could not breathe in this sewer and made his way up on deck where he could smell the sea and feel the wind upon his face.

He stumbled to the rails on the starboard side of the ship holding tightly to the rail as the ship lurched and dipped over the great swells. He focused his thoughts and spoke out into the night, "Hear me, hear my words old man of the sea. Calm your wrath and quiet your waters. We ask only for safe passage this night. Bring us safely to dry land."

Chapter Eight

The Ghost of Wick

The first stop after Aberdeen was to the fishing village of Wick to unload cargo and bring on supplies, and more MacDonalds if any were to be found. Maitiú jumped at the chance to stand on dry land and Dónal accompanied him mostly out of concern.

Wick was not a large village, and it was less crowded and much cleaner than Aberdeen. In their walking they found an abandoned church.

The abandonment appeared recent as parts of the wooden roof remained intact. The interior was stripped bare and the statues and paintings defaced. Certainly John Knox's or Luther's doctrine had reached here, as well as the most ancient doctrine of greed. While quietly praying in what Maitiú and Dónal still considered consecrated ground, Dónal caught sight of an elderly woman wearing a threadbare black shawl, slinking through the shadows of the dilapidated building. She moved like a ghost and it unnerved him.

Maitiú seemed not to have seen her, so deep was he in prayer. Dónal thought it best not to mention the ghostly soul as it may add to his father's anxiety.

While heading back to the ship, Dónal discreetly inquired at the local ale house about the old woman he had seen in the church.

"She be a whore and a witch," the barman said. "She served that wretched papist priest before we ran him off. More than likely, she was his concubine. She frightens the local children who go ta that ruin ta play. She curses at 'em in a strange language and no one knows what she be sayin'. It be not Gael or Northman. The people shun her, but she be otherwise harmless. Lives in that ruined church she does and eats from garbage scraps like a pig. Watch out though, stranger," the publican sneered and chuckled, "as she might put the come hither on ya!"

Dónal was disgusted at the callousness and cruelty of this man. Throughout his campaigns he had seen the old and innocent suffer at the hand of religious and political tyrants. No one should have to suffer such disgrace. He left the ale house with a heavy heart. Someone must make amends to that poor woman.

Dónal saw his Da back to the ship. It was leaving with the next tide, which gave Dónal about four hours of time.

He ran to the local baker and purchased a fresh loaf of barley bread and then ran to the old church.

He called out in the broad Scots but got no response. He called out in the Gaelic of Scotland - nothing. Latin, he thought. He called out in Latin, "Dear woman, I have bread for you."

He heard a faint reply and found the old crone curled up in a corner of what was once the vestibule of the church. She was shivering. He approached and could see she was gasping and struggling for each breath. She was dying. Her face was gray and emaciated, her teeth rotten, and she smelled like death and stale urine. He broke off a piece of the bread and soaked it in the ale he had in his flask.

It was then she asked Dónal in perfect Irish Gaelic, Munster Gaelic, "Why would ya be helping me young man? Your kindness be much appreciated, but alas, ya be too late for me. But I am happy to be going. I just wish I had a priest for the final anointing."

Tears welled up in Dónal's eyes and he held the woman to his breast and said, in Latin, "O, my God, I am heartily sorry for having offended thee, and I detest all my sins. For I fear your just punishment, but mostly because it offends you, my dear God, who art all good and deserving of all my love. I firmly resolve, with the help of your grace, to sin no more and avoid the near occasions of sin. Amen."

The old woman reached her withered hand up gently to caress Dónal's face and she handed him her rosary. Then she fell limp in his arms. Dónal was weeping when he felt a hand on his shoulder. It was Maitiú.

"May her soul and all the souls of the faithfully departed, through the love of Christ, rest in peace." Then he said, "A Dónal, a mhic, mo ghrá, mo chroí, ya are a true Catholic Christian gentleman. Tá grá agam duit."

"Da, how did she know I be from Munster?"

"I guess we will never know," Maitiú said with a shrug.

The vault under the altar was ajar, no doubt from the looting and they lowered her frail body into the vault and pushed the stone over it. Then they quickly ran back to the ship. Maitiú said a word of thanks that his seasickness and weakness had left him.

Philip was pacing in front of the gangway as the two came up in a sprint. "Where in God's teeth have you two been?"

Dónal gasping for breath replied, "We were giving someone a good send off."

Philip, in exasperation said, "Well, let us all have a sendoff from Wick."

As he turned around to bound up the gangway with his Irish servants he felt a twinge deep in his gut and sensed an urgent concern for Katie on Skye.

From Wick most ships sailed for Orkney, a fair and beautiful group of islands known for their rich farmland, excellent beef and ancient stone circles. But instead of heading for Orkney the MacDonalds on board had pressed the captain to take the ship through the treacherous waters of the Pentland Firth. The currents were turbulent and rapidly changing in the Firth. Even the most seasoned captain and crew were reluctant to sail these waters. Sailing around Orkney was generally safer and more profitable, but that was cast aside by the MacDonalds, intent on reaching Skye with all haste.

About three o'clock in the afternoon, one day out of Wick, a massive storm came up suddenly. The deck of the ship pitched violently this way and that. Massive waves were breaking over the sides. One of the sails ripped in the gale force winds before it could be brought in and the helmsman had to be replaced every half hour because of the exposure to the frigid sea water.

Below decks Maitiú's respite from sea sickness was over and he was back to nearly constant retching. Philip, swinging in the hammock next to Maitiú, was staring off in a corner seeing nothing but the face of his dear Katie. Dónal could endure it no longer. He went up to the First Mate and asked, "Let me take the helm."

"What experience have ya had?"

"I can handle the wheel, Captain," Dónal assured him. "Let me take a turn while ya warm up yer best man, then he can relieve me."

Hesitantly, the Captain gave his consent. When Dónal staggered up on the slippery deck to the helm, the previous occupant fled below. The sea was raging on all sides and the clouds would open and close revealing, at times, the sun that appeared more like the moon. So dark was the sky it was hard to tell if it was day or night. From his experience on ships on the Mediterranean, Dónal knew to turn the boat into any big waves and a big one was coming, bigger than any he had ever seen. This was surely it he feared. He never thought that this is how his life would end. He had always hoped he would die in the heat of a battle for a just cause or in his sleep as an old man. But not like this.

"Into your hands I commend my spirit." He began to recite his own Act of Contrition in preparation for his own death when he heard a woman's voice reciting it with him. Since there was no woman in the ship's company, Dónal gasped and looked around. Turning his eyes back to the bow and the approaching wave he saw, in the fleeting sunlight, a young woman wearing a thick, black shawl, facing the last wave with him. He was clutching the old woman's Rosary when the wave suddenly died before him. He stared in awe as he watched the sea turn into a calm sheet of glass. The woman with the black shawl was gone.

The next helmsman ran up to relieve Dónal and some of the other sailors came up on deck as the noise of the raging sea was suddenly gone. Looking at Dónal, the helmsman said, "What happened, boyo? Where did the storm go?"

Dónal shrugged his shoulders and said in Irish, "Níl a fhios agam, I do nay know," and looking into the sky he said, "Dona Nobis Pacem," give us peace.

For the rest of the voyage, the weather was unusually near perfect with favorable winds. The MacDonalds took it as a good omen and that their mission was blessed. The storm that was now coming was on Skye, and it was in the form of human conflict.

As the ship glided smoothly toward Skye on the calm ocean, the MacDonalds on board held a council in the cramped Captain's quarters. They discussed where on Skye they should land. Since Philip was well known and respected among all on board, he was invited to sit in and perhaps say a few things himself should the need arise.

While the council took place below decks Philip's two Irish servants sat on the aft portion of the deck enjoying the warmth of the sun. Quietly, and with a calmness that denied the terror of the previous day, Dónal told his father about the vision of the young woman who prayed with him as he manned the helm.

"Do you believe me, Da? I am not sure I believe me. She recited the Act of Contrition in perfect Irish."

After a pause, Maitiú replied with complete sincerity, "It could have been the woman in the church. She spoke Irish, did she not?" Dónal nodded.

"But I have another idea," Maitiú continued. "Do you remember when you were a wee lad and you had nightmares about that pointed nose dog?"

"You mean Giraffee? He was a devil." Dónal recalled.

"I know. I believe ya. But who saved ya?"

"It be a woman with long dark hair and freckles. She be beautiful."

"I always believed that was me mother, yer Mimi. She died years before ya were born."

"In Hebrews it says we be surrounded by a 'Cloud of witnesses'." Dónal said.

"That be right, boyo. It be the communion of saints. Love lives beyond death."

Down below decks an ugliness was emerging. While MacDonalds appeared united in the immediate face of the enemy, when that focus was off they argued and bickered with one another.

Some wanted to land in the south of Skye at Sleat, a MacDonald stronghold. Others were for landing at Staffin, another MacDonald strong-hold recently captured from the MacLeods.

One of the MacDonalds spoke up, "I never trusted the Staffin people. They have mixed blood. The have mixed with the MacLeods and I question their loyalty."

This talk made Philip uneasy as his own wife was a MacLeod and while he was loyal to the MacDonalds, his love for Katie was beyond measure, trumping any clan loyalty. It was then Philip reminded the council of his Staffin cousin, Sandy Óg MacLeod of Garafad.

"Who can doubt my cousin Sandy MacLeod." Philip exclaimed. "He has stood by and campaigned with us on many occasions. He be married into the MacDonalds, and be cousin to me wife. His father was a great friend of mine and he has always helped me in times of need."

Lines of loyalty to a cause can be blurred by a greater call to love of family. Sandy loved a MacDonald and Philip loved a MacLeod. If they could land in Staffin and meet up with Sandy perhaps he could count on his help to retrieve Katie.

"I vote for Staffin!" Philip bellowed.

While many of the MacDonalds seemed swayed, Sorley Boy MacDonald voiced his descent. "Staffin be MacDonald in name only. Like me friend said earlier, these people have mixed with the MacLeods, just as our warrior-poet has pointed out!"

"Do you doubt me loyalty?" roared Philip with his fists clenched in rage.

Alarmed by the warrior-poet's vehemence, McDonald backed off a bit, "Now, now laddie, let me finish. These people have also mixed with the MacRanalds of South Uist and a fair number of Irishmen as well. We MacDonalds of the Glens of Antrim know the vileness and treachery of the bogtrotters as we have dealt with them for years. So I say vote for Sleat, where loyalty has never been in doubt."

The captain of the ship spoke at last. "We have been blessed by God almighty with this fair weather we have today. Tomorrow may bring a return to what happened yesterday. Now I be a hired man here, and will do the biddin' of this assembly, but let me point out that beside the threat of weather, if we sail around to Sleat the MacLeods will see us. We may be raided by MacNeil pirates or even O'Malleys up from Sorley Boy's old sod. I say Staffin be yer best choice. If you want Sleat, I still be yer Captain, but Staffin makes more sense ta me."

So when the vote was taken, and it was close, the council voted for Staffin. It was from the north that the assault on Dunvegan was to occur. The question was how to send a messenger to coordinate the attack with the Sleat men.

Philip stood up saying, "Send me and me bogtrotters. No one will suspect me since I be a traveling poet." All greed that Philip would carry the message.

When the boat made shore the crew disembarked and made their way to Duntulum Castle. It wasn't really a castle as the Irishmen knew castles. It was more like a Norman keep or strong house used to repel small bands of raiders, reivers and thieves. It was never meant to repel a large army. Years ago the MacDonalds took it from the MacLeods. Now the MacDonalds hoped to take Dunvegan from the MacLeods as well.

In the close confines of Duntulum the MacDonalds of Staffin, who were led by one Angus Óg (young Angus), although well into his seventies, assembled with the newly arrived ship's company.

When the ship's company was introduced, Dónal discreetly leaned over to whisper in his Da's ear, "If this be Angus Óg, I wonder what Sean Angus looks like." Maitiú snickered, drawing the unwanted attention of the assembly to the Irishmen. Philip cast them a sharp glance, irritated by their carelessness.

With an angry voice Angus Óg inquired, "Who be these gobshites?"

Sorley Boy sneered, "They be the Irish servants of Philip MacAlasdair. Who cares what names they have, they be Irish bogtrotters after all."

Angus persisted, "They have names. Let them speak!" That directed even more attention toward them.

It was then Dónal spoke up, "I be Dónal Murphy of Wexford and this be me Uncle Maitiú, also a Murphy."

Angus squinted at them. "Me eyes are nay as sharp as they once were. Ya remind me of a grey merchant I once knew from Waterford, one Roibeard de Faoite."

Quickly Philip interjected, trying not to reveal his growing alarm, "Roibeard de Faoite was indeed a Waterford man as you say. These men are from Wexford. Ya know how they all look alike."

The entire assembly laughed and returned to the subject at hand—how to get word to Sleat that they had 150 fighting men, when the ships complement was combined with the castle's contingent.

The ship's captain piped up saying, "MacAlasdair has volunteered to do the deed."

Angus Óg was old enough to remember Philip MacAlasdair as a young scout and how he once, and somewhat miraculously, got word across Skye in a previous Clan skirmish.

"Very well then," he said. "Rest tonight and be off, you and your bogtrotters. Mind you, I will spare no horses for your trip as they be too dear to me."

As everyone agreed and disbanded to find lodging in the village nearby, Sorley Boy gave the two Irishmen an intense stare. He wondered where he had known the name, de Faoite.

After receiving Angus Óg's blessing, they started off across Skye. Looking from the castle windows, watching the three jog away it occurred to Sorley Boy just who the elder Irishman was and, in a loud voice directed to no one in particular, proclaimed, "That be Maitiú MacRoibeard de Faoite! I know that running gait well. I watched him run across the Glens of Antrim for days."

When Angus Óg heard this he laughed, "Almost as clever as his sire, that one."

Chapter Nine

Sandy MacLeod

They did not have too far to go and as they walked along, Maitiú turned to Dónal, "Murphy, why did ya say we be Murphys?" he asked.

With a wry smile, Dónal calmly replied, "It be the most common name in Ireland. They be everywhere ya know."

"Then ya said we be from Wexford. Our accents tell them we are not." Maitiú added.

Philip interrupted, "These Skye men can nay distinguish a Waterford accent from a Wexford, ya just sound Irish to them. On the other hand, if Dónal had said Waterford, Angus would have made the connection to your own Da, and Sorley Boy would have remembered ya. I be a bit concerned he might know ya even now. Did ya see how he eyed ya both when we left?"

After a brief stretch of their legs MacAlasdair and his two Irish servants arrived at Sandy MacLeod's cabin. A mud wall cabin was a humble abode. The floor was dirt. The windows were small and filled with cloth at night to keep out the cold. There was a hole in the center of the thatch roof to let out smoke from the fire that was used for both cooking and heat. The animals of the farm shared the living space for safety and the additional heat their presence provided.

Three children spied them as they approached. Two boys and a little girl whose ages appeared to range from six to ten. When they saw the three men coming their way they ran inside the cabin.

Within a few minutes Sandy MacLeod and his son, Neil emerged with the children following close behind. Once Sandy recognized Philip, the travelers were welcomed with open arms.

"Good Marrow MacAlasdair, what brings ya up Staffin way? Bad time to be wonderin' about the Isle," Sandy said as he reached for Philip's hand.

"'Tis good ta see old friend, I come on most urgent business," Philip replied.

Sandy gave Maitiú and Dónal a once-over glance. "And who be these two lads?"

Philip introduced his Irish companions who graciously bowed their heads saying, "It be our honor sir, peace be with ya."

"What manner of business would cause ya ta risk bringin' two Irishmen ta Staffin. Ya know how the MacDonald's feel about the Irish, Philip." Sandy warned.

"Aye, that we do. We've just come from Duntulum, sailed in on a ship full of MacDonald's bound fer Dunvegan. Old Sorley Boy be leadin' 'em in. They charged me with the task of getting' a message ta their men in Sleat," Philip explained.

Sandy looked questioningly at Philip. "Takin' up their campaign are ya?"

"Nay me friend," Philip replied. "Sandy, the Lairds have taken Katie and Andrew ta Dunvegan. I've come ta get her out. If I deliver Sorley Boy's message, I can sail with the MacDonald's from Sleat straight in ta Dunvegan and ta Katie."

Dónal and Maitiú exchange a troubled glance. This was the first they had heard of an actual plan of action from Philip, and they didn't like it.

Sandy looked at Philip shaking his head. "Come lads, come and rest yerselves, we have much to talk about."

Maitiú and Dónal were introduced to Ana, Neil's wife, and Deirdre, Sandy's wife. They were given a fine evening meal and as the day grew darker everyone gathered together near the fire to share stories. Sandy and his wife told some local stories. Then it was the guest's turn to entertain.

Philip repeated some of his classics, like the Argyll satire, that had Sandy and family laughing uproariously. Then Philip turned to Maitiú, "Tell them how the Argyll satire almost got us killed."

"Which time, a chara? There be too many to name." Maitiú asked.

"About the time before Shane O'Neill," Philip replied.

"It be a long story and Philip said you tell it so well," Dónal added.

"Ah yes, Shane the Proud," Maitiú recalled. Looking toward the children Maitiú asked, "Do ya all know about Shane, the thorn in the English queen's side?" They nodded.

Maitiú winced in feigned distress, "Me throat be so dry, I can nay tell the story."

Sandy leapt to his feet and grabbed a jug off the wall, "Here be the cure for that, Irishman," he said with a big smile.

Maitiú took a big draught and a let out a wheeze saying, "Oh, that be grand!"

Then he began to tell the tale of how he and Philip came to Ireland, how their ship was attacked by O'Malley pirates off its west coast, and how they landed and made their way across Ireland until, at last, they found themselves face-to-face with one of the most ruthless men in the country, one Sorely Boy MacDonald.

The children listened with wide eyes, smiling and laughing as Maitiú told his tale of Sorley Boy. When the story was done, they clapped their hands saying, "More, more!"

"Philip, tell them your story about the soft horse," Maitiú prompted.

The legend of the soft horse was known throughout Skye by MacDonald and MacLeod alike. It was Philip's story and he told it to Maitiú on a fireless night sneaking through the bogs of Ulster.

Dónal also knew the legend of the soft horse as he had heard it as a wee lad sitting on his papa's knee. Dónal recalled the story his papa had told him so long ago.

A fisherman and his son were out fishing one day, far from their village on the coast of Staffin. The boy was said to be 'touched' with an incredible and detailed imagination that persisted well into his manhood. He claimed to have a pet he called the soft horse that no one could see. Well, one day the father slipped, fell and broke his leg while on the rocky shore of the of one of the islands hunting seals. At the time, the lad was too small to man the curragh, and the chance that another fishing boat would come along and find them was slim. So the boy told his father he would ride the soft horse back to the village for help. This angered his father who scolded him about his wild imagination in the face of real danger. Yet the son, assuring his father of his immediate return, disappeared, leaving the curragh behind. One day later his son appeared with men from the village. When questioned how he got to the village without the curragh he said, "I rode the soft horse, Da."

Dónal's papa always liked to tell that story. It reminded him not everything that happened in the world could be explained.

Philip took his turn from the jug and started his story about the time he saved their grandfather so long ago and how the soft horse helped him do it. Finally, he ended his story with a far-away smile. With that everyone in the cabin applauded.

It felt good to Maitiú that he could still spin a tale that brought joy, especially on this most trying journey.

It was getting late. Deirdre stood up and softly clapped her hands calling an end to the evening's festivities. The children moaned and groaned, begging for one more story. But their pleas fell on deaf ears. She led the children off to their beds. Maitiú and Dónal went to their beds in the other far corner of the cabin.

The lanterns were dimmed, the fire was raked and soon the only sounds heard were the snoring of men and beasts. Philip could not sleep so he stepped outside the cabin and prayed, in his own way, for help finding Katie and taking her home. Perhaps the old ones were listening. He was praying, but hearing and feeling nothing. Philip knew the Aes Sidhe were there, but why did he not feel them?

So deep in thought he was, he did not notice Sandy come up behind him.

"Philip, what ya be thinkin' man?" It startled Philip when Sandy spoke.

"Do ya think they be about, Sandy?" Philip lamented. "Why do I nay feel their presence? I need them, but I can nay feel them."

Sandy shook his head in disappointment, "Because ya've placed limits of yer own making on the power of this place. The old ones be not at yer beckonin' call, Philip. Can ya nay see those two Irishmen ya brought with ya? They followed ya without question. Are they not the sign of true friendship and love?

"Aye, I suppose," Philip conceded.

"And yet yer heart be nay with them. Ya pray fer magic ta help ya instead of trustin' in yer friends," Sandy warned. "If ya care fer these men, do nay take them on this trip. Ya be puttin' them in danger."

"I need ya Sandy, help me! Help me find Katie!" Philip begged.

Sandy looked at him shaking his head. "Ya know full well I can nay go with ya, Philip," Sandy replied. "I be a Macleod who married a MacDonald woman. Me and me family, we walk a fine line between the Clans. I can nay take one side over the other." Sandy walked around to face Philip. "Katie will be safe at Dunvegan. The Lairds have taken them there to keep them safe. Do nay bring yer Irish friends with ya on this journey, man. Ya'll only get them killed.

Perturbed, Philip said, "I will bring them, for the love of Katie, I will bring them. I need their swords. And should the Aes Sidhe or the soft horse come ta me, then I be goin' on without them."

"And what would yer Katie say if she heard that out of ya? Ya be lost man, lost in yer pride and selfishness. Should the Aes Sidhe come, 'twould be to them, nay you. Fer the love of Katie, send these Irishmen home," Sandy pleaded.

"Should it come ta battle, I be needin' their swords. If ya will nay help me Sandy, then I pray ya, leave me be!" Philip snapped.

Sandy did just that and walked silently back to his cabin.

Morning arrived too quickly and the whole cabin awoke in a state of drowsiness, except for Philip, who had not slept at all. When Maitiú wished him a good morning he did not return the pleasantry. He simply said, "We need ta get movin'."

While the women prepared a hearty breakfast of rashers, eggs, and porridge, Maitiú and Dónal laughed and played with the children. Dónal played the shell game with them using the shiny stones he had brought from Sterling.

Philip was becoming more and more annoyed with every minute. Every laugh and giggle scraped on his nerves. His companions' lack of urgency and concern for their journey irritated him, and he did not take kindly to the attentions paid to them by Sandy and his family. He rushed them through their meal with hardly a word spoken.

Maitiú and Dónal somberly gathered their belonging. They thanked Ana and Deirdre for their meals, and Sandy for sheltering them for the night. They walked out of the hovel, with the children on their heels, leaving Philip to say his goodbyes to the family.

Philip and Sandy grasped forearms as Sandy said, "Stay on the coast road, Philip. "Twould be safer fer you and yer friends. I pray ya think twice about goin' on this journey, man."

"I thank ya fer yer kindness and yer counsel, Sandy. Fare thee well," was all he said as he left the hovel.

When Philip was gone, Sandy looked to his wife. Deirdre looked at him with eyes that said, *Do nay let them go.* Sandy came to her, taking her in his arms as they both looked toward the open door. "May God be with them all," was all he said.

Chapter Ten

The High Council

The great hollow of the Tuatha de Danann was bustling with the Fey warriors who had been called to the pools to help defend Dunvegan against Clan MacDonald and protect the great relic of the Aes Sidhe.

Nestled at the foot of the Black Cuillin Mountains, the pools lay near the shire of Glenbrittle. The hollow had been a gathering place of the Aes Sidhe for centuries. Hidden from the eyes of men, as all Sidhe mounds are, the entrance to the great hollow was veiled by a magnificent waterfall.

For centuries, the Braolauch shi—the Fairy Flag—had been preserved in the keep of Dunvegan Castle, an heirloom to the Chiefs of Clan MacLeod. A simple piece of saffron colored silk fabric imbued with the magic of the Fey, it is a powerful talisman and a relic of great importance to Clan MacLeod, a relic to be protected at all costs. For should it fall into the wrong hands, it is not known what misfortunes might befall Clan MacLeod or what powers it could wield in the hands of a rival clan, particularly Clan MacDonald.

As Shalynn passed behind the roaring water, before her lay a pathway of ancient stones covered in deep green moss. The pathway led to a circular opening draped in ferns and vines. The cave inside was, in fact, a foyer to the hollow. At the back of the small cave was an enormous arched doorway. The edges were adorned with beautifully carved symbols and writings of the Aes Sidhe. At the top of the arch was the carving of the great stag of the forest, the symbol of the Tuatha de Danann.

The door itself was a carved representation of the rowan tree. At the base of the tree, a large emerald had been imbedded. Shalynn placed her hand upon the stone and the door to the hollow opened to her.

The hollow was a serene and beautiful place. Huge trees provided the support for the entire cavern. The crystal clear Loch Brittle waters that fed the Fairy pools ran through the center of the cavern. Natural skylights provided light during the day and fireflies lit the trees at night. All manner of life inhabited the hollow. There were birds, rabbits, red deer, butterflies and reptiles; the hollow was their sanctuary as well.

She was late arriving to the pools. She knew the other members of the High Counsel would already be gathered.

There were seven members of the High Counsel including Shalynn, who was the youngest member to sit with the elders.

They were the most ancient of the Fey: Anu, Mother of the Tuatha; Diancecht, the great physician; Eochaid, the horseman; Erin, one of the three Queens; Macha, a war goddess, ancient and wise; and Airmid, daughter of Diancecht and Shalynn's mother.

Making her way through the hollow, the workers and warriors bowed their heads to her as she passed. She hurried to the chamber of the council.

The elders were gathered around the council table discussing strategies and evaluating the scouting information being brought in by the warriors. As information came to them, they moved and positioned small replicates of ships, soldiers and horses across a huge map of Skye and Dunvegan.

Shalynn approached the table and stood before Diancecht.

She had tried to prepare herself for this exchange with her grandfather, for she knew he would not be pleased that she had returned empty handed. As she waited to be recognized, she glanced around the table looking for her mother, hoping for bit of motherly backup, but Airmid was not there.

Diancecht was a regal man who possessed the wisdom of the ages. Taller than most of the Fey men, his lean frame was clothed in leather in preparation for battle. His long, grey hair was braided and tied with leather wrappings.

When he finally raised his emerald green eyes to Shalynn, he did not greet her.

"Where is the youngling?" he demanded.

Instantly irritated with his lack of affection and courtesy she replied, "I am well, thank you. She travels to Badenoch with the one called MacPherson."

"Badenoch?" he muttered. "She is needed by the council, you know this!"

"I do your Grace," Shalynn snapped. "But she is not ready. She must be trained."

Diancecht grumbled in exasperation and turned his back on Shalynn. She moved around to the other side of the table to confront him, "Please your Grace, believe me when I tell you that her gifts are much greater than the Watcher before her, but she is innocent of them and she must not be pushed."

"Pushed?" he challenged. "For nearly twenty years of men the Braolauch shi has been without its sworn keeper, who we now know to be dead; and the young Watcher lost to Aes Sidhe. Dunvegan faces a massive assault by Clan MacDonald, and you know as well as I that only the Keeper or the Watcher can unfurl the flag and raise it for Clan MacLeod."

"I do," Shalynn concurred. "Do not worry, she will come of her own need. Her love for her friends will bring her back to the Isle, it will not be long, I promise you."

"See that she does Shalynn, and see that she is protected until her return to the Isle," Diancecht warned.

"She will be Grandfather. My soft horse is with her

and the sentries follow her path. They will guide her home," Shalynn assured him.

"Make sure that they do," he restated. "She is the only one who can raise the Braolauch shi, she must be protected at all costs. Bring her Shalynn, bring her back and take her to Dunvegan. Time runs short and battle draws near—make sure she is ready."

He turned his attention back to the council table, effectively dismissing her. She bowed to him respectfully and left the chamber.

Making her way up the stone staircase Shalynn saw her mother, Airmid, coming toward her. As they embraced, Airmid spoke into Shalynn's ear, "I take it he was not pleased?"

Shalynn gave her a weary smile, "No Mother, he was not. I do not know what else I can do."

Airmid released her daughter from her embrace, "You will find a way, you always do," she said reassuringly. She stepped back and looked at Shalynn from head-to-toe shaking her head, "Why do you dress for battle Shalynn? You are a healer like your grandfather, not a warrior."

"I am both, Mother. If I am needed in battle, I will go," Shalynn said in her own defense.

In truth, she much preferred her leather breaches, jerkin and boots to the flowing, silver-threaded gowns of the Fey women. It was just not Shalynn's way, a characteristic of her personality that annoyed her mother to no end.

"What will you do now?" Airmid asked.

"I will wait here for the youngling. She will come, I am sure of it." Shalynn replied. "And while I wait for her to arrive, I will make sure that those she holds so dear remain safe."

Chapter Eleven

A Touch of Magic

The three messengers, Philip, Dónal and Maitiú, trekked toward Sleat with the sea on their left and the Trotternish Ridge on their right. If everything went well, and this was a big if, they expected to cover the necessary distance in a couple of days at most.

"Philip, why do we not head along the coast road, it be relatively easy to travel?" queried Maitiú.

With a tone stained with impatience Philip snapped, "Too many people and too many eyes!"

Dónal countered, "If we stay close to the ridge the travel will be slower and we will still be seen. When we are seen, it will raise more questions and suspicions."

Maitiú added, "While more will see us we will stand out less and we can always say the great poet MacAlasdair be stayin' close to his patrons." Maitiú waived his hand high in the air as if to be a herald announcing the great warrior-poet. Philip was not amused.

"No, ya bloody gobshites, enough with yer tomfoolery. This be me country and I know it better than you. I be goin' this way! Keep up if you can!"

Dónal tried to continue the debate, "This be yer wife's country and..." But Maitiú cut him off with a wave of his hand across his throat. Dónal shrugged and he and Maitiú endeavored to keep up.

The deer and goat tracks were all they had to follow in this otherwise trackless landscape of mud, loose stones and sheep dip. Philip strode on oblivious to the terrain. When they did encounter a shepherd or farmer, Philip grunted a brief acknowledgement while Maitiú and Dónal tried to provide a more hospitable address only to rush after Philip with strained smiles and shrugs.

After a little while Dónal and Maitiú made another attempt to slow Philip down or at least make a change in their path.

"Philip, at this pace we make Sleat in a day, fer what?" Maitiú pleaded. "We'll be exhausted, hungry, thirsty, and in no shape to fight, if it comes to that."

Philip pivoted abruptly and moved in two steps to just inches from Maitiú's face, "You? You fight? Ya do nothin' but play games and sing songs. Ha! Ya bog mouse! Ya be no fightin' man. Ya have no balls for it. Ya be an Irish capon!"

That was more than Dónal could take. With his fists clenched he pushed Philip back away from his father. "I care nay who ya be, ya will nay speak to me Da in that manner!"

Maitiú grabbed Dónal by the shoulders and pulled him saying, "Easy there, boyo."

While Dónal and Maitiú were off balance, Philip seized the opportunity to push them both back, and together they fell backwards twisting to break their falls. The result was Dónal with a sprained left ankle and Maitiú with a wrenched right knee. They tried to regain their feet only to fall again in a groaning heap.

When the heat of the moment passed, Philip realized what he had done. Instead of regret, Philip, overwhelmed by his single-minded focus on Katie, looked down with disgust. "Eejits, how will ya both keep up now?"

Maitiú trembling with rage snarled, "Póg mo thóin! We will nay keep up! After all we been through together and you, ya have yer head so far up yer arse ya have to remove yer shirt to see! Go on without us and bad cess to ya!"

Philip felt only anger, disgust, and the overriding anxiety for Katie that underlined it all. He stood there briefly without words.

After a long moment of silence, Dónal, turning his head from Philip, saw an old, white nag with a sagging back standing in the opening of a stonewall where a wooden gate once stood.

"There be your soft horse gobshite!" Dónal exclaimed. "Why do ya nay ride off on that shite covered beast and be gone. Go hilfrinn leat, go to hell!"

Philip saw the horse and looked at his Irish companions lying in a soggy dip in the land. A small voice in his head told him to help them up and put them on the horse. But an even louder voice urged him to go. He opened his mouth to speak but no words came out. With no apology, he walked purposely but slowly over to the horse so as not to frighten it and, grabbing it by the mane, threw his leg over its back and rode off toward Sleat without looking back.

After a distance, beyond the sight of his friends, guilt told him to go back to help them. But his legs squeezed the horse and his heels kicked its flanks.

Between his thighs, the bony flesh of the old nag was transformed into a cool mist and he started to fly. He was flying!

"Jesus, Da, he be truly gone. What are we goin' to fookin' do?"

"Let's see, a mhic. Your left ankle and my right knee, there must be one good leg between the two. Let's bind them together for support and walk."

Dónal grinned, "That just may work. It be better than sittin' in this mucky Scottish hole waitin' to be rescued."

Once they gained their feet, legs strapped together, they tried to take a step and immediately fell backwards again.

"Ah, damnation!" Maitiú bellowed. As if on cue, rain began to pour.

"See Da, see what yer cursin' has done!" With that Dónal threw his brat over their shoulders and after one more unsteady attempt they began to stumble toward the nearest village, wherever that was.

As they staggered along they began to count in order to smooth out their rhythm and stay in step. "A haon, a dhá, a thrí, a cheithir; one, two, three, four," they said together.

A couple of lads watching over their flock of sheep heard the strange voices and ducked behind a big boulder to see what it was. To their dismay, right out of the scariest of stories they had ever heard, came a three legged, two headed giant from Éire. The giant did not see the lads and once past, the wee lads fled to find their parents.

Less than an hour of walking through the trackless rolling heather the Irish giant came across a small pond.

"Da, I could use a drink."

"Let's hope it be a spring and not a brackish pool of bog water, boyo," Maitiú replied.

When they got to the edge of the water, Maitiú farted and started laughing. "I guess Scottish food does nay agree with me."

"It does nay agree with me either, Da." With that Dónal flung off the brat and the sudden movement caused them to fall on their arses again at the side of the pond. Looking at each other they burst out in laughter as it was either that or cry.

Looking at Dónal, Maitiú said, "Well a ghrá, mo chroí, I guess we be truly fooked."

"At least we will nay be thirsty," Dónal replied after catching his breath from laughing.

Unbinding their legs, they cupped their hands and drank from the pond, the best tasting water they could remember since Ireland. Looking around, they could tell from the numerous tracks that this pond would eventually be visited by a shepherd tending his flock. They just had to wait. Dónal rooted around in his sparán looking for something to eat. He found nothing but the smooth marble stones he had picked up from the river bed near Sterling.

"I do nay know why I kept these. They seemed important at the time. We sure had fun rolling dice for them." Dónal commented.

Then absent mindlessly he began to pitch the stones into the middle of the pond. Maitiú said to his son, "Since we be in the magical isle of Skye, I be wary of throwin' stones into the pond. Ya might summon up some fairy folk that be 'round about."

"I wish we could," Dónal replied. "We could use the help. Ach, do ya really think the Fey folk would help such devout Catholics as ourselves?"

"And why would they not?" was the reply from a strong female voice that echoed from somewhere behind them. Startled, both Irishmen jumped up unsteadily and quickly crossed themselves. Turning around, they saw a young woman with dark hair, wearing a green shawl and a brown bog dress, walking toward them. She was speaking in a dialect of Gaelic they struggled to understand.

"My name is Shalynn. You need help, yes?"

Maitiú looked hard into her face and then his eyes lit up.

"I know ya. Have I nay seen ya before in the Wycked Aye? Ya be Maureen MacLeod's friend."

Recognizing Maitiú's voice, Shalynn switched to perfect Munster Irish.

"You have and I am. Please sit down, before you fall down. You would be Maitiú and this young man?" she asked turning to Dónal.

"Me son, Dónal, M'lady; how would it be we be meetin' here?" Maitiú asked as he and Dónal sat back down near the edge of the pond.

Shalynn smiled and replied, "I heard tell of a three legged, two headed, Irish giant hereabouts. I have not seen one of those in a very long time. I suppose now, that was you two? You are in need help, yes?"

Dónal looked up at her with hope in his eyes, "Shalynn, if ya be a healin' woman, we could use yer help. Me Da's knee and me own ankle are hurt pretty bad."

Shalynn knitted her brow and said, "I do have a bit of skill in that area. Let me see if I can help."

Dónal watched her closely as she came to sit down on the grass next to him and carefully began to remove his boot. She appeared to be near Maureen's age, maybe a bit younger. Her long dark hair was braided around her head and woven with ribbons. Her big, dark eyes held his gaze and he found himself staring at her, not hearing the questions she was asking him.

"Eh? I be sorry Shalynn, I did nay hear what ya asked," Dónal said.

"She asked ya if it hurts ya big oaf," Maitiú said as he smacked Dónal on the back of the head. A faint smile crossed his face when he saw a faint glimmer in his son's eyes he had not seen before.

Dónal winced a bit when his boot slid from his foot. Shalynn gently pulled his woolen sock over his foot to reveal an ankle that was swollen, dislocated and badly bruised. Although it was cold outside, her hands were warm and soft against his skin. She seemed so young and fragile, yet her manner was strong and confident. There was something about this young woman that caught his eye.

After a brief examination Shalynn said, "Lie on your stomach Dónal and bend your knee." She cupped Dónal's foot and ankle in her hands and gave a sudden thrust. There was a loud snap.

"Mary, Mother of God!" Dónal cried out and rolled over to grab his ankle. Holding it for a few seconds he said, "Shalynn, ya be brilliant!" He rolled his ankle around, right and then left. "Good as new!"

"Put it in the pond Dónal and let it rest now." Shalynn instructed.

She then looked at Maitiú who immediately said, "Oh no darlin', ya'll nay be snappin' me knee like a twig."

"No Maitiú, just slip your leg into the pond."

Maitiú removed his boot, rolled up his breaches and plunged his leg into the pond. "Jesus, Mary and Joseph, this water be cold!"

Shalynn waited until Maitiú could stand the cold no longer. When he pulled his leg from the pond, she took hold his ankle and gave a quick pull—another snap.

"I think that hurt, but I can nay feel a thing." Standing up cautiously at first, he took a few measured steps and then began to gingerly walk around. "Me knee feels grand. Goraibh míle matih agat, Shalynn. Ya be magic fer certain!"

"Well, some people may think so." Shalynn continued, "To answer your earlier question, I am here about visiting my kin. Now that your injuries are tended to, where are you off to?"

"Home," Maitiú announced. "No offense ta yer homeland Shalynn, but we've had enough of this place. We were helpin' a friend, but he turned on us. We've no further obligation to him now. How do we get home?"

Shalynn pointed toward the ocean. "You might pick up a boat back to Ireland in Portree. There are many ships there and you will find work if you need to eat."

Maitiú asked Shalynn if she would accompany them as far as the coast road and she agreed. They walked slowly as both men still had a noticeable limp to their step.

"So it be visitin' kin ya are Shalynn?" Maitiú asked. "Would ya know Sandy, Sandy MacLeod? We were just visitin' him, his wife, and bairns, as you Scots call them."

Shalynn smiled at him but did not respond. Maitiú persisted, "Were you visitin' him as well? Why did we nay see ya roundabout?"

"Oh, I was roundabout," she replied. "But I saw Sandy had guests and did not want to disturb him just then."

Maitiú shrugged. He knew she was avoiding his questions. He decided it best to simply let things be. For whatever reason, she had come to them and he was grateful for it. He didn't need to know anything more.

When they reached the coast road, fog was rolling in and Shalynn said, "It is time for a parting of the ways. I am going to Staffin and you are going to Portree."

"Shalynn, ya be careful now," Dónal said as he stepped close to her, putting his hands on her shoulders. "Staffin be full of MacDonalds and their blood be up."

"I will be careful and good journey to you both." She took both their hands in farewell and walked off. They watched as a mist began to form along the edge of the road and then she just disappeared into the fog.

The two Irishmen turned and limped their way toward Portree and, hopefully, back to Ireland, Philip be damned.

Chapter Twelve

St. Johnston

Heber and the two women left the stone house early. No one had bothered them during the night and all seemed quiet as they rode out. The journey to St. Johnston would take most of the day. At least at the end of this ride, their small company could look forward to a warm inn, a soft bed and hot food. St. Johnston would be their final stop before crossing into the lands of Badenoch and the safety of Clan Chattan.

The day's journey was filled with conversation of MacPherson family memories and visiting with others making their way along the road. As they approached their destination, one could feel the wind blowing in from the Firth of Tay.

St. Johnston was an ancient city that sat on the west bank of the River Tay in Perthia. There had been a settlement there for as long as anyone could remember.

Arriving late in the afternoon, they left Meg at the inn to secure a room for the night. Maureen and Heber took their horses and the cart to the stables for boarding.

Maureen pulled her father's sword from the cart and slipped her doe-hoofed dagger into the sheath on her belt. Heber pulled his sword from Gunnar's saddle. As he walked past Maureen, he tapped her dagger with his fingers and said, "Boot girl, put that in yer boot." She did as he asked and swung the scabbard with her father's Claymore across her back.

As they walked passed the other stalls toward the door of the stables, two draft horses caught Heber's attention. Both big Clydesdales, they were the same two horses he had seen the night before—the gallowglass

109

were here.

They had only a short distance to walk to the inn. As they came through the center of town, Maureen saw what was left of the St. John's Kirk. Once a beautiful church named for St. John the Baptist, it had been completely destroyed by John Knox and his followers. The sight of it stopped Maureen in her tracks. Heber had walked ahead of her not realizing she had stopped.

"Come along girl," he called back to her. "What be done can nay be undone."

The main hall of the inn was bustling. They found Meg and settled into their room. The women immediately poured basins of water to wash away the grime from the day's long ride.

They found Heber in the dining hall at a table to the back of the inn with his back to the wall looking out over the entire room.

"Once a chieftain, always a chieftain," Meg remarked. Heber had ordered a fine meal and they were all enjoying the food and warm fire when Heber spied a nobleman moving through the hall.

Meg knew Heber well and she knew that look on his face, "Heber, what be wrong?" she quietly asked. Maureen stopped eating and looked at his face as well.

"Seems we have company, Meg," Heber said as he shifted his glance in the direction he wanted Meg to follow.

When she spotted the man in the crowd, she gritted her teeth, "Bothwell."

Maureen was not sitting in a position to see the man Meg and Heber were watching. She started to turn around when Heber stopped her, "No lass, be still. Let's just see who the good Earl be dinin' with this night."

Heber watched as Bothwell took a seat across the hall near the fire. It was not long before the two gallowglass entered. They waited at the door, scanning the patrons and gauging the room. Heber watched as their gaze came toward them, they spotted Heber immediately.

"Damn it to hell!" Heber growled under his breath. Both women looked at Heber questioningly. "Those be the two from last night, we've been seen," he whispered.

Without thinking, Maureen turned to look in the direction of the two gallowglass. When their gaze met, the look in their eyes sent a cold chill down her spine. She felt like a rabbit, spotted by two birds of prey.

From under the table Maureen felt Heber kick her in the shin. "Ouch, M'lord that hurt," she whined as she turned back around.

"For the love of Christ girl, are ya truly that thick?" Heber snapped.

Bain and Cavan Moffet got a good look at the prize they had been sent to retrieve.

"Well, well. Would ya have a look at that," Bain said. "Seems like he's brought her right to us."

"Aye, that he did," replied Cavan. "We be takin' her on the north road on the marrow. Come now brother, let's go see the man and collect our pay."

The two men cast a snide glance in Heber's direction and then proceeded to join the Earl of Bothwell at his table.

Heber was furious with Maureen. They sat in silence finishing their meal as Heber slowly fumed. He knew the gallowglass would not waste any time in trying to take her. They knew now that he was traveling with only two women – no fight at all for two gallowglass.

After a long silence, Maureen whispered, "I be so sorry M'lord. I did nay think. I wanted to see them."

"Sorry does nay help much, does it lass? Well, ya've

111

seen them now and they have seen ya as well. I be pretty damn certain ya be seenin' 'em again, and soon," he warned. "We need to go and get some rest. We be leavin' before dawn."

They left the table and went straight to their room. Maureen started to speak to Heber, but Meg stopped her, "No more tonight lass, let it be," she warned. "Ready yerself for bed now, we nay have much time to rest."

Heber wedged a chair up against the door and weapons were placed by each of them. As they lay in their beds, Maureen whispered, "M'lord, I be truly sorry."

"I know lass," he replied. "Now go to sleep."

But sleep would not come. She reached down and felt the pouch of Rowan leaves in the pocket of her underskirt. She waited until she knew Meg and Heber were both asleep and then quietly crept from her bed. She took the basin from the washboard and filled it with water.

If she could see what the gallowglass had planned she could warn Heber. She had never tried to use her gift at her own bidding before. She took the basin to the window and cracked open the shutter. The full moon was casting a bright light across the river Tay. She pulled her pouch of Rowan leaves from her skirt pocket. Glancing back into the room, she checked to make sure the other two were still sleeping and then she dropped the leaves into the basin.

As she swirled the leaves with her fingers, they began to spin on their own. She waited, trying to relax and concentrate on the water. The leaves began to find their way to the edge of the bowl.

She saw a long road leading away from St. Johnston. A road that led to the edge of a forest and beyond that was a small loch. Just inside the perimeter of the forest sat the two gallowglass. That is where they would try to take her; that is where they would be waiting. She was just about to look away from the water when the vision began to change.

She saw Dunvegan, but this time it was inside the castle walls. People were running in chaos, soldiers were wielding weapons and fires burned all around the castle. She saw Katie running towards the gates, she was yelling for someone to come and help her. Maureen tried to see the other person, but she could not. Was it Philip? Would Philip find her?

The vision began to fade from the castle to another place, somewhere out on the moors. She did not know this place. Her heart was racing as she watched and waited. An image began to form and she saw her two dear friends, Dónal and Maitiú flat on their backs near the edge of a pool, not moving.

She put her hand to her mouth so as not to gasp out loud. She could look no more. This gift was becoming a terrible burden. She did not know how to understand what she was seeing. She hung her head in frustration, she was completely helpless. She removed the rowan leaves from the basin and tossed them out the window, then carefully and quietly placed the basin back on the washstand.

Through barely open eyes, Heber watched as she made her way back to her bed. She sat down on the edge of the bed and placed her head in her hands.

Heber raised up and said, "Tell me what ya saw girl."

Somehow, his voice did not startle her at all. She simply replied, "They wait in the forest at the end of the north road."

"Be that all that ya saw?"

"Nay M'lord, there be more," she whispered. He did not question her further. As he lay back down on his bed he simply said, "Go ta bed now, lass."

It was near midnight when the two gallowglass took their leave of St. Johnston. They had their money. Hepburn had paid them well indeed.

They came through the stables and pulled their horses from their stalls. Olaf, Gunnar and the ponies were boarded just a few stalls down. Olaf had his head over the gate to the stall and was snorting and tossing his head.

When the men passed by with their horses, Bain walked up to Olaf and grabbed him by his mane.

"Come tomorrow you and that knife carryin' little bitch will belong to me, ya black devil. Oh, we heard all about ya, and ya will nay be gettin' away with her this time."

He laughed releasing Olaf's mane and then foolishly turned his back on him. Olaf dropped his head over the stall gate and head butted the man clean off his feet.

Bain scrambled up off the ground, grabbed his own horse's reins and whipped Olaf across the face.

"Ya fookin' devil horse! If I could, I'd run ya through and eat ya fer dinner!"

"Come on now brother, quit playin' with that damn horse," Cavan said with a grin. "We need to be on our way."

Heber woke them well before dawn. They quickly gathered their belongings and left the inn. The streets of St. Johnston were dark and deserted. They moved quickly down the center of town to the stables.

As they walked through the stables, the two stalls that held the big Clydesdales were empty. Which meant the two gallowglass were gone. Heber's plan to beat the

114

two ruffians out of town was not to be had. Now they were truly the hunted.

Heber was confident that the gallowglass would not harm either Meg or him. But he was not certain he could protect his young charge from being taken.

They began to pull the horses from their stalls to hitch the cart and saddle the stallions. Olaf was very anxious and almost pushed his way out of the stall. Maureen had a hard time holding him still to saddle him up.

"Whoa boy, hold on now," she said as she tried to settle him down. She had never seen him this agitated.

With the horses ready to ride and the cart packed, Heber put his sword through the scabbard on his saddle. He then handed Maureen's single hand broadsword to Meg.

"Heber, why ya be given me this?" Meg asked nervously.

"Ya remember what I taught ya now. Ya may be needin' that," he replied.

Maureen had already sheathed her battle sword and the doe-hoofed dagger was in her belt. She struggled to mount up as Olaf danced in circles.

"Olaf, settle down now," she said sternly.

"Get a hold of that horse, girl," Heber commanded.

"I be tryin' M'lord, but somethin's got him riled for certain."

She finally got him calmed down and turned in the right direction. She reached to her chest to touch her cross for comfort and felt the medallion Shalynn had given her. Suddenly, she remembered Shalynn's words, *Should you be in need of help or shelter, let this be seen and help will find you.* She pulled the medallion from under her chemise and let it hang in full view.

And so they began their journey out of St. Johnston and down the North Road to Badenoch. What lay ahead,

115

they did not know. But it would not be long until they found out.

After about two hours of riding, they pulled the horses off the road near some trees to rest and take drink. The edge of the forest was just up ahead and they were probably being watched as they sat beneath the trees.

Being watched they were. But not from the forest up ahead. The two Fey sentries, sat comfortably on the limbs just above them waiting patiently for the right moment.

Heber sat down next to Maureen and asked, "Tell me lass, what else did ya see?"

"Katie, I saw Katie. She be inside the walls of Dunvegan. I saw her running to the gates, tryin' to get away," she said quietly.

"Be that all?" Heber pressed.

"Nay M'lord. Maitiú and Dónal, I saw them out on the moors alone, layin' flat on their backs, side-by-side near the edge of a pond, not movin'. I fear the worst has befallen them."

"Can ya say that fer certain?" Heber prodded.

Maureen shook her head, "Nay M'lord, I can nay be sure. I do nay understand all that I see as yet."

"And the gallowglass?" he asked.

"That I be sure of M'lord, just up ahead to the back of the tree line."

Heber nodded his head in understanding, gave her a pat on the knee and then got up and walked back over to the cart where Meg was waiting.

Now was their chance. As Maureen rested up against the tree trunk, the two sentries jumped down behind her. Maureen heard them hit the ground and turned to see two Fey warriors standing behind her, one with very light hair, the other dark. They both bowed respectfully to her and then stepped back behind the tree trunk.

"Greetings My Lady, my name is Fiann, and this is Séamus. If you please, turn back around and act as if you see nothing."

Maureen did as he asked and then he continued, "You signaled for help, we have come to help you. The ones who hunt you wait up ahead at the back of the forest. We shall see you through safely," Fiann explained.

She sat facing away from the tree, watching Meg and Heber as they took their rest. Who were these two men? Who sent them? Were these the eyes she had felt watching them all along? Were they to be trusted? And what of Meg and Heber, how could she ever explain the appearance of these two men?

She whispered back to them, "Master Fiann, how am I ta explain ya ta me friends?" Maureen asked.

"There will be no need My Lady, they will neither see us nor hear us. But we must move quietly through the forest. We will lead the horses, do not fear." Fiann instructed.

Maureen slightly turned her head back toward him and whispered, "Many thanks to ya Master Fiann, I be most grateful fer yer help."

"There is no need to thank us My Lady," added Séamus. "It is our honor to be called to the service of the Watcher."

The Watcher? She was puzzled by Séamus' words. But before she could question either of the Fey sentries they both vanished back up into the tree. She glanced over to Heber and Meg as they readied the cart and horses to move on. Then cast her gaze up into the tree. Shalynn must have sent them. She needed the sentries

117

help and she must trust them now.

It was not long before Heber called to her to mount up and soon they would be on their way once more.

As she pulled Olaf's reins from the cart, Heber came to her side, "I do nay know what will happen in the forest lass, but you and Olaf should be ready to run, ya hear me now?" he warned.

"The way Olaf's been feelin' today, I do nay think that will be a problem M'lord. But there be no need ta worry over it." She glanced up to the trees and smiled, "We have help."

Heber looked to the trees and then back to Maureen with a questioning glance.

"Trust me M'lord," she said. "If we move quietly through the forest, we be fine. They will nay see us."

Heber looked back up to the trees as he spoke, "Just the same, keep yer weapons close and be ready to run." He walked over to Gunnar and mounted up, casting another cautious glance into the trees.

Meg was aboard the cart and had the ponies on their way. Maureen swung up into her saddle and headed Olaf toward the boundary of the forest.

As they passed under the first grouping of trees, down from the branches dropped Fiann and Séamus, landing on the back of each of the ponies. The two Connemaras, Hope and Grace, startled but just for a moment. They seemed quite at home with the two sentries on their backs. Heber and Meg did not notice a thing.

Olaf immediately trotted up next to Fiann. The sentry reached over and patted Olaf on the neck and whispered, "Hello my old friend, it is good to see you once more."

Fiann turned to Maureen, "tell them to be quiet now My Lady and to drop their reins."

118

She turned back to Heber, "We must be quiet now, drop your reins and let the horses go."

He did not question her directions. They all let their reins rest and the two sentries began to lead their company through the forest.

The gallowglass had been sitting in the forest for hours.

"Where the bloody hell can they be?" asked Bain.

"Do ya think they stayed in St. Johnston brother?" replied Cavan.

"I can nay say, they should 'a been here by now."

He got up and walked back to another tree to relieve himself.

A few moments later, Cavan heard the sounds of hooves coming down the forest road. He picked up a rock and threw it at his brother, hitting him square in the back.

"Shake it off boyo, they be comin'," he yelled at Bain.

The two men moved quickly and quietly, readying their horses and weapons. They lay silently in waiting, behind a thick cluster of brush and trees listening to the sound of hooves drawing closer and closer.

Their mounts were well trained war horses and they stayed completely still waiting for their rider's single kick to send them running.

Their dogs lay on the ground patiently waiting for the horses to advance.

But when the sound of hooves made its way into the clearing, all the two gallowglass saw was a small herd of cattle lazily moving through the forest.

Bain was completely gobsmacked and sat up straight and tall in his saddle, giving away their position.

"What the bloody hell be this now?" he yelled.

Maureen turned quickly to Heber and Meg, putting a finger to her lips signaling them not to speak.

Both Fiann and Séamus were poking each other and quietly laughing, taking great pleasure in their trickery and enjoying the confusion of the two humans.

"Where the fook are they?" Bain cursed.

"They must 'a stayed in town brother, or gone another way," reasoned Cavan.

"There be no other way, ya amadan! This be the only road north to Badenoch," Bain snapped at his brother. "They must have stayed. Come on boyo, we be headin' back to St. Johnston."

And with that, they kicked their steads into action and headed south out of the forest and back down the forest road.

Fiann and Séamus continued their mirage for a bit longer until it was clear that the men were not coming back.

Meg was the first to break the silence, "Oh dear God, what a relief," she exclaimed. Why did they ride off like that Heber, 'twas like they never saw us at all?

Maureen cast a faint smile in Heber's direction and turned back to the sentries. Fiann motioned to Maureen to pick up her reins. As she did, Heber and Meg followed suit.

"Will we reach Badenoch this day M'lord?" Maureen asked.

"Nay lass, not this day," Heber replied. "This night we shall rest at the home of an old friend. Tomorrow we shall reach Badenoch and the manor house of the MacPhersons."

"Ah, home at last," added Meg.

"You are safe now My Lady," said Fiann. "The road ahead is clear of danger. You may rest easy. We will ride

120

with you to the next grove of trees and then we will leave you to your journey. Hide the medallion – use it only when you are in great need. Should you need us, we will come." Séamus nodded his head in agreement.

Maureen did not speak, but slightly bowed her head to them in thanks and then tucked the medallion back under her chemise and out of sight.

They picked up their pace and soon approached a grove of trees surrounding the entrance to Loch Tay. As they passed under the first few branches, Fiann and Séamus stood up on the backs of the Connemaras preparing to depart up into the trees.

"Fare thee well, My Lady," said Séamus. "We shall meet again." In a flash they were gone.

As they rode on, Maureen kept looking back to the trees behind them. Heber watcher her as she anxiously kept looking back.

"What be wrong lass?" he questioned.

She wanted desperately to speak with the two sentries once more. "M'lord, if ya please, go on ahead without me, I be right back I promise ya." And with that, she turned Olaf and kicked him into a gallop back to the edge of the trees.

She jumped down and walked frantically under the branches calling quietly up into the trees, "Fiann, Séamus, are ya still here?"

They appeared from behind a tree nearby and walked up to her, "What is it My Lady?" asked Fiann.

"Before ya go Master Fiann tell me, who sent ya?" she asked

The two men looked at each other and then Séamus replied, "Lady Shalynn of the High Council."

"So, 'tis Shalynn that ya serve?" Maureen questioned.

Both men bowed gracefully to her as Fiann replied, "We are the Sentries to the Fáidh of the Tuatha. We serve the Watchers; we have always served the

Watchers."

In a brief flash of light, the two men vanished up into the trees. They were gone. Maureen leaned her head back and let out a deep breath in exasperation. "Aahh, bloody arse fairies!"

She turned to Olaf and put her arms around his neck and held him close. "Oh Olaf, what would I do without ya. I feel like a bloody puppet bein' passed from hand-to-hand. I do nay know what be goin' on here me beauty, but I know one thing for certain, we must go to Skye. Will ya take me there me old friend?" She whispered.

The great horse laid his head on her back and nudged her to his chest. She leaned up against him for a few moments. "I knew ya would," she said as she patted him on his chest. "Come, let us catch up with the others. Our day's travel be not yet done. We will go to Badenoch as our master wishes, and then me beauty, we be goin' ta Skye."

Chapter Thirteen

The Halls of Clan Chattan

Heber sat quietly before a warm hearth in his own home, on his own land. And although his journey was over and he was back in his family's home, the home where he planned to spend the rest of his days, something was missing, and that was Fionnula.

He had sent his missive to his beloved wife a few days before his departure from the Wycked Aye Tavern. Surely by now Fionnula would have received it and would be on her way back to him.

Meg entered the great room with mugs of tea and whisky. "Good to be home, eh?" she asked.

Heber took a sip from his cup, "Aye Meg, 'tis indeed."

A silence fell between them as they sat before the fire, each consumed in their own thoughts. Meg sensed Heber's melancholy and knew something was troubling him.

"Troubled are ya, Heber?" she quietly asked. He did not answer, but continued to sit watching the flames of the fire. Seeing that he would prefer to be one with his thoughts, she decided to retire to her own chamber and got up to leave the room. She placed a comforting hand on his shoulder saying, "Do nay worry cousin, she will come home."

Heber watched as Meg left the room. Drawing a long deep breath, he laid his head back against the high-backed chair, trying to clear his mind, for troubled had been his heart of late.

They had just arrived in Badenoch and now he wanted desperately to travel to Invernlochy and wait there for Fionnula to arrive. He did not want to spend another day in this house without her.

But his longing for his woman was not all that

weighed heavy on his mind.

He was feeling uneasy over the vision his young charge had shared with him. Maitiú MacRoibeard de Faoite and his son, Dónal were loyal and trusted friends. These Irishmen had been fully prepared to journey halfway around the world on Heber's behalf to bring him home. Was Maureen's vision true? And if it was, then somehow the Irishmen and MacAlasdair had become separated. Maitiú and Dónal were strangers to Skye, and Heber could not just leave the lads to their fate with a clan war brewing. But he could not make such a journey alone, nor could he involve clan MacPherson in a dispute that had nothing to do with them.

Though Heber wanted to believe Maureen, he was uncertain about her gift. She had been right about the gallowglass in the forest, but what about the other visions? Was she right about them as well?

The girl was his charge, his responsibility. He brought her here to protect her. She was adamant that the Irishmen would need her help to see their journey through and return home safely. If she was right, keeping her from going to Skye could cost the Irishmen their lives. Should he force her stay, or let her go? He took another sip of his tea and whisky, contemplating his options. It was getting late and the fire was dying down when Maureen entered the room to bid Heber goodnight.

She came at the end of the day to sit with Heber and talk for a bit before retiring to her room. Being at the manor house was not like working at the tavern. She much preferred the hustle and bustle of the tavern to being a chambermaid. She did not like being inside all day and longed for the open air. She had not been riding with Olaf since they arrived and she missed him.

But most of all she missed William. She longed to

hear his voice and feel his arms around her. But she knew she would see him again. When all this was behind her, she could go home to William.

Heber took his feet from the footstool and scooted it next to his chair so she could sit with him before the dwindling fire.

She took her seat next to him, leaning forward and reaching her hands toward to warmth of the hearth.

Heber could sense her unhappiness; it was not what he wanted for her. He reached over and put his hand on her shoulder. He could feel the bones of her shoulders beneath her chemise. She was not as strong as she pretended to be. She was slight of build and not as tall as most women. How she had ever survived on her own for so long was beyond him. If he could, he would take her back to Dunbartonshire and match her to young Macaulay. Macaulay would see to her happiness and keep her safe, but that would have to wait.

"Ya seem tired lass, how was yer day?" Heber asked.

"Chores of the household seem to be never endin' M'lord. Meg be a fine mistress, but I miss the open air," she replied.

"Well, I believe I can do a little somethin' about that." Heber teased.

Maureen turned to face him waiting with great anticipation.

"I've decided to journey to Invernlochy. Ya know I sent word to Fionnula before we left the Wycked Aye. She should be arrivin' anytime now, would ya be willin' to accompany me lass?"

Maureen's heart jumped for joy, "Oh aye M'lord, I would fer certain."

"And on the marrow, let's take the horses out for a ride, shall we?" he added.

She knew it was not her place, but she could not help herself. She gave Heber a big hug and placed a kiss upon his cheek.

"Thank ya M'lord, thank ya," she said.

"Off ya go ta yer chamber now, lass," Heber directed. "Sleep well me girl."

She leaned over and placed another kiss upon his forehead. He watched as she left the room with a lightness to her step that she did not have when she came in. A smile crossed the big man's face for his little, green-eyed wildcat had truly found a place in his heart. He loved the girl as if she was his own, and he would not allow any harm to come to her. Taking her with him to Inverlochy was much safer than leaving her at house MacPherson. It would not take long for Bothwell's gallowglass to find their way to Badenoch.

On the marrow he would take her to the Halls of Clan Chatton and present her as a MacPherson.

As they rode along, it became clear to Maureen that Heber had a destination in mind and this was not a simple ride through the woods.

"M'lord, where we be goin'?" she asked.

"To the Halls of Chattan, the manor house of Lachlan Mackintosh, Chief of Clan Chattan." Heber explained. "I be in need of his counsel and I wish ta present ya ta the Chiefs of the Confederacy as me ward and heir."

Maureen was mortified. She was not dressed properly to be presented to anyone. She was in her riding clothes and boots, not her good Sabbath skirts and bodice. But there was nothing she could do about that now.

"What be the matter ya seek counsel for M'lord?" She asked as she brought Olaf up next to him.

Heber looked across at her. "The vision ya had of our

126

Irish friends be weighin' heavy on me mind girl. They be true and loyal men and we can nay just leave them on a strange Isle in the middle of clan war now can we?"

Maureen was gobsmacked, "Will ya be askin' fer men ta go ta Skye, M'lord?"

"I be asking fer counsel lass, nothin' more," he cautioned.

Maureen brought Olaf to a halt. Was he actually considering going to Skye after Maitiú and Dónal? She did not want to jump to any conclusions, but she could not help herself from entertaining the possibility of Heber going with her to Skye.

Heber saw she had stopped and turned to urge her along.

It was not long before Maureen could see the manor house of Lachlan Mackintosh. They turned the horses onto a long, stone carriageway that led up to the main house. A massive stone pond sat before the entrance to the manor.

Footmen met them as they dismounted and took their horses to a nearby fenced pasture.

Maureen looked around at the beauty of this fine manor. Gardens surrounded the house with trees all dressed in their autumn colors. The pond in the middle of the carriageway contained huge statues of two rampant lions. Never had she seen such a magnificent place.

Heber looked back to see her gazing about at the wealth and grandeur before her.

"Come along lass," he called to her.

She turned and followed him up the steps, brushing the dust from her skirts and trying to make herself as presentable as possible.

They were ushered through a long passageway by the house mistress.

"Wait here sir, if ya please," she said as she directed

Heber to a long couch upholstered in rich, deep green velvet. She did not look or speak to Maureen. It was clear to her that Maureen was nothing more than Heber's servant girl, and not worth her recognition. She went through two double doors, leaving them to wait.

Heber motioned for Maureen to come and sit next to him, but she nervously shook her head from side-to-side, no. Her skirts were covered in horsehair and dusty from the ride. She did not want to be held responsible for soiling a fine piece of furniture. She had been severely punished by the mistress of the Armstrong household for the very same thing and would not make that mistake again. She stood behind the couch, next to where Heber sat and waited.

Finally, the house mistress returned. Heber stood up to follow her into the great hall. As he motioned for Maureen to follow, the house mistress stopped him.

"Only you, sir," she instructed. "Yer servant girl can wait."

"It be alright lass, I will nay be long," he said trying to put Maureen at ease.

She watched as they entered the great hall and the door closed behind them. She stood for a moment, staring blankly at the closed doors. Within a few minutes, the house mistress emerged and began to walk back down the hallway. After a few steps she turned back to Maureen and said, "Do nay let me find ya sittin' on any of the furniture, wench."

Lachlan Mackintosh sat on a fine couch before a grand hearth with two other men seated in large leather chairs.

There were two purposes to Heber's meeting with these men of Clan Chattan. One was to gain protection for his young ward against the Armstrong Clan. The other was to see if the Confederacy would approve of a journey to Skye on behalf of the two Irishmen.

As Heber approached the small council, Lachlan rose to greet him. They joined forearms and patted each other on the back as men do.

"MacPherson, good ta see ya home and well old boy. I see our ten gold sovereigns to bring ya home was successful," Lachlan said. "What brings ya to us this day?"

The mention of the confederacy's funding of ten gold sovereigns on Heber's behalf was a subtle reminder that he was already indebted to the council and to ask more at such an early stage would not be looked upon kindly.

Heber began telling the men of how young Mistress MacLeod came to the tavern and his taking her as his ward. He told them of the killing of old Ian Armstrong and Robert MacLeod, and the vengeance of Armstrong's son, Logan. He spoke of the clan war brewing on Skye and of his desire to help his trusted Irish friends who had been abandoned on the Isle. When he finished, he stood silent waiting for the men to respond.

"Come Heber, take a chair and pour yerself a wee dram," Lachlan said.

As Lachlan began to discuss the situation with the other two men, Heber took a chair near the hearth and listened.

It was then that he realized there was one very important fact he had failed to make privy to the council, and that was the involvement of James Hepburn, Fifth Earl of Bothwell and the Lord High Sheriff of Scotland.

"Lachlan," Heber interrupted. "There be one more thing ya need ta know. The gallowglass sent to take the girl were paid fer their services by the Earl of Bothwell."

The mood of the room changed immediately. All three men sat up in their seats and faced Heber. "Ya be sure of this MacPherson?" Lachlan pressed.

"Aye, I be certain of it; watched 'em meet with the good Earl at the inn in St. Johnston to gather their wages." Heber confirmed.

"What the bloody hell would the Lord High Sheriff care about a worthless servant girl?" asked one of the other men.

"I can nay say," Heber replied. He lied, he had no choice. He knew exactly what Bothwell and Logan wanted.

The men excused themselves from Heber's presence and moved to the back of the hall. It did not take long for them to come to a decision. Before they returned to Heber, Lachlan sent one of his footmen out of the room.

"The Confederacy will nay take a position against the Lord High Sheriff, MacPherson, and we can nay back a campaign into the middle of a clan war on Skye." Lachlan announced. "If ya be choosin' to venture to the Isle, ya go of yer own accord."

The doors to the great room opened and the footman returned with Maureen following behind him. He walked her up in front of the men and pointed to a spot where she should stand.

Lachlan looked her over and then turned to Heber. "How can it be that such a waif of a woman-child can cause so much trouble."

Heber rose from his chair by the hearth and stood next to Maureen.

"I believe I be throwin' this little wench back MacPherson." Lochlan said. "She be too small to keep. Get yerself one with a pretty face who can fill out a bodice better than this one."

Lochlan and the other men began to laugh at her. Heber saw Maureen lower her eyes and drop her head, humiliated by harsh and careless words from an arrogant man of higher station. He could tell Lachlan's words had stung like a whip.

130

"This young woman be no servant of me household Lachlan, and I will nay have her addressed in such a manner." Heber growled. "She be me charge, me ward. She be Maureen MacLeod MacPherson—me daughter."

It was as if time had stopped. Maureen raised her eyes to Heber and he met them with a smile. Daughter, he had called her his daughter. It was a moment of happiness she had never known before.

Heber put his hands on her shoulders, "Go now lass, wait fer me outside. We be on our way very soon."

She obediently bowed her head to him and turned to leave the room without any acknowledgment to Lachlan Mackintosh or the other men of the council. They did not matter and she cared not what they thought of her.

The footman saw her to the main door and closed it firmly behind her the moment she was out of the way. She walked halfway down the great steps, turned and stuck her tongue out at the closed door behind her, then wandered across the carriageway to the pond. Taking a seat at the edge, she stared into the water watching the reflections of the trees and clouds above as they seemed to float across the pond. She reached her fingertips into the water and gave a leaf floating by a little push. The water was cool and crystal clear. She put her hand back into the pond and began to sweep the water around the edge.

The water began to move. Not by her hand, but on its own. Faster and faster it went until the entire pond was swirling like a maelstrom. She laid out on her belly across the edge of the pond and reached both hands deep into the water.

"Show me, show me," she whispered. "What do ya want me to see?"

The water cleared and the entire pond became a looking glass under the watchful eyes of the stone lions.

She saw a merchant ship full of warriors armed for

131

battle. Before them stood a tall, thin man with flaming red hair. In one hand he held a long bow, in the other a sword. He was clearly their leader that much she could tell. But who was he?

The image began to change. Dunvegan Castle materialized across the pond. A great battle was going on. Many dead lay upon the grounds of the castle.

The tall, red haired man was standing at the castle entrance holding a flag of sorts and waiving it above his head.

This was the clearest vision she had ever had. But where were Maitiú and Dónal? She did not realize she was speaking out loud when she asked, "Maitiú, me dear friend, where are ya?"

She pushed her hand through the water and waited for it to clear. There, there they were, running through the gate at Dunvegan and away from the castle. She saw them run down a long gravel road, and under an old stone bridge covered in moss and ivy heading toward the edge of the forest.

Suddenly, Maitiú fell to ground, his legs crumbling underneath him. She watched as Dónal came to his father's side. She saw him looking back to the stone bridge. There, standing on the bridge stood the tall, red haired man with bow in hand.

Maureen yelled at the water, "Nooo!" She took her hands and splashed away the vision from the pond for she could not bear to see any more. She slapped at the water, angry at the painful sight it had revealed to her.

When Heber emerged from the Halls of Clan Chattan, he found her weeping by the side of the pond, her cloths soaking wet. He sat down beside her, pulling her to him, "What is it girl, what be wrong."

"Our friends be in grave danger M'lord and we be powerless to help them," she said as she buried her face against him.

"Fetch our horses!" Heber barked to the footmen. "Come lass, we have plans to make."

He helped her up on to Olaf's back and they rode like the wind back to house MacPherson.

Chapter Fourteen

Invernlochy

Maureen did not speak any further of the vision in the pond. She had told Heber everything she had seen when they returned to house MacPherson from the Halls of Clan Chattan.

One thing that concerned Heber was the red haired man. He questioned Maureen again and again as to any more details she could recall about him. But there was nothing more she could tell him.

Maureen had other concerns and she was troubled by this vision, for she had not called her gift and she had not used the leaves of the great Rowan tree to awaken the water. Her gift was changing and she needed help understanding it. She needed Shalynn.

Heber had been busy preparing for the journey to Invernlochy. It seemed to Maureen that he had abandoned the quest to Skye and had chosen not to challenge the wishes of the Confederacy. How could he leave Maitiú and Dónal when he knew they were in danger?

Maureen's mind would not rest. She was consumed by a driving need to get to Skye. She knew in her heart that she must go to Maitiú and Dónal. She must meet Shalynn at the pools of Dunbrittle as Shalynn had instructed, and then make her way to Dunvegan Castle.

Her plans were set firm in her mind, for she too had been preparing for the journey. She would travel with Heber and stay with him until they met Fionnula. But she would not return with them to house MacPherson. From Invernlochy she would take Olaf and make her way to Skye.

For the next few days, Maureen struggled to get through her daily chores. Her anxiety over Maitiú and Dónal grew with every passing moment. But one thing bothered her more than anything else, where was Philip? How had the three of them become separated? And why had she not seen him or Katie? Were they together and safe? Was she only seeing those that were in danger? She had so many questions.

"I be speakin' to ya lass, what ya be doin' standin' out here?" She suddenly realized that she was standing in the middle of the second floor hallway and someone was speaking to her.

Meg snapped at her, "Stop yer day dreamin' and get to it girl."

She did not know how long she had been standing there, but she quickly regained herself and went on about her chores.

That night she met with Heber and Meg for their evening meal and joined them before the hearth to talk of their journey to come.

"How long will ya be gone Heber?" Meg asked.

"I can nay say fer certain Meg."

In truth, Heber was not completely sure Fionnula would even be coming into Invernlochy.

"How will ya find her Heber? Do ya nay think that if she be in Invernlochy she would 'a sent word by now?" Meg questioned.

"I can nay explain it Meg, but I feel she be there soon. Fionnula always had a way about her ya know. If she has nay already arrived, she will be there very soon." He said. "I know she will."

Maureen had been quietly listening and could hold her tongue no longer, "And what of the Irishmen?"

"If ya be thinkin' I be givin' up on our two lads, ya be mistaken lass. We be doin' what we can once we get to Invernlochy."

He could see the relief on her face as she gave him a weak smile. The fire was burning down as they bid each other good night.

As Maureen made her way to her chamber she thought to herself, two more days, just two more days and they would be on their way to Invernlochy, and then to Skye.

Heber had the fine carriage readied for the trip. The weather was changing and making the journey in an open cart would not be safe or comfortable by any means. After all, this was Autumn in Scotland and it rained more often than not.

They would be leaving on the marrow. Heber was filled with anticipation of seeing his beloved Fionnula once more and Meg was busy readying the manor house for her arrival.

Maureen took Olaf out for a ride early that afternoon. Ever since Fiann and Séamus had met them on the north road to Badenoch, the great horse had become more and more restless. She had trouble holding him still to saddle him, he seemed agitated and he just wanted to run.

After a bit of a ride, she brought him up to the edge of the river Spey and dismounted. She walked up and put her arms around his neck, "I know where ya want to go me beauty, I want to go there too. But ya must be patient a bit longer. We be on our way soon; I promise ya."

They walked along the river bank for a while and then made their way back to house MacPherson.

That evening in her chamber as she lay awake in her bed, her thoughts went to William. Closing her eyes, she reached back in her mind to try and feel his touch once more, to remember the warmth of him.

She sat up in her bed, looking around her chamber. Other than her bed, a washstand and a small table, the only other item in her room was her small trunk. It held very little for she had placed most of her belongings in her saddlebags. Her swords were leaning up against the trunk, ready to go. She had no idea what lay ahead. As she laid back down she whispered to herself, "I be home soon William, I promise."

Heber was waiting by the carriage with Collin, one of the stablemen, when Maureen rode up on Olaf. It was a cold, damp morning. She was dressed in her leather riding dress and wrapped in her cloak. Heber walked up to meet her and took Olaf by the bridle for it appeared he had no intention of stopping.

"What this be about lass?" He asked as he looked Olaf over. He could plainly see that her saddlebags were pack and her blades were sheathed. He could see her father's claymore slung across her back beneath her cloak.

He knew then that her mind was made up. He could no longer hold her or protect her. Her path was set.

"Ya never know where the road might lead, M'lord," she replied.

Heber did not reply, he simply nodded his head to her, released Olaf's bridle and took his place on the carriage.

"Well then lass, let's be seein' where this old road

takes us," he said.

He gave Collin a nod and he snapped the reins, putting the horses in motion. Maureen gave Olaf a little nudge and together they began their trip to Invernlochy.

They arrived in the quaint little harbor in the late afternoon. They secured the horses and carriage, and found lodging at a small inn near the docks.

The loch was covered in fog and the quay was clear of any ships. They made their way to a tavern nearby. It was nothing like the Wycked Aye. It was a stone building with low beamed ceilings and a single hearth. The tables were long plank tables with benches to sit on. The tops of the tables were rough and sticky from spilled ale and food. It was smoky from the fire and dimly lit with only a few scatter lanterns and candles. Heber immediately began asking for Fionnula. But no one had seen her or knew of anyone waiting at the inn.

Collin took his leave and made his way down to the docks to listen to news from the deckhands. Maureen and Heber found a place at a table near the hearth and were brought bread, ale and bowls of fish chowder.

She sipped her ale and nibbled at the bread. As she pushed her spoon around in the bowl of chowder, a gruff, heavy set woman stopped next to the table. Her sleeves were rolled up above her elbows and her soiled apron was tied high over her full belly. Her kerchief was loose and her greying auburn hair stuck out in every direction. When Maureen saw her she thought how Chieftain Sara would never allow such a presentation in the Wycked Aye.

"Ya do nay like yer soup lass?" she barked. Before Maureen could answer Heber interjected.

"She just be a bit tired from our travels. We thank ya

fer yer hospitality and this fine meal. Would ya be so kind as ta bring us both a wee dram of yer finest?" He asked.

Maureen looked questioningly at Heber as the woman went off to the bar.

"Whisky lass, one thing this place be know fer be whisky." He explained.

The woman returned with the whisky and poured them each a small cup. She gave Maureen another glance that suggested she damn well better eat the chowder, then she left them alone at the table.

"Now, swallow down that chowder lass," Heber directed.

Maureen rolled her eyes at him like a temperamental child and said, "But M'lord, it be horrible."

"I know," he replied. "That be why we have the whisky."

They choked down their meal and then sipped on their whisky.

Maureen put her hand to her mouth, "I believe I'm goin' ta retch."

Heber chuckled at her and said, "Come lass, we need ta get some sleep."

They headed back to the inn and met Collin along the way.

"What did ya find out lad?" Heber asked.

"Two ships due in M'lord, one on the marrow, the other the day after. One from Ireland, one from England," Collin reported.

"Well done, well done Collin," Heber said as he patted him on the shoulder and handed the man two schillings for his task. "Have yerself a fine evenin', boyo. Check in on the marrow won't ya?"

"Many thanks, M'lord," Collin said with a smile as he tossed the coins in his hand.

Heber and Maureen returned to their rooms for the

evening. Maureen changed to her chemise and took her rosary from the pocket of her underskirt.

As she knelt on the floor, her room lit only by the light of single candle, her thoughts were with Maitiú, Dónal and Philip as she prayed the rosary. She asked the blessed virgin to bring Fionnula to Heber safely. Finally, she asked God to watch over Katie and keep her safe from harm.

She curled up in bed and pulled the covers tightly around her. She thought of William and longed to feel the warmth of his body and lay in the comfort of his arms.

Tomorrow she would start asking her own questions of the local folk and deckhands on how to get from Invernlochy to Skye.

Heber lay awake in his bed. His body wanted desperately to rest, but his mind would not let it. He was excited at the news of the ship from Ireland. There was a good chance Fionnula would be on it. But if she was not, how long could he wait? If Fionnula did not arrive, should he stay and wait, or go on to Skye? He knew full well that Maureen would not wait much longer. He could sense the urgency in her manner.

Her last vision had caused Heber great concern. For if the red-haired man she saw was who he thought he was, then trouble lay ahead for them all.

Sorely Boy MacDonald was a powerful clan leader and had a strong influence with clan MacDonald. And although he was brash, careless and impulsive, his campaigns on behalf of his clan had been mostly successful. Bloody, but successful. The man was ruthless to say the least.

Maitiú and Sorley Boy had a bit of a history between them, bad blood for certain. Maitiú had shared that story with Heber after he and Philip had returned from their last trip to Skye. Maitiú swore he would never go back to the Isle.

Heber rolled over and pulled his bed covers up around him. Everything hinged on Fionnula for now. He would sleep and see what the marrow would bring.

They woke the next morning to rain on the rooftops. It was cold, wet and dreary. Maureen dressed in her leather bog dress, one chemise, one underskirt and a warm knitted wrap that Katie made for her. It would be a day of sitting by a warm fire, letter writing, needle work and conversation.

It was mid-morning when they hurried through the rain to the tavern for their morning meal. The rashers of pork, eggs and cheese were far more satisfying than the fish chowder from the night before.

Maureen sat with pen and parchment, working on a missive to Chieftain Sara at the Wycked Aye. It was just before eleven and already the tavern was busy with deckhands and dock workers staying out of the rain and waiting for the ship to arrive from Ireland.

It was not until just past noon when the call came from the docks, "Ship on the loch!" The workers quickly downed their ales and headed for the dock.

Heber immediately sprang to his feet with excitement. Maureen watched as he fumbled with his brat and hurried to pay for his food and ale.

"Stay here lass where it be warm and dry. No need fer ya to be waitin' out in the rain," he said as he threw his brat around his shoulders.

He gave her two schillings to pay for whatever she needed in his absence and then flew out the door to the docks. Maureen watched him hurry out the door and pass by the tavern windows. She hoped he would not return disappointed. He seemed so confident. Somehow he knew she was coming. Fionnula always had a way about her, she had her own kind of magic.

Heber stood under an overhang from a small storage shed just near the end of the dock. He could see the tall sails of the ship coming up the loch through the rain and the mist. It sailed silently across the loch with only the occasional sound of water lapping against the hull. As it neared the quay, deckhands began scurrying about dropping canvas and securing lines. Finally, Heber heard the order to drop anchor and the vessel slowed to a halt.

He watched anxiously as the ship was secured and the dock workers raised up the gangplank to begin unloading the ship.

For over an hour Heber watched as barrels of ales, bags of wheat and barley, and bolts of textiles were unloaded from the vessel. In between the runs of cargo, passengers made their way to the docks as well. When it appeared that no one else would be coming off the ship, he turned to head back to the tavern, pulling his cloak over his head and tight around him. As he passed by the gangplank a voice called out from the top of the ship.

"Will ya not wait fer me husband?" Fionnula said.

He turned to see her standing on the deck of the ship next to a small trunk.

"I do nay believe I can carry this trunk all by meself," she added.

Heber bolted up the gangplank and took her in his arms.

"God love ya woman, I been lost without ya," he said.

Fionnula cupped his face in her hands, "I thought I lost ya Heber." She said as tears of joy began to flow. "I thought I lost ya."

A deckhand came up to them and gave the trunk a kick with his foot, "Ya goin' ta be movin' that trunk?"

"Come wife, let's get out of the good lad's way and out of this rain."

Maureen had finished her letter long ago and had grown restless just sitting in the tavern. She found herself a tray and began helping out serving ale and food. As she moved from table to table she casually mentioned her traveling to Skye and asked of any news of the clan war.

The old woman who had served them the night before grabbed her by the arm and pulled her aside, "Listen here now girl, ya be careful who ya be talkin' to about the trouble on Skye." She lowered her voice and leaned closer. "There be a band of MacDonalds gatherin' here. They be waitin' on that Irish ship comin' in today fer passage to Armdale. Mind yerself now, ask no more questions." She pushed Maureen away, "Go now and wait fer yer master by the fire."

As Maureen turned to walk away, the old woman called her back, "If ya be set on getting' to Skye lass, go north by land to Glenelg. Stay off the ships."

Maureen could see that the old woman was not as harsh and gruff as she appeared. In a few seconds the old woman had given her the information she had been fishing for. She thanked her for her advice and then went to wait by the fire.

It was late afternoon when Heber and Fionnula returned to the tavern. When Maureen saw them come

143

through the door she could not believe her eyes. How in the world did he know she would be there? It was a bloody miracle. And though the weather was wet and miserable, their faces were filled with love and joy. Maureen hurried to the door to greet her. They embraced each other with tears streaming down their faces.

She looked as beautiful as Maureen remembered. Her red hair was neatly braided as always and her blue eyes were sparkling. They held each other until Heber said, "Come on now wife, let's get ya settled and then we can all warm up by the fire and catch up."

Maureen returned to the table by the fire. As she sat waiting for their return she came to realize that she was at a crossroad. Now there would be no delay in returning to Badenoch. Maureen knew that Heber would not venture on to Skye. With Fionnula home, he would not leave her now. She remembered the day at the tavern when Heber told her and Sara that he was done fighting other people's battles, it was why he returned to Badenoch in the first place.

From here, she would be on her own. She knew that now, and she believed Heber knew it too. Time was running short and she suddenly found herself torn between following her plan to go on to Skye and leaving Heber and Fionnula behind.

In the few hours they spent together at the tavern, Maureen felt as if her family had finally been realized. Heber had taken her as his own, the three of them were now a family.

Having Fionnula back in her life filled a place in her heart that had been empty for such a long time. Each of them had been longing for the other in different ways. Now they were together. They were complete, they were happy.

As they ate their evening meal they talked of Fionnula's journey, the manor house at Badenoch and the plans to leave promptly on the marrow.

They did not speak of Heber's disappearance or the horrors he suffered in Morocco. They did not speak of the troubles with clan Armstrong. Those were conversations for another time, a private time between Heber and Fionnula.

They returned to the inn and retired to their own rooms. As Maureen lay in her bed, a sick feeling rolled through her body and this time it was not due to bad fish chowder. This was uncertainty and fear. She did not know if she had the strength or courage to follow the road that had been placed before her, and she truly feared what she may find on Skye. She placed her hand to her chest and pulled the Fey medallion from beneath her chemise. As she ran her fingers across the silver medallion, she knew what she must do. She needed help and she knew just where to find it.

The storm passed during the night, and although the weather was still cold and damp, at least it was not raining. The sun was doing its best to break through, casting occasional burst of light through the breaks in the clouds, but the remaining clouds and fog seemed to be winning the battle.

Collin was waiting in the common room of the inn when Heber came down the hallway to meet him. Together they headed to the livery to harness the carriage and prepare to leave Invernlochy.

"It should nay take long to get the horses ready M'lord. We be on our way by mid-morn me thinks," Collins said. "I fear the roads may be a bit sloppy after the storm, could be a bit of a slow journey."

Before Heber could reply they heard the sound of men speaking and shuffling about just up ahead near one of the dock sheds. Heber put his hand to Collin's shoulder to stop him.

"Wait up lad, wait up," Heber cautioned. They stepped to one side of the road and casually leaned up against the side of a building and waited.

Within a few moments a large group of twenty or more men came out from one of the storage shelters at the dock. They were fully armed with swords, bows and targes. Dressed in leather armored chest plates, they headed directly for the Irish ship at the dock.

Heber turned to Collin, "Do ya know who they be Collin," he asked.

Collin turned his head away from the marching warriors and whispered, "Aye M'lord, they be MacDonalds bound fer Sleat on the Isle. Overheard a few 'em spoutin' off last night after a few too many ales.

"Come on, boyo. Let's get the horses harnessed and get the hell out of here. I do nay need to be snatched on to another ship headed fer nothin' but trouble," Heber replied.

The men waited until the MacDonald warriors had made their way onto the quay, then hurried past them and on to the stables.

When they opened the stalls for Hope and Grace, the two Connemaras were anxious and fidgety. The men managed to get them harnessed in short order and the carriage was ready to go.

But when Collin opened Olaf's stall the great stallion was almost uncontrollable. He headed immediately for the end of the stable and tried to push his way out through the doors. It took both men to corner him and get him saddled. But neither one of them could get a bit in his mouth and bridle him. He simply would not have it.

"Stay here with him Collin," Heber directed. "I be goin' ta get Maureen, maybe she can handle him."

When Heber came to her room, Maureen grabbed her cloak and immediately went to her beloved stallion.

Heber was right, the great horse was frantic. He was pacing up and down the middle of the stables. When she went up to him with the bit and bridle he shook his head at her in anger.

"As ya wish me beauty," she said to him and she put the bridle away. "I think ya could use a bit of a run before we start back," she whispered to him.

"M'lord, let me take him out for a bit of a run. He be calmin' down after that. We will nay be long, ya have me word," she asked.

He did not like the idea of her going out alone on a ride in unfamiliar land, especially with the MacDonalds gathering. She could tell by his hesitation that he did not want her going alone.

"We be fine M'lord; we will nay go far." She assured him.

"Ya have no reins lass, if he decides to run...," Heber warned.

"I be fine. William taught me how to ride without reins, and Olaf will listen to me, I know he will."

"Very well, lass," Heber relinquished. "One hour, no longer, and stay within sight of the loch, ya hear me now."

"I do M'lord, will ya give me a lift up?" she asked.

He laced his fingers together and lifted her into the saddle. She wrapped her cloak around her and then laced her fingers into Olaf's mane. Olaf was ready to run.

"Open the door won't ya Collin?" Maureen asked. Collin unlatched the big door to the stable and Olaf shot past him like an arrow. As they flew past, Collin came up to Heber.

"I do nay think that be a good idea M'lord," Collin mumbled.

Heber looked at Collin and chuckled, "If ya know of a

good way to stop her Collin, I be interested in knowin' just how ya'd do that."

As soon as they cleared the dock, Maureen reached around her neck and pulled the Fey Medallion from beneath her chemise, letting it hang in clear view. They were heading north along the loch on the same road they came in on.

It was not long before the road began to turn east back toward Badenoch. Just up ahead was the junction for the road that turned north. But before they could reach it, Olaf turned north on his own. They were running through a field of tall meadow grass and were coming to the end of Loch Lochy. Olaf was running like the wind. Maureen had to lean forward and hold tightly to his mane with both hands. Heber had warned her to stay along the loch. She looked up and could see the shoreline and just past it was the edge of a large cluster of trees that surrounded the end of the loch. Olaf was heading straight for it.

When they reach the trees Olaf slowed to a trot, and as he came underneath the branches he raised his head and let out a loud neigh. Within a few moments, down from the trees dropped Fiann and Séamus. Maureen leaned over and whispered, "Ya knew they were here the whole time."

Olaf trotted right up to them. Both Fiann and Séamus bowed deeply before him and Olaf dropped his head to them in return.

"Good to see you again old friend," Fiann said as he patted Olaf on the neck. "It will not be long now; you are almost home."

Séamus looked up to Maureen and offered her a hand down. All three of them were wrapped in cloaks with hoods pulled tight. The remaining clouds from the storm and the fog had left the trees of the forest damp and dripping. It was strangely quiet beneath the branches of the trees and the smell of earth rose from the damp forest floor.

When Maureen dismounted both men took a knee before her and bowed their heads.

"Why do ya do this?" She asked.

"We are here for you My Lady," Fiann replied.

She looked at them, confused, "I do nay understand, Master Fiann."

"You will soon. Lady Shalynn awaits your arrival. Are you ready to return to the Isle of Skye?" Fiann asked.

"You will take me, Master Fiann?" she said as she took Fiann's hands in gratitude.

He held her hands tightly, "Yes, My Lady. We are here to take you home."

All of the fear and apprehension she had been feeling was suddenly lifted from her mind. The sentries would take her to Shalynn. From there she would find her friends and bring them safely home to the Highlands.

It was then that she realized she must return to Invernlochy. Heber was waiting and she needed to collect her belongings.

"Fiann, Séamus, I must go back to Invernlochy to gather me own things. Wait fer me at the cross-road won't ya?" she asked of them. They nodded in agreement and waited for her to mount up before disappearing back up into the trees.

She turned Olaf and headed back to Invernlochy. She could hardly control her excitement. They rode back at a good pace but it was nowhere near the speed that Olaf had reached before. She had never seen him run like that.

As they came back into the stables, Heber and Collin were just finishing putting Fionnula's trunk on the carriage.

"Ya got that stallion under control lass?" Heber yelled to her as she rode in.

"Aye M'lord, he be just fine now. We both be just fine now." She replied.

"Fionnula be waitin' at the inn. Gather yer things and take care of yer needs. We be leavin' shortly."

As she came through the door to the inn, she met Fionnula on her way out. They hugged and gave each other a loving peck on the cheek.

"Hurry now lass," She said. "Heber be ready to leave."

"I be right behind ya, Fionnula." Maureen replied.

She hurried to her room, pulling off her cloak as she went through the door. She donned her belt and scabbard, and cinched it tight around her waist. She sheathed her battle sword and then strapped her father's claymore across her back, putting her cloak on over the top to conceal it as best as she could. She slipped the doe-hoofed dagger into its sheath on her belt. She grabbed her saddlebags, her single-hand sword and turned to leave.

But when she got to the threshold of the open door, she stopped. This was it. The crossroads were just a thirty-minute ride at most and then she must leave behind two people she loved so much.

What would she say to them? How could she explain the urgency of her leaving when she didn't truly understand it herself? She suspected Heber knew she would be going on to Skye, but Fionnula knew nothing of any of this. How could she explain? How could she say goodbye?

She closed her eyes and prayed that when the time came the words she needed would come.

Maureen rode alongside the carriage next to Collin while Heber and Fionnula sat inside. Most of the early morning fog had burned off and only a few scattered clouds remained, along with a few patches of low mist laying near the tree lines on the forest floor.

The crossroads were just up ahead. Maureen began to look around for the sentries, but there was no sign of them. All she saw was an old white mare grazing in the grass near the trees.

When they reached the junction to the north road, Olaf came to a stop. The carriage continued down the road until Collin finally realized that Olaf was no longer walking beside him. He pulled back on the reins and brought the ponies to a halt.

"What be wrong, Collin? Why have ya stopped? Heber called from inside.

"It be the lass M'lord, she stopped." Collin replied.

Maureen watched as Heber stepped out of the carriage. He looked back at her and then looked out across the small meadow toward the trees. Fionnula looked out of the carriage door and Heber offered her his hand to help her step down.

Maureen drew a deep breath and dismounted. She turned to Olaf, "Go me beauty, go meet them. It be time fer me to say goodbye fer now." She patted him on his neck as he turned and began walking across the meadow toward the old mare.

Maureen stood alone on the road as Heber and Fionnula waited at the carriage. *Courage girl, courage*, she said to herself as she straightened her back, raised her chin and walked up to meet them.

"Maureen, what are ya doin' girl?" Heber asked as she approached.

"I have to go on to Skye, M'lord. I can nay put aside what I be seein' any longer."

"It be far too dangerous lass," Heber said shaking his head, "No, no lass, I can nay allow ya to go alone."

Maureen looked toward Olaf and the old white mare,

151

"I will nay be alone M'lord."

He followed her glance out across the meadow.

"Maureen, me girl, what be happenin' on Skye be no cattle raid or little skirmish. It be a clan war, girl. Not even *they* can protect ya from that," he said as he tossed his head toward the trees.

She walked up close to them and the three of them wrapped their arms around each other.

"I love ya both more than I can say, and I be back, I swear it," she said. "I be comin' home to ya very soon. And when I do, I be bringin' Katie, and Philip, and those two bloody Irishmen with me." Then she raised her eyes to Heber, "I beg ya, let me go. Let me go so I can do what I need to do."

Heber pulled her back into this arms, "I do nay want to lose ya girl."

Fionnula did not understand what was happening. As Heber held her, Fionnula cupped Maureen's face in her hands saying, "What are ya thinkin' girl. Yer comin' home with us. There be no more talk of this now."

Maureen put her hands over Fionnula's and kissed her lovingly on her cheek. She slowly backed away from their embrace and took a step back.

"I love ya and I be home soon, I promise." Then she turned and began to walk out across the meadow. About half way out, she turned back to see them watching her walk away. As tears began to flow, she pulled her hood over her head and hurried across the meadow to the edge of the forest.

Fionnula turned to Heber, "Where she be goin', Heber?"

"Home," he replied. "She be goin' home."

Holding each other, Heber and Fionnula watched as Maureen, Olaf and the old white mare walked into the forest mist and were gone.

They stood for a few moments staring silently into the

152

forest, then turned and walked back to their carriage.

Collin snapped the reins and started the ponies on their way back to Badenoch. After a few minutes of sitting quietly in the carriage, Fionnula turned to Heber and asked, "Husband, what in God's name be goin' on here?"

Heber turned to her and said, "We have much to talk about."

Maureen rode through the forest for a few minutes then she leaned forward and spoke to Olaf.

"Wait, please wait me beauty, just fer a moment." Olaf came to a halt and turned back to toward the forest's edge. Through the trees, Maureen could see Heber and Fionnula's carriage pulling away down the road back to Badenoch.

"Oh God, what have I done?" she whispered aloud as she covered her face with her hands.

"You must not worry My Lady," Fiann said as he and Séamus rode up next to her. "We will see to your safety. Come now, Lady Shalynn awaits us. We must go. There is a mound just up ahead. We will travel through and it will bring us to the edge of the sea. This way."

Chapter Fifteen

Lock Dunvegan

At dawn, Katie walked down to the edge of the sea. She had wrapped her belongings in her satchel and was ready to make the journey to Dunvegan Castle.

The guardsmen were just beginning to move about, gathering the horses and the small herds of livestock left at the village.

She had plenty of time to pay her last respects to her dear Andrew. When she got down to the cove, the waters on the loch were calm. There was no sign of the curragh or Andrew. The sea had taken him and now it was time for Katie to move on and find her way home to Philip, to Dunbartonshire and the Wycked Aye Tavern. She tossed a small bunch of wild flowers into the sea and blew a kiss to the memory of Andrew James MacLeod.

It would be a little more than a half day's journey to the fortress of Clan MacLeod. Katie was beginning to believe that there was no threat of a clan war at all. She had heard the guardsmen talking and they believed the assault would come from the south toward the castle. But there had been no sign of such an assault. Where were the warriors of Clan MacDonald?

The Lairds had sent out scouts to the south, but they came back with nothing. No sign of MacDonalds gathering or moving north to the castle. It appeared to Katie that they had been forced on this journey for no reason at all. That the Lairds had been wrong and there was no threat. It angered her to think that Andrew's last days had been painful and away from his home for nothing. Bastards! She would have nothing more to do with it.

Oren was waiting for her when she reached the top of the path. He knew where she had been and why.

"He be at peace now Katie," he said as he offered her a hand up from the path.

"I be in yer debt Oren. I do nay know if I can repay the kindness ya have shown me. Ya'll always have a place at me table and a bed under me roof should ya need it," she promised.

Soon they were all assembled by the guardsmen and the journey to Dunvegan Castle had begun. Katie walked along with Oren as they helped to drive a small herd of goats. They talked quietly about the clan war as they walked.

Oren agreed with Katie and he too had no desire to continue on this path. He did not want to fight a clan war. He was a big, strong man, but he was a farmer, not a soldier, and he had no stomach for battle or taking the life of a man he had no quarrel with. It was not his way. It was then that he and Katie decided that together they would find a way out and leave Castle Dunvegan behind.

When they arrived at the castle it was utter chaos. Soldiers and horses were running everywhere. Reinforcements were being made to the entrances and weapons were being posted along the castle walls. The smith's fires were burning hot and everywhere you could hear the sound of hammers on steel.

The castle was massive and could easily shelter the people who had been brought there for safety. The villagers were taken to a lower part of the castle that was obviously servant's quarters. These accommodations were far better compared to the squalor of the village from which they had come. Even though the living quarters were greatly improved, to Katie it still felt like imprisonment and servitude. She longed for the peace and tranquility of her own cottage and her own hearth.

Although they were by no means being held as prisoners, the Lairds did not want any of the villagers leaving the castle and being taken by Clan MacDonald. These people were simple folk, farmers mostly, and if they were taken they would be harmed for whatever information they had.

Upon their arrival, William MacLeod, MacLeod of MacLeod, Chief of Clan MacLeod spoke to all the people as they had gathered in the courtyard of the castle. He told them that Dunvegan Castle had been the stronghold of the Clan for all time, that it would never fall to Clan MacDonald, and they would be safe in the castle. He assured them he and his men would see to their needs, and that when the threat was over they would be free to return to their homes.

Oren and Katie were not moved by the Chieftain's words. They were set on leaving this place as soon as possible. But for now, they would have to wait. Wait for the right time when they could slip away, sight unseen.

Oren was quickly recruited by the castle guard. But to their dismay, this man of great stature had no skill with bow or blade, and was not well suited for battle. To send Oren out into combat would be signing his death warrant. Much to Oren's relief, he was sent to the curraghs to fish Loch Dunvegan and watch for any signs of Clan MacDonald moving around the shores of the Loch.

Katie was sent to the castle kitchens. The women worked long and hard. Katie and Oren would meet at night after their day's chores were done. Oren would bring the day's catch to the kitchen and they would share an evening meal and make their plans.

"How shall we meet Oren," Katie asked. "I do nay know how I will be able to get past the guards at the front gate, and I do nay know me way around the castle well enough to find another way out."

But Oren knew of another gate that went straight down to the shore and the boats. It was the gate he and the other men went through each day instead of going all the way around through the front gate of the castle. Many of the women met their men there when they returned from the Loch. It was the perfect way for him and Katie to slip away.

"There be another way Katie," Oren whispered. "The fishermen use another gate to go down to the loch. We can go out that gate and sail one of the curraghs through the loch and around the point."

Katie drew in a deep breath and Oren could tell she was uncertain and nervous in carrying out this plan.

"Do nay worry Katie. Walk with the other women down to the boats for the next day or two and meet me there when we come in. They will think ya be one of the wives and they will nay stop ya."

Katie nodded her head in reluctant agreement and said, "Very well, Oren, but once we be out on the loch, how will we see our way at night. I have no skill as a boatman and as ya well know, I can nay swim. I fear the water somethin' terrible."

Oren gave her a comforting smile, "In three days' time it be full moon. If it be a clear night, we will be able to sail by the moonlight and see our way around the point."

Katie reluctantly agreed and the plan was set.

That night in her chamber Katie could not sleep. She desperately wanted out of this place, but what about Philip? If he was coming for her, he would come to

Dunvegan Castle. That is where he would expect her to be. But she could not be certain he had even received her missive in the first place. He may not even know about any of this. No, she would leave with Oren, and find her own way home. She closed her eyes and thought of Philip, it had been so long since she felt his arms around her. She just wanted to go home.

For the next two days Katie walked with Oren down to the boats along with the other men and their women. Thinking Oren had found himself a woman of his own, the guards said nothing to Katie as she came to the gate each day and walked down to the water to meet him.

On the morning of the third day, Katie packed a satchel of food and a jug of fresh water for Oren to place in the boat. She worked her full day in the castle kitchen and slipped a bit more food into another pouch before she left. Her stomach was in knots as she prepared to leave her station for the day.

It was just dusk when the boats came in off the loch. Katie met Oren on the shore as his curragh came in. When the other men had walked away, she placed the pouch of food down in the bottom of the boat. There was barely enough light to see their way back up to castle as they walked with the others to the sea gate, lagging behind at the end of the line.

Just before reaching the gate, Oren and Katie stepped aside and slipped down a side path that led back down to the water. They moved quietly down to the edge of the shore and waited until everyone was through and the gate was closed.

Since everyone had been expecting Clan MacDonald's assault to come from the south, the north side of the castle had been left sparsely guarded. It was a clear, cold night and the full moon shined bright upon the water.

Oren helped Katie into the curragh and had her pull the sail canvas over her head. He pushed the boat out and hopped in. Quietly he rowed out onto the loch. The wind was in their favor and soon they would be well away from Dunvegan castle and on their way home.

When they were well out of sight of the castle quay Oren asked, "Katie, are ya still under there girl?" Katie peaked her head out from under the canvas. "It be alright, ya can come out. No one can see us now."

The wind across the loch was cold and bit at her skin. Katie pulled her dark cloak up tight around her face. She looked out across the dark water. It seemed endless. To the west, she could just see the shore of the loch in the moonlight.

Oren stood up and raised the sail on the single mast. The sail flopped around for a moment, then caught the wind and snapped tight. The curragh jumped forward and quickly picked up speed as they headed toward open sea.

Katie began to relax as it seemed Oren had complete control of the curragh and they were safely on their way.

It was cold, very cold. Oren noticed Katie shivering as she sat with her cloak pulled tightly around her. He took an extra piece of canvas from the bottom of the boat and wrapped it around her.

"'Tis very cold out here in the dark, Katie." Oren said. "But as soon as we make open sea and come around the point we can make shore on the peninsula. I be getting us to land as soon as I can, I promise."

Katie nodded her head but did not speak. She had her cloak hood pulled tightly across her face so that only her eyes were showing. She was becoming uneasy, for the closer they came to open sea the rougher and choppier the water became.

The night sky was clear and the full moon cast a bright shine across the water. As they approached the point, Oren turned the curragh away from shore and out to open sea. There was a small island just off shore that they would need to navigate around before reaching open water.

One of the sail lines came loose from the rope cleat. The sail slipped on the mast and began to flap in the wind. Katie jumped and gasped, startled by the noise of the sail.

Oren put a hand on her shoulder, "'Tis alright Katie, do nay worry." Oren moved carefully to the mast. He pulled the sail up tight and began to secure the line on the port side of the curragh.

"There we go now, good as new," he said trying to reassure her and make light of the situation. He glanced back to see Katie sitting with her head down, trying to keep the freezing wind from her face. He could plainly see that she was scared to death.

"We be coming around the point now," he said as he finished tying down the sail. "There be not a thing to worry over and...."

It took a few moments before Katie looked up, as Oren had gone silent. He stood holding tightly to the sail canvas.

"Oren?" she called. "Oren, Oren!"

But he could not respond. The arrow had pierced his side and gone into his chest. He stumbled against the sail, trying to hold himself up. Katie looked to the shore and there on the small island stood three warriors with bows in hand. She looked back to Oren as he turned to face her.

He tried to speak, but could not. He slid back against the sail and tumbled over the side of curragh. Katie watched in horror as he silently slipped below the icy blackness of the sea.

She threw herself on the bottom of the curragh as two more arrows flew across the stern of the boat. She did not know if the warriors were from Clan MacDonald or if they were MacLeods from the castle.

It mattered not. What did matter was that she was alone and adrift on Loch Dunvegan, and heading out to sea.

Chapter Sixteen

Captain Craig

Portree was considered the unofficial capital of Skye and its major port. It was similar to Wick in size, but the traffic in and out of the port had not the volume of Aberdeen. Yet, there was work to be had for any able bodied man who desired it. This was especially true in times of turmoil and clan unrest. Two foreigners walking along the coast road with willing hands would be hired with no questions asked.

While waiting for a ship that might carry them on their way back to Ireland, the Irishmen immediately found work loading and unloading cargo. The Hebrideans working alongside of them sang shanties that almost made the hard work pleasurable. When there were breaks between ships, Maitiú and Dónal had time to talk about recent events.

"Da, did ya nay find it strange how out of nowhere and in the middle of Skye Maureen's friend Shalynn appeared? There be somethin' magical about Skye, aye?"

"Dónal, how and where Shalynn appeared may seem magical, but what she did to heal us was not. Skillful, aye, but it was nay magical. I've seen English bone-setters do similar work in Waterford."

"Yer point be well taken and yet I think there be magic in the air of this place. That, or it is all a strange coincidence!"

"Dónal, I have heard it said that coincidence is God's way of remaining anonymous."

Two more ships came in with the tide and one had a familiar look to Maitiú. When the captain pulled up and called out to the harbor master for laborers, Maitiú heard a voice well-known to him from the past.

"That be the voice of that blaggard Craig Coleman. We were brewery apprentices together with old Murphey in Cork City years ago. Let's go surprise him."

Craig Coleman had a brewery in Cork that he acquired from old Murphey when he married one of Murphey's homely daughters. He and Maitiú were professional rivals but personally held one another in high esteem. In a loud voice for all to hear Maitiú called out, "There be a cluasánach— fat head— from Cork! Ya had to travel far to find a market fer yer sour and vinegary swill be it?"

The surprise was complete. Coleman was stunned into silence, a rare condition for a Cork man.

The effect was brief. Coleman called out, "Be there no place safe from ya ugly bollocks!" Craig jumped from the boat to the docks and ran up to Maitiú and gave him a hearty handshake.

This dramatic greeting drew a small crowd of curious onlookers. Dónal, standing next to one of the workers, leaned over and spoke the obvious. "I think they know each other."

The harbor master walked into the middle of the reunion to break it up, announcing, "Let's be unloadin' this ale now or I will nay pay any of you bastards, and there will be no Irish ale for any of ya!"

Never have thirsty men worked with such diligent efficiency. With work done and pay distributed there was a mad rush to the pubs.

Craig, Maitiú, and Dónal found a table near a window looking out at the harbor. With pints in hand they had to lean in and nearly yell at each other to be heard over the rambunctious noise of the tavern.

"Maitiú, we lost half of our stock on this trip. Between the O'Malleys, the MacNeils, and the fookin' clan war I had to bribe me way here. This may be a break-even proposition at best."

Then looking over to Dónal, Coleman smiled, "And the last time I saw you, ya were this big," looking to the space between his thumb and index finger. Dónal smiled and nodded with respect. Coleman continued, "Pray, what are ya two doin' here, truly?"

"A Craig, a chara, it be a long story," replied Maitiú.

"It appears we've not but time," Craig said. "There'll be no more work out of this lot today. But mind ya, come tomorrow, these Hebrideans will be back hard at work, hangover or no. We be loadin' up with barley here and again at Staffin, and eventually makin' our way back to Cork. This six-row barley from Skye makes a most delicious ale."

Maitiú smiled, "Well, Craig, 'tis not too bad, for Cork swill. But we could use a way out of this place." Pausing, Maitiú continued, "Staffin be a salty place right now. Do nay ask how I know this, but the MacDonalds be gatherin' there for an assault on Dunvegan."

Craig grimaced, "You and Dónal be welcome on me ship but I have to stop at Staffin for the rest of the barley. By the way Dónal, ya be too handsome a man to be the son of this ugly fooker."

The three of them laughed, threw back their pints and returned to the ship to prepare for the next day.

The sun was not up but for minutes when the Hebrideans lined up with massive hangovers to work at loading Coleman's ship. By midday, with the grain on board, the Cork-man's ship was sliding up the coast to Staffin.

When it pulled up to the docks at Staffin, Maitiú and Dónal's hearts both skipped a beat. The Aberdeen ship was there. Thanks be to God, none of the crew were anywhere to be seen.

The Staffin harbormaster stood by himself waiting to receive Coleman's vessel on what appeared to be deserted docks. After disembarking, Coleman cautiously inquired of the harbor master, "Where be yer men, kind sir?"

The harbor master hung his head with regret and said, "I be so sorry, good sir."

With that, out from behind containers and through the open doors of nearby buildings, came two dozen MacDonalds armed to the teeth.

"We be seizing this ship for Clan MacDonald. Upon the finishing of our needs we will compensate ya. But for now, this ship and your crew are bein' pressed into our service," shouted the leader of the group.

"I suppose I have no say in the matter?" Craig questioned.

The MacDonald man slowly shook his head, no.

Some of the MacDonalds boarded the ship and forced Coleman's crew out on the docks to line them up for inspection. Maitiú thought that surely he and Dónal would be recognized. Both of the Irishmen stood with heads bowed and caps pulled down to the brow. Maitiú had a brat draped over his head to further obscure his continence.

The leader of this group of MacDonalds came out from behind his men and looked over the crew nonchalantly, and with disdain said to Coleman, "Where did you get these bilge rats?"

"They be able bodied seamen, from Cork mostly. Their loyalty be to me and me alone. They have no dog in this fight of yours and will defend this ship regardless of the task that lies before us. If that be nay good enough, then staff this ship yourself."

The MacDonald captain looked Coleman up and down then stood inches from his face. "They'll do, Paddy. Now you get these deck apes to do as I say, and ya'll keep yer head on yer shoulders."

"No need to threaten, Jock. We be doin' what ya'll have us do. Should me head be separated from me shoulders, so will yours. Sound fair enough to ya, Jock?"

As the two men stood toe-to-toe, a MacDonald lieutenant interceded, "Mind not me captain Master Coleman, he's had the screamin' shits since we pulled out of Aberdeen a week ago. His arse be on fire."

With mocked concern, Coleman sneered to the lieutenant, "Ah, poor creature."

The barley from Portree was dumped and the MacDonalds boarded for a trip around the tip of Skye. They traveled by night to reduce the chance of being spied from the shore. As they sailed there were strict orders to maintain silence. About an hour before dawn, with the light rising in the sky, the crew could see the outline of Skye on the port side. It was then the MacDonald captain informed Coleman, "Our original plan was to land north of Dunvegan and assault the castle from there, but these waters and this coast are too treacherous and I will not risk my men in such an uncoordinated attack. So we be headed to Sleat and we be joinin' our clan there."

Just as the sun rose, a curragh appeared in the water off the port bow. There seemed to be but one person on board and a woman at that. The MacDonald commander looked to Coleman and said, "I hope the bitch drowns." Dónal and Maitiú were above deck and peered over the side to see into the curragh. They stared straight into the eyes of Katie MacLeod.

Katie looked at her Irish friends and began to yell but Maitiú signaled her to hush. He leaned over and whispered something in Dónal's ear. Dónal bounded across the deck to where Coleman and the MacDonald stood. Turning to Dónal Coleman said, "Aye sailor, what be it?"

"Captain, when I served in the Mediterranean with the Portuguese fleet the Turks would send out picket boats to count our ships and men. What better disguise for the MacLeods to send out a woman in a curragh."

The MacDonald looked over his shoulder at Dónal saying, "Thank ya son," and turning back to Coleman said, "Pull alongside and haul her on board for questioning. When we have extracted from her what she knows, we be throwin' the whore over board to feed the sharks."

Katie was hoisted on board and was interrogated roughly by the MacDonalds with a knife to her throat. Satisfied she knew nothing important he signaled she should be thrown over-board. Maitiú spoke up in a panic, initially stuttering for a loss of words, then it came to him.

"Wait, wait, I know her. She be a bar wench from a tavern I used to frequent near Dunbartonshire called the Wycked Aye. I used to ship out from there and I was in that pub all the time." Looking slyly at Coleman, Maitiú continued, "They serve the finest Irish ale there. From Waterford I think."

The MacDonald commander, annoyed said, "Never mind that! Pitch her in the sea!"

"But sir," Maitiú pleaded, "the pub be run by Heber MacPhearson of Clan Chattan. I happen to know he values her for many reasons, if ya know what I mean," as he winked at both men.

Katie gave Maitiú a swift kick in the shins.

"Shite woman, that hurts!" Maitiú whispered between clenched teeth. "MacPhearson will pay a ransom for her return. She has some value. Ya be throwin' away coin if she goes overboard."

167

"Very well, sailor, restrain her and take her below. Maybe we can salvage some profit out of this trip," Coleman said as he looked out to sea.

Maitiú and another sailor tightly tied Katie's hands behind her back and Maitiú hustled her roughly to the hold. Right before he pushed her below decks Maitiú whispered in Katie's ear, "That really hurt!"

With a half-smile, half-sneer Katie whispered back, "You're welcome."

Chapter Sixteen

For the love of Maureen

It was just before dawn and William stood in the stables staring at empty stalls. The only horse left was old Molly and she was in no shape for such a journey.

He turned and went straight to his father.

"Where are they Da?" he yelled as he entered his father's chamber.

Séan Macaulay sat up from his bed, and turning to his son said, "Say that again?"

Where be all the horses Da?" William repeated with great irritation in his voice.

"There be no horses to be had at this hour. They all be spoken for," Sean replied nonchalantly. "Mayhaps ya should wait until evenin' when some of the riders return," he said as he lay back down on his bed.

William was livid. It was clear to him that his father had intentionally sent out all of his riders so he would not be able to ride out with Braden and Connor. William stormed out of his father's room. He grabbed what few belonging he needed for the journey and left to meet Braden and Connor.

William found Braden and Connor in front of the tavern finishing saddling up.

"Where the hell's yer horse?" Braden asked as William walked up to meet them.

"I do nay have one," Williams said. "Me Da sent out all of his riders and...."

Braden glanced over to Connor who shook his head telling Braden that they could not wait for him.

"I be afraid we can nay wait on ya lad, we need ta be our way and we...."

Cutting Braden off in mid-sentence William snarled, "There be no need to wait – we go now, I'll follow, on foot."

Now Connor had his say, "On foot be it? Are ya daft man?"

William was a big man, lighter and leaner than Braden and Connor with the legs of deer. He was also blindly driven with the concern for his woman and bringing her home.

"Well, I be goin' on. I can nay wait any longer," William said.

Knowing they could not leave William to his own in his current frame of mind, the big men shrugged. They mounted up, and down the boreen Connor and Braden trotted with William running behind.

They must have been at it for two or three hours with only a brief stop to piss. William managed to keep Braden and Connor in his line of site although they sometimes got ahead by one hundred yards or more.

It was at this point that Braden leaned over to Connor tapping him on the shoulder and pointed back in William's direction. They brought their horses to a stop.

"Christ almighty, he's going ta run himself ta death." Braden said.

He be crazy in love that one," Connor replied. "I can nay blame him; I'd do the same fer me own woman."

It was at this point Braden called up to William, "Slow down man. If we be findin' these blaggards that be after Maureen, ya'll be too played out to fight!"

"I will nay be!" William bit back as he came to a stop, bending over and leaning on his knees.

"Ya might try thinkin' with yer brains and nay yer stones boyo. Braden be right," Connor countered.

Deep inside William knew that too, he could not continue like this. He prayed to himself while Connor and Braden turned their horses and rode back to meet him, "Oh God, let us find some horses; please dear God, horses."

170

As the two big men rode back to William, they decided to take turns riding double and rest for the evening on the edge of river Firth.

It must have been close too mid-afternoon when the trio spotted a group of horsemen in the distance heading down the road from St. Johnston. As the horsemen came closer, Braden called out in a panic, "Jesus, Mary and Joseph, it be fookin' Bothwell. Look at the colors on those horses. It be Bothwell fer certain and he cares not who knows."

Connor, looking to his mates, asked, "Do we hide and let him pass?"

William, who was emboldened by love said, "Nay, let's see if he be willin' to sell us one of those horses."

The lads were certain they would not be recognized so they stood erect at the side of the road in plain sight with hats in hands and nowhere near their swords. Nevertheless, one of Bothwell's retainers galloped up quickly, gave them a once-over look and returned immediately to the oncoming Earl, speaking to him out of earshot of the lads.

With an arrogant, beaming smile Bothwell called out in a jovial voice, "What have we here? By the look of ya, I'd say ya three fine strapping lads appear to be in bit of a hurry and short one horse."

Bothwell continued, "If ya be MacDonalds know that Skye be off in the other direction."

William glared at him and was about to speak his mind when Bothwell saw William's glare and returned it with one of his own, silencing him immediately.

Seeing what was afoot, Braden quickly spoke up saying, "Me Lord Earl, me friend Liam here be in a hurry to St. Johnston. It be his mother who be ill ya see."

Bothwell gave a sarcastic and insincere smile and said, "Ah, poor creature! You will nay be making St. Johnston this day on foot boy." Looking back on his

171

retinue he said, "Be there anything I can do to help? I have some spare horses if ya have coin and be willing to buy."

Chieftain Sara had funded her two warriors before they left and they carried a fair amount of coin between them.

Connor turned to William, "How much coin do ya have boyo?" he asked quietly.

Sadly, William only had enough for food and lodging, not nearly enough to pay for a horse. He was forced to take only what he had saved on his own and not ask his father for help. William turned his back to Bothwell's entourage and whispered to Connor of the sad state of his own purse.

Connor, who fashioned himself quite the hard bargainer stepped forward to commence the negotiations.

"And which piece of horse flesh would ya be offerin' up M'lord?" Connor asked.

Bothwell signaled to one of his men who brought forth a massive Clydesdale draped in the colors of Clan Hepburn. And so the bargaining began.

Unfortunately, the wily Hepburn emptied William's purse, and a good portion of Connor's as well. They obtained the horse, but at great cost.

As they parted, Bothwell turned to one of his bodyguards, "'Twas was a pleasure shearing those sheep of their wool. From their voices, they sound like culchies from Sterling way. Did you recognize them?" The bodyguard nodded no. Bothwell shrugged and rode on, smiling as the coins jingled in his sporran.

William seethed, "Did ya see that arrogant, rotten bastard?" Turning to Connor his eyes flashed with anger, "And you, ya gave him damn near all our coin."

"We be pressed now fer enough coin fer food and shelter. What will we eat and where will we sleep?"

Braden asked Connor.

William turned to the men and humbly replied, "There be a croft just down river from here. I stay there now and then when I ride fer me Da. They be good people, they'll give us shelter and food. We'll have to sleep under our plaidies but we will nay be cold or hungry."

He walked up to the big Clydsdale and as he started to mount up he turned back to Connor and Braden, "Me apologies to ya men, this be me fault. Now let's get goin'."

The next morning, Connor pulled some of the sashes and banners Bothwell's horse was wearing and placed them on the other two horses. The three men mounted up and made haste to St. Johnston.

William rode behind the other two men. The long ride gave him time to think about his hasty and foolish actions. He needed to mind himself now. Connor and Braden had been more than patient with him and he would not be a burden to them any longer. They were skilled Highland warriors and he would take their counsel from now on.

In silence they rode into St. Johnston, arriving just before sunset. Braden wondered to himself how they would pay for livery.

Connor wondered aloud, "How will we be findin' them two blaggards who be after Maureen? How do we know they be here at all?"

William just stared off into the distance down the narrow streets, in the dimming light of day, toward the site of a ruined church.

Connor went on, "If we ask a lot of questions it may cause suspicion. Bothwell be a wealthy man with great power."

"I am going to ask the stable to put up our horses," William offered. "If we can nay pay the bill on the marrow the stable master keeps me horse."

They dismounted and walked up to the stable. One of the stable hands came out and walked straight to the horses, ignoring William, Connor, and Braden.

"Ah, my beauty, back so soon?" he said to William's mount. He looked at the three men and the banners on the other horses. Assuming that the men were in Bothwell's employ he winked and said, "Yer two mates be in Mackintosh's tavern across the road. By the way, what be old Bothwell up to with the five of ya all in town?"

Connor laughed and patted the stable hand on the shoulder saying, "If we told ya boyo, we'd be obliged to kill ya."

The stable hand laughed until he looked William in the eye, then he hesitated, "I assume ya'll pay up on the marrow, eh?"

Connor said, "Aye...aye, indeed. On the marrow it be." Then the three of them walked toward Mackintosh's Tavern.

Watching them walk away the stable hand patted one of the horses on the neck and said, "That tall, lean fellow, well, his stare goes right through ya, eh?"

As they walked up to the tavern door Braden asked the obvious, "How are we to know which two are 'our mates'? This place be packed."

As if on cue, they heard two voices squawking out the song, *By the Banks of the River Clyde*. The three looked at each other and nodded. Braden continued, "Who would sing that song about that river who was not from there?"

William started toward the gallowglass when Connor grabbed William's arm saying, "Easy, Willy, we'll wait for them outside. There are too many eyes and ears in here now." The three of them backed out of the door and receded to a nearby stoop, watching and waiting for the lowlanders as darkness fell.

As the night dragged on it started to drizzle and by midnight it was pouring. With little coin for drink, the three could not go in for warmth and refreshment, so they pulled their plaidies over their heads and waited. After a while Connor got up to stretch and Braden followed his lead. Braden groaned, "I am so fookin' sore and stiff and cold and hungry."

"Well then, you should be in a good mood to fight." Connor replied.

William said nothing. He just stared intently at the tavern door and waited. Hours passed and while the rain let up the wind began to blow.

Braden moaned to Connor, "I am shaking so bad I think I be dancin', not shiverin'."

"Let's hope these fookin' sots are so drunk that our being cold, wet, tired, and hungry will nay matter." Connor replied.

William stood up quickly, erect with hand to sword. In the light of dawn, Bain and Cavan Moffet came swaggering out of Mackintosh's door. Cavan swayed a bit, stooped with his hands on his knees, and spewed out a copious amount of whisky and ale. Bain laughed, "What a waste of coin, that!"

Cavan wiped his mouth and laughed, "That be nothin' brother, watch this." He proceeded to emit another stream of vomit.

William, seeing this, thought this was the perfect time to advance, but in his haste forgot to tell Braden and Connor. William threw off his blanket, grabbed his sword and flung his sheath away. Braden and Connor barely had time to react, racing after him.

As William advanced, Bain and Cavan instantly regained sobriety. Their swords came out without panic and they faced the oncoming William holding their swords in front of them with tips down. This was a very good defensive position for, if William advanced, with a flick of their wrists, he would have six inches of lowland steel through his ribs.

William wisely stalled his advance giving Braden and Connor time to join him. Connor on his right and Braden on his left.

Bain spoke to Cavan without turning his eyes from his foes, "Cavan, laddie, it appears we have some sport this fine mornin'. These be friends of yours?"

Cavan replied, "I thought they be yer friends, brother. Did ya cheat these fellows at cards? Those two big fellows look scary but it be the tall, lean fella in the middle that means business."

William snarled, "If ya've harmed Maureen I'll cleave you in two!"

With a quick glance to Cavan, Bain said, "'Twould Maureen be that bar wench ya had go a with? Did ya nay pay her for her services?"

Cavan said, "No brother, I think he be referring to the wee lassie Bothwell wants." Addressing William, he said, "Oh, no, big fella, we want her alive. Bothwell wants her alive. Although, we might want to have a bit of fun with her first."

William was wild with anger and wanted to attack but he had no room to maneuver. Connor and Braden moved up next to William. "Mind yerself boyo," Braden said as he nabbed William by the back of his shirt. "They be tryin' ta bait ya boy, get a hold now."

Everyone stood still—eyes fixed, muscles taunt, swords drawn. What must have seemed like minutes were surely only seconds.

Suddenly, Bain moved toward Braden, and Cavan toward Connor. Each struck at the thighs of their respective foes. Connor was just barely able to block

Cavan's sword but Bain, taking advantage of Braden's stiffness from the cold was able to slice a large gash on Braden's leg.

Braden howled out with pain. He was through. His wound was not fatal, but had rendered him ineffective in the fight. The best he could do was stagger off to the side, with his dirk in hand, and wait.

It came down to Bain and Cavan facing off against William and Connor. Between breaths Bain called out, "Brother, you take that stout fellow and I'll take this tall lean one."

Instead, both men made a thrust at William that had him take a quick half step back causing him to slip on the muck in the road.

Cavan then locked swords with Connor doing what every good fighter knows: When fighting a big man, keep him in close. Then, with a skillful flick of his arm, Cavan shucked Connor's sword aside and popped him on the gob. Connor's knees buckled and he dropped to the ground like a rock.

The three on two advantage had quickly evolved into a two on one disadvantage for William. He was on his own against men who fought for a living.

The Moffet brothers were in no hurry. But the adrenaline of the initial assault was starting to wear off and they were quickly becoming aware of the fact that they had been drinking all night.

They began to circle slowly around William, like big cats moving in on their prey.

Cavan said, " Come now big fella, let us go now."

But William was not having it. He was resolved but was thinking to himself how this might be a bad day for his father, Séan, and his love, Maureen.

Suddenly, Bain lurched forward dropping his sword. In the dim morning light, William and Cavan watched as Bain began choking and coughing up blood.

177

Cavan screamed, "Brother, what?"

Bain slowly turned, pivoting toward where Braden stood, then with knees buckling, he fell to the ground. Braden's dirk was sticking out from Bain's back just below the shoulder blade. Thrown hard and from a short distance, the dirk had pierced the gallowglass' lung.

Cavan circled around, sword pointing to William until he reached his fallen brother. Bain mouthed something that neither William or Braden heard, but Cavan heard his brother's words perfectly and understood. Cavan burst into tears, threw down his sword and held his dying brother in his arms. In moments, Bain was dead.

At that moment, something too died in Cavan. He and Bain had been together all of their lives. Orphaned together when young, they came into the service of the Hepburn's as gallowglass. Without Bain, Cavan was a man with a broken spirit. There was no longer any fight in him.

William drew his sword high, in a position of wrath and prepared to separate Cavan's head from his shoulders. Cavan turned to look William in the eyes with an expression that plainly said, *you have already killed me, what more do you want*?

What William saw haunted him. Suddenly he remembered his father's words: *Please son, tell me ya have nay killed a man.* He lowered his sword and brought the tip of the blade to Cavan's throat.

"Where be Maureen?" he asked quietly.

Cavan did not respond. William slowly raised the sword, putting pressure just under Cavan's chin and repeated his words, "Where be Maureen?"

Between sobs Cavan said, "We could nay find her. We were headin' up Badenoch way to see if we could catch her there. But there be no point now. Me brother be gone and no amount of gold can replace him." He turned back and buried his head in his dead brother's chest and wailed.

"I'll nay kill ya, ya gobshite, and I will leave ya ta yer grief if ya swear ya'll leave us be," William warned.

Cavan said nothing and with his arm waved William away.

William went over to Braden, "Ya saved me life me friend." Taking him under the arm they staggered over to Connor who was just coming to.

"What happened?" Connor said. Then holding his head asked, "Who be doin' that God awful wailing?"

"Braden killed one of the blaggards with his dirk and the other one be weepin' over him," William replied.

By now some people from the nearby tavern had begun to gather. The barman came out to the road and seeing the carnage said, "Quickly, get him inside before the bailey comes. I want no trouble. It be bad for business." He turned to the few onlookers, "Nothin' to see here folks, off ya go now."

The barman helped Cavan carry his dead brother off the street. Connor and William followed with Braden under William's arm. A few of the onlookers tried to follow them into the bar.

"The bar be closed now, find yer way home." The barman said turning them away.

Once inside the tavern he closed and barred the door. He moved from Connor, then to Braden, and then to Cavan. He then went over to quietly speak to William.

"The big fellow," pointing to Connor, "he'll be fine but I'd like to keep an eye on him for a day or two. The other big fellow," pointing to Braden, "he be hurt pretty bad. Needs to have that sewn up. If he does nay come down with the fever, he should be ready to travel in a fortnight." He then looked over at Cavan.

"That one there, he be a broken man. I've seen it happen many times after a battle where comrades are killed. More than his brother died in that fight."

William was not sure what to do next, and stared at the barman with a lost look. "We need to go on to Badenoch," he said, thinking out loud.

"I be lookin' after yer lads and this broken one as well," the barman said trying to reassure William. "Ya go on now to wherever ya be goin', and say nothin' more to me. If someone asks me, I can say I do nay know and it be no lie." He paused for a moment, "Oh, and I be keepin' the horses and most of the coin to pay fer me troubles." Then winking at William he said, "And tell Heber MacPhearson that he be once more in the debt of Cluney Mackintosh of Perthshire."

William sat down with Braden and Connor. "I do nay know what ta say," he offered. "This be me fault lads."

"Do nay worry about us, William. Go to Maureen now, make haste." Connor said.

He be right boyo, go on now." Braden concurred. "We'll head back to the Wycked Aye in a day or two and let Chieftain Sara know that the MacPhersons be safe."

William got up to leave and then he did something that surprised even himself. He put his hand on Cavan Moffet's shoulder saying, "I be truly sorry fer yer loss man."

With a note from Mackintosh, William returned to the stables where he was greeted by a different stable hand than the one from the night before. This man read the note and in less than ten minutes returned with a beautiful, brown horse with a white face, saddled and ready to ride. William thanked the stable hand saying, "This be a fine mount."

"A friend of Cluney's be a friend of mine." The man replied.

William mounted up and rode out, up the north road in the direction of Badenoch and MacPhearson country.

As he rode along the track to what he hoped was Heber's dwelling, William's heart was pounding. Not from the exertions of riding but from the thought of seeing Maureen again. He could see her in his mind's eye, he could feel her warmth, her gentle touch. And aye, he could smell her hair and taste her lips. So consumed he was by his imaginings that he failed to see a low hanging branch and was nearly knocked off his horse.

"Jesus man, where's yer head at?" he said out loud to himself. The near miss refocused him on the present, which was timely, for not ten paces later he met face-to-face with an archer with a knocked arrow.

"Greetings stranger. What brings ya to the land of the MacPhearsons?" The archer asked.

William caught the movement of two other archers also with knocked arrows on his right and left.

"I be William Macaulay from down Sterling way, and I seek an audience with Heber MacPhearson."

The archer spoke in a most formal manner, "Do nay dismount, friend. Stay as ya are. I be sendin' someone up ta the house to see if anyone up there knows ya. If they do nay know ya, then we will be shootin' ya."

The archer waved to someone behind William, whom William had not yet seen, and a fleet-footed youth ran up the boreen toward a clearing where William assumed the strong house of the MacPhearson's stood. While he waited the guard queried further, "Macaulay be it? That be a Skye name, aye? I hear ya be havin' a bit of a fuss over there. I hope ya are nay bringin' any of that trouble here."

"I want no trouble, just ta speak ta Heber

181

MacPhearson." William replied.

In a moment, the young lad returned, short of breath.

"Himself said to have this one dismount, remove all of his weapons, then bring him up. If he be who he says, he be welcome. If not..."

"Then ya be shootin' me," William cut in.

A big broad smile broke over Heber's face when he saw William approach. When he wrapped his arms around William, the archer leaned over and said quietly, "I suppose this means I'll nay be shootin' ya, Skye boy. Welcome to Badenoch."

Immediately after Heber released him, William said, "Maureen, where..."

"She nay be here, son. She be headin' back to Skye." Heber could see the hope drain out of William's face only to have it refill with frustration.

He turned away from Heber, taking a few steps and then abruptly turned back, "How could ya let her go? How could ya, man?" he said as he stepped back toward Heber.

"Easy now lad," Heber said sternly as he placed a hand on Williams chest, backing him off. "I had little choice in the matter. There be somethin' about that girl."

"Do ya think I do nay know that?" William snapped.

In frustration Heber said, "'Tis not what I mean William." Heber put his hands on William's shoulders and said, "Come in, rest yourself, eat, drink, sleep. On the marrow, with a fresh mount and the company of those fine fellows ya met on the road here, ya'll be off to Skye."

He led William to the great room of the manor house and two big leather chairs in front of the hearth. Heber caught the attention of one of the house servants and sent him for food and drink.

"What I mean, William," Heber continued, "Is there be things about Maureen that be special, of a spiritual sort. The girl has gifts from beyond the world as we know it. With those gifts comes a responsibility, a callin' of sort. All I can tell ya lad be that I had to let her go."

William hung his head in frustration and, as his anger left him, the exhaustion from the journey began to take its toll. All he could think of was his bonny lass riding alone into the middle of a clan war. Tears, at last, welled in his eyes.

Fionnula entered the room and both men rose to greet her. When she saw William's face, her heart ached for him.

"Oh William, God love ya." She said as she took his hands. "Please sit now, and rest yerself." She took a seat on the couch next to Heber's chair.

Heber continued, "Lad, she loves ya somethin' fierce, this I know. She needs ya, especially now. She said she could nay put aside all she had seen, that she had to go on to Skye."

William looked back to Heber overwhelmed. "Which way did she go?" he asked.

"North," Heber replied. "She rode out alone toward the forest and the north road to Glenelg followed by that old white mare.

Hearing this, William slowly raised his eyes to Heber, "An old white mare ya say?"

"Beg pardon husband, but she was nay alone," Fionnula interjected. "There be two young lads on the back of that old white mare."

Both men turned to her in astonishment. They both just stared at her until she could stand their silent gaze no longer.

"What?" She asked. "'Twould it nay be better that she

be ridin' with someone than goin' alone?"

William sat up straight as the tension seemed to drain from his body, "Aye, M'lady. 'Twould indeed."

After a fine meal and a dram of Heber's finest, William told Heber of all that transpired since he and Maureen left for Badenoch. Finally, when he finished telling what happened in St. Johnston, William said, "Oh, and Cluney Mackintosh gives ya his regards and says ya be once again in his debt."

Heber smiled, "Bothwell thinks he has influence with all his coin to throw about. His coin pales to the love and loyalty of Chattan. The richest man be not the one who has the most coin. The richest man be the one who has the love of his mates and his kin. Good old Cluney."

They showed William to Maureen's chamber to sleep for the night. As he closed the door behind him, he saw her small trunk sitting in the middle of the room. He opened it to find only a few of her belongings left. Her good chemise and bodice that she wore to Mass, some pieces of embroidery, and the Sabbath apron Katie had insisted she have. In the bottom of the trunk was the bed quilt that had covered them on their last night together in her cottage. He pulled it from the trunk and put it to his face. Her scent still lingered and he could smell her faint fragrance of lavender. It sent his head spinning.

He laid back on the bed with the quilt in his arms and thought about his next move. Fionnula's words had awakened something in his memory. He remembered how his gran would tell him stories of the white horses of Skye. He had seen them grazing near his gran's house when he was a boy.

He would go on to Skye. He did not know where Maureen would be, but he knew someone who would.

As Heber and Fionnula retired to their own chamber for the night, Heber turned to his wife.

"The two men ya saw ridin' off with Maureen, ya be sure of that wife?" he asked.

She looked at him curiously, "Aye, I be most certain. Ya did nay see them, Heber?"

He shook his head, "Nay me love, I did not."

Chapter Seventeen

The Mound

The horses turned together and headed through the forest toward the base of the foothills. Just behind a cluster of Rowan trees was the opening to the mound. Fiann and Séamus went through first; Maureen and Olaf followed closely behind.

The entrance to this mound was much different from the one that led to the sacred circle of rowan. This was a narrow, cobblestone path with deep green moss growing between the stones. The path was bordered on each side with tall, tightly spaced trees that formed a canopy above them. A mist filled the air and a faint light glowed behind the mist, softy lighting their way. It was strangely still and completely peaceful.

As they moved down the path Maureen began to see small flickers of light in the trees and could hear the murmur of voices. She knew their arrival was being announced, but to whom? Up ahead of Fiann, she could see that the mist was beginning to clear, and the tree canopy was coming to an end as they approached another entrance. She looked back behind them to see an endless path of mist and trees with no apparent end. She had no idea in what direction they had gone, how far they had traveled or how much time had passed.

When she turned back around, she saw that her two sentries no longer rode on the back of an old, dirty mare, but sat upon the most beautiful pure white horse she had ever seen. This horse was as big as Olaf with a long flowing mane and tail. Her eyes were silver blue, like the sea on a sunny day.

"Now that be a fine bit of trickery Fiann," Maureen said.

"It is not my magic My Lady, it is theirs," he replied.

As they entered the mound, before them lay a great meadow, and like the sacred circle of rowan, the meadow was teaming with life. Animals of all kinds walked side-by-side with the Aes Sidhe who inhabited this mound and bird songs filled the air. Beautifully adorned tents bordered the tree line at the edge of the meadow. The mound seemed to be a type of small shire or way station with places to rest and eat, and care for the animals.

As they made their way into the meadow, the Aes Sidhe abandoned what they were doing and came to the side of the path, kneeling before them as they passed.

"They pay ya honor," Maureen commented to the sentries.

"It is not us they pay homage to My Lady, they bow to the horses," Séamus replied.

They rode up to one of the tents and dismounted. As soon as they stepped away from the horses, two men came up to Olaf and immediately removed his saddle. The horses then turned and walked together to a pond nearby to drink. The men followed them, bringing fresh hay and oats, and brushed them down as they fed.

Fiann walked to the tent and pulled back the flap, "Come My Lady, we will take rest and food, and then we will go on to the pools."

"Can we nay go on now, Fiann? Ya said Shalynn be waitin', surely we have time to get at least halfway to Glenelg before nightfall. It be early and the horses be well rested," Maureen asked.

"Darkness has already fallen outside the mound. We must spend a short time here before we can move on," Fiann explained. "Please My Lady, rest now. When we leave this mound, we will be at Glenelg."

She bowed her head in acceptance and passed through into the tent as he asked. Inside she found

187

herself surrounded by fine silken curtains, a feather bed and a hearth that burned warm but needed no chimney.

A carafe of mead along with a plate of bread, cheese, nuts and fruit sat upon the table.

"Thank you, Fiann," she said as he closed the tent door.

As the two sentries walked toward another tent, Séamus took Fiann by the arm and stopped him as they walked.

"Did you see them, Fiann? Did you see them? She carries the sword and the doe-blade as well."

Fiann nodded his head in acknowledgment, as he had notice the hilt of the ancient sword beneath her cloak immediately.

"Yes my friend, I saw them, the sword hilt bears the great stag but I must see the blade to be certain."

"Do you think it is her, Fiann? Séamus asked.

"I do not know my friend. But if it is, our job just became far more important than it was before. We must get her to Lady Shalynn as soon as she is rested," Fiann replied.

Maureen removed her cloak and took her father's claymore, laying it up against the bed. She pulled her belt and blades and laid them down as well. The floor of the tent was covered in deep, green grass. She sat down on the bed and reaching down, pulled a few blades of grass. She put them to her face, taking a deep breath. She reached down and took off her boots and socks. The grass was cool on her feet.

She took a piece of bread and cheese from the table, and walked barefoot in the grass as she moved around the tent.

A large stone basin filled with water sat near the head of her bed with two fine linen cloths and a small bottle of lavender water sitting next to it.

The opportunity to wash the trail dust from her face and hands was so inviting, but as she reached for the basin she stopped and pulled her hands away. She was afraid to touch the water. She turned her palms toward her and clinched her fists.

"Not now do ya hear me, not now! I do nay wish to see, not now!" she spoke out loud. She unclenched her fists and slowly immersed her hands in the water. Nothing happened. Relieved, she soaked one of the cloths in water and washed the dust from her face. She unlaced her bodice and ran the wet cloth over her body. She splashed a bit of the lavender on her chest and neck, and then went to the table and poured herself a cup of mead. As she sat on the edge of the bed sipping the mead, she suddenly became a bit dizzy and very tired. She slumped back on the bed, dropping her cup to ground, and fell fast asleep.

Fiann pulled back the flap of her tent and peered inside. He could see the young Watcher asleep on the bed. *Good*, he thought to himself. He quietly entered the tent and went straight to her father's sword. Checking once more to make sure she would not wake, he pulled the sword from its scabbard. When Fiann saw the markings on the first few inches of the blade, he did not need to look any further. He gently slid the blade back down into its scabbard and slipped unnoticed from the tent.

"Well?" Séamus asked as Fiann entered their tent.

"It is the sword of the Keeper. We must move her quickly my friend," Fiann warned. "We will let her sleep a bit longer and then make the jump to Skye."

Maureen woke to the sound of voices and rustling in her tent. Two Fey women waited just on the other side of the silken curtains. On the end of her bed sat two brown rabbits, a small fawn sat curled before the hearth and a large grey squirrel was helping himself to the nuts on her table.

The women moved forward immediately upon her waking. They were both dressed in light flowing gowns wrapped at the waist and wrists with leather strapping. They carried a fresh change of clothes, ribbons and leathers for her hair, a wool cloak and new boots.

They laid the clothes on the bed and turned to Maureen, waiting for her to rise from her bed and remove her clothing.

"I thank ya ladies, but I be fine dressin' meself," Maureen said as politely as she could, for she had no intention of undressing in front of them.

Séamus came into the tent as Maureen was doing her best to tell the two women she did not need any help, but they were insisting on dressing her.

"They are here to help you My Lady. They dress you for High Counsel," Séamus explained.

He spoke to the women in a dialect of Gaelic she did not understand. They proceeded to spread out her clothes on the bed, and then went to stand behind the silken curtains with Séamus.

"They will help only at your request. Dress quickly, we must be on our way," he said.

"How long have I been asleep?" Maureen asked.

"Just two of your hours," he replied. "Fiann has the horses ready, we must go now." With that he left the tent, leaving Maureen with her two helpers.

The clothing was not what she had expected. Instead of bloomers, skirts and corset she found suede breeches, a leather bog dress that laced up the sides, a long sleeve linen shirt and knee-high riding boots.

Maureen turned her back to the women and managed to get into most of the clothes on her own, but did need their assistance to lace up the sides of her dress, if it could be called a dress. It was more like a tunic or jerkin, laced to the waist and split for riding.

They had not dressed her for High Counsel, this was a disguise. *Who are they hiding me from?* she thought.

They braided and tied her hair with the leathers and ribbons. She donned her belts and blade, and put the Claymore across her back. Together the two Fey women placed her cloak over her shoulders.

"Fáidh," they both said and then bowed to her as they backed away.

Fáidh, Maureen knew that word. Seer, they called her seer. She thanked them as best she could, and then hurried out of the tent.

Fiann and Séamus were waiting with the horses. When Maureen saw Olaf she could not believe her eyes. His coat was glistening and his handsome, flowing mane nearly touched the ground. He stood at least two hands higher than before and his frame was thick and strong. He was the biggest, most beautiful horse she had ever seen.

"Olaf, what has happened to ya?" Maureen whispered to her beloved companion as she ran her hands down the sides of his magnificent head. "Would this be who ya truly are?"

There were no saddles or bridles on either of the horses. Many of the Aes Sidhe stood by them, petting them and giving them small offerings of food as they waited for their departure.

"It is time my old friend, you are almost home," Fiann said to Olaf. The two horses knelt down for their riders.

The small company mounted up and began their journey out of the mound.

"We shall be at the pools very soon My Lady," Fiann offered.

They rode down the stone path toward the opposite end of the mound in silence. When they were away from the other Aes Sidhe in the mound Maureen turned to Fiann.

"What happened to the horses Fiann, why did they change like that?" Maureen asked.

"They are going home My Lady," he replied. "They are going home."

Chapter Eighteen

Armdale

Coleman's ship was waiting for the tide to slide into Armdale. Katie was safe in the hold of the ship and Dónal was sleeping like a baby beside Maitiú. Maitiú stared out across the dark water, watching as the first hint of sunlight peaked over the horizon.

This time of day always haunted Maitiú from as far back as he could remember. The hours before dawn were always the coldest and the darkest. He remembered his mother telling him years ago that it was the hour when most people died. He remembered when he and his mother were caring for some of the people in his village outside of Clonmel who were suffering from the plague. He always helped his mother care for the sick. But in this memory, he could not tell if it was he who was sick. Maybe his mother was wiping the sweat off of his forehead and encouraging him to hang on and wait for the coming of the sun.

He could see her face in the dim candle light. Next to him lay his sister and his baby cousin Gwen, both fast asleep. They were sleeping just as Dónal was now.

How he wished his mother was here to encourage him and give him hope. But she had been gone for many years, dying long before Dónal was born, on a bleak October morning. Dying at the time when most people died.

Dónal stirred, snorted and farted loudly in his sleep. When he was a wee babe he would stir in his crib about this time.

Maitiú half closed his eyes and prayed, "A Mháthair, pray for Dónal, Katie and even that bastard

193

MacAlasdair. They be in trouble and I be not able to help them as much as they need. I be needin' God's help. Mayhaps, as ya be up there, ya can get His ear better than me. Mamaí, where are ya now? I need ya."

An unusually warm breeze blew across Maitiú's face and he saw a single gray-leg goose fly across the sky honking plaintively.

Dónal reached up and touched his father's arm, "Da, why are ya cryin'? 'Twill be fine."

Turning to Dónal, wiping his eyes, Maitiú said, "Ah boyo, ya've yer Mimi's spirit in ya."

"I was seein' Mimi in me dreams Da," Dónal whispered. "She told me to tell ya that it will be fine, that she loves ya and she be proud of ya."

Maitiú's eyes teared up again and, patting his son's shoulder he said, "Get a little more sleep mo chroí. I be goin' ta see if Coleman's awake."

Maitiú got up slowly and walked to the Captain's quarters. The night watch nodded to him as he crept by them in the pre-dawn light. Coleman was indeed awake.

"A word Captain," Maitiú requested.

"Ach, sure man, what be on yer mind?"

"When we disembark in Armdale, we need to get word to that fooker, Philip MacAlasdair, that his wife be on board."

Coleman nodded and asked, "Why do you nay tell him yerself, Maitiú?"

"I be afraid if I visit him again, it would be a flyin' visit. Dónal might give him even worse."

Coleman sat up from his bed and pulled a chamber pot to him. "Fret not, I'll send a crewman to ask fer the warrior-poet. We'll see if he can get his wife out of trouble."

Maitiú nodded and turned to leave. As Coleman finished filling the chamber pot he called back to Maitiú, "What about ya, lad? Will ya remain on board? We could use ya. I can get you and yer boy back to Waterford, and then we be brewin' beer together again, drinkin' pints and watching Cork kick Waterford's arse in hurlin'."

Smiling, Maitiú said, "Bad cess to ya Coleman. May it be as ya say, but with Waterford victorious."

Philip was in his glory riding the soft horse. The Aes Sidhe had heard his pleas. He would ride into Armdale on this majestic steed to the amazement of all.

But when the soft horse returned to the earth, Philip's vision was not to be had. The horse landed in a secluded meadow. She walked into a copse of trees outside of Armdale, and returned to her disguise as a shit covered, old, white nag. As the sway-backed nag wobbled within sight of the stronghold of Clan MacDonald, she bucked Philip off rather unceremoniously and trotted off over the hills and out of sight.

The MacDonald's manning the ramparts laughed derisively at MacAlasdair's return to Armdale in Sleat.

"Who goes there?" one of the guards cried out in laughter.

"I be Philip MacAlasdair with word from Staffin.

The guard's laughter died away and MacAlasdair was quickly ushered in, "Do enter sir and follow me. Make haste."

Philip reported his news to the command of Clan MacDonald.

"If we could coordinate the attack, we could pinch Dunvegan like a boil and pop the MacLeods like the pus they are," spoke the Taoiseach, the leader.

His second in command, the Tánaiste, turned to Philip, "Could you return with word of when to attack?"

Lying without hesitation, Philip replied, "Nay, the horse I rode broke down."

"Then we be gettin' ya another one." He returned.

It was then the Taoiseach interjected, "No, we be sendin' word by ship. Are any ready to sail?"

The Tánaiste replied, "There be a ship from Ireland just outside the harbor. They have some lads that have come late to Staffin and missed the deployment. We can send them back after we offload that ship of its Irish ale. We can keep those lads on board to keep the rest of those Irish apes in line.

When Coleman's ship pulled in and its cargo of confiscated Irish ale was unloaded, Maitiú and Dónal moved inconspicuously next to Katie as she waited to be taken off the ship.

"Do nay ask me how I know this for I am nay sure meself, but yer man be here." Maitiú whispered. Katie turned to face him.

"Katie, ya be safe now. Dónal and I be stayin' with Coleman and be getting' the hell out of here." He gave Katie a big hug and Katie returned his embrace.

"We may never see each other again. God speed to ya Katie MacLeod." Maitiú released his embraced and began to walk away, when he turned back to her, "One more thing, when ya do see Philip again, tell him I said he can go fook himself!"

Katie took a step back, gobsmacked by the strong curse coming out of the mouth of a man who had always been a dear and loyal friend to Philip.

Maitiú seeing her reaction continued, "Let him explain it to ya." Dónal nodded politely and then Katie was led away. Maitiú and Dónal remained on board with every hope of finding their way back to Ireland.

Philip was sitting on the roof of the strong house, leaning against a battlement. He sat in silent remorse as he thought back over his actions that had brought him to this place. So much had gone wrong and he knew his behavior was the reason.

He had become so obsessed with finding Katie that he cast aside the help and advice of Dónal, Maitiú and Sandy.

He rode the soft horse and it was glorious. But he was bucked off and humiliated, he was rebuked. He could hear Maitiú telling him that his head was so far up his arse he would have to pull up his shirt to see. To see, all he wanted to see now was Katie.

He was so consumed in his own despair that he did not hear the messenger at first. Then he heard someone call out for him.

"Philip MacAlasdair, a message fer ya, sir."

Philip bounded to his feet and ran down the spiral stairs connecting the roof to the ground floor of the strong house.

Standing at the entry way to the strong house was a young MacDonald page, his voice the high pitched tone of a youth, standing stiffly with his shoulders drawn back at attention. The lad was taking his task quite seriously.

Philip walked up to the boy, "I be Philip MacAlasdair, what news, lad?"

"Katie, yer woman, she be at the docks, sir. She be just off an Irish ship. She be askin' fer ya," the boy announced.

Philip started to run toward the docks, then turned back to the boy patting him on the shoulders, "Thank ya lad, thank ya!" He ran to the docks not feeling the ground beneath his feet.

When he approached he nearly ran over some MacDonald soldiers who grumbled and snapped at him when he flew past. When he turned the corner and came around the warehouse he saw her. He stopped dead in his tracks. It was her, it was really Katie. She was staring at the ship pulling out and did not see him approaching.

"Katie!" he yelled at the top of his lungs.

Katie turned to see him running toward her.

"Oh, darlin', me dear, sweet Katie!"

She swung around as Philip pulled her into his embrace. He held her tightly, running his hands over her hair and around her face. They separated just enough to gaze into each other eyes and then gently and passionately kissed.

Some of the sailors and guards standing by began to hoot and holler. Philip began to speak but Katie's loving smile transformed into a frown.

"Husband, ya have some explainin' ta do."

Chapter Nineteen

The Pools

The path out of the mound opened just off the edge of the sea. It was just before dawn and no one was moving about. Maureen looked out, and there, just across the water, she saw for the first time, the mysterious Isle of Skye.

The sight of it took her breath away. The mountains that rose from the shoreline were surrounded in a blanket of mist, as the early morning fog hung low over the land and sea. The peaks above the ring of white fog seemed to be covered in deep green velvet. The shoreline of Skye was so close to Glenelg you could swim to it.

The horses seemed anxious and Olaf shifted his weight back-and-forth, dancing on his front hooves. Maureen chuckled as she remembered Dónal teasing Olaf about his "happy feet".

The sentries scanned the shoreline and the trees that grew around the edge of sea. They seemed uneasy and restless, just like the horses.

"Lean forward and hold tightly to his mane, My Lady," Séamus instructed. "When the horses hit the water, they will make the jump."

Jump? Maureen thought to herself. *Jump where? There be no boat, or barge, or bridge.*

Fiann leaned over to Olaf and said, "Take her home, Mo Ri."

Before Maureen could say anything, Olaf reared up high on his hind legs, stretched his head toward the sky and let out a neigh like she had never heard before. When his front hooves touched down, he bolted toward the sea with the sentries right behind.

The moment the horses touched the waters of Skye they leaped forward. Maureen leaned into Olaf's mane, burying her face and holding on for dear life. She braced herself and waited for a cold, wet landing smack in the middle of the sea.

After a few moments, she realized they were still rising and not descending into the water at all. She turned her head slightly and slowly opened one eye, venturing to look around her.

"Mary, Mother of God!" she exclaimed.

They were surrounded by mist. She could see glimpses of the sea below them. Before them, she could see the peaks of Skye.

They were moving at incredible speed. She found the courage to free her face from Olaf's mane and gazed in astonishment at the beauty and magic before her.

It was not long before the horses began to descend and return to the earth, coming to rest at the base of the Black Cuillin Mountains and the Fairie Pools of Dunbrittle.

Shalynn waited on the ridge above the entrance to the great hollow. Olaf walked up and dropped his head to her. She patted him on his nose saying, "Welcome home my old friend."

He knelt down and Maureen swung her leg around and slid down off his back. When she looked at Shalynn she saw that the woman was dressed exactly as she was; in breaches, boots and a leather jerkin. She wore no shirt beneath her jerkin, only wrist guards and shoulder armor. Her skin markings showed clearly on her face and arms, and her hair was tied back with silver and black lacing. She was dressed for battle, not high counsel.

"Shalynn, a stór, a chara," Maureen said, greeting her properly. "I be so glad to see ya. I be in great need of yer help."

"And we are in great need of yours as well." Shalynn replied. "Come child, we have little time to waste."

They walked along the edge of the pools toward the path that led to the entrance to the hollow. Fiann and Séamus follow closely behind, with the horses behind them.

The beauty of the pools was spellbinding. Never had Maureen seen such a place. Waterfalls flowing half way around the pool. Water so clear and calm you could barely tell it was even there. The bottom of the pool was covered in beautiful colored stones that looked as if God had painted and placed them Himself. It was the most peaceful and enchanted place she had ever seen.

They made their way behind the water falls and entered the outer room to the hollow.

Shalynn went forward to open the massive door before them. She pressed her hand to emerald stone set in the intricately carved door. The door swung open and Maureen stepped forward when Shalynn stopped her.

"Wait," she said as she stepped aside, followed by Fiann and Séamus. Now Maureen understood why there was such a large door to the entrance to the hollow. They waited as Olaf and Rhea entered first and moved forward to stand side by side on the massive stone platform inside the hollow.

As they waited for the horses to pass through, Maureen noticed the carving of the stag of the forest above the door, and the markings around the outer edge. Strange and ancient carvings, yet somehow they seemed familiar to her. But before she could get a better look, Shalynn ushered her through the door.

Maureen threw back the hood from her cloak and tossed the sides of the cloak back over her shoulders. The hilt of her father's claymore showed plainly as she strode forward, walking up between the waiting horses. Shalynn took her place by Olaf's side and directed Maureen to stand next to Rhea.

The Fey of the hollow were clapping and cheering at the return of the soft horses. Before Maureen took her place, she turned to Olaf and whispered, "Well, me beauty, looks like ya be too important fer me now, eh?" Olaf lowered his head and gave her a little nudge toward Rhea.

"Alright, alright, I be goin'," she said and gave him a kiss on the nose.

They walked together down the huge stone steps and into the meadow of the hollow below. People began to gather around them just like in the mound near Badenoch. But there was no time for pomp and circumstance. Time was running short.

"Come child, this way," Shalynn said.

They left the horses behind, and made their way to the council chamber. The people of the hollow bowed to Shalynn and Maureen as they walked through the mound. Many pointed at Maureen and whispered to each other as they passed by. Most of them were dressed for battle as well. Like Shalynn, they wore no other clothing beneath their jerkins and armor. They were truly a handsome race of beings. They all bore markings upon their bodies, just like Shalynn's. Most resembled the plants and leaves of the forest, but many bore the same symbols that Maureen had seen on the door to the hollow.

Maureen was growing anxious. She needed Shalynn's help to get to Dunvegan and find Katie. She knew Maitiú and Dónal would be there as well, and she knew they were in danger, she had seen it.

Diancecht had been alerted to the arrival of the young Watcher the moment the soft horses had returned to the Isle. The counsel had immediately gathered and now waited for her arrival. Now they would see what fate awaited them at Dunvegan.

The council members were gathered at the far end of the table when Shalynn and Maureen entered the room. The sentries came to Maureen to remove her cloak and take her weapons. When Fiann tried to remove her father's claymore she reached for the hilt and said, "Nay, leave it."

Diancecht had recognized the blade the moment she came into the room. "There is no need to worry, child," he said as he came forward. "We will arm you with a more suitable blade. It will be kept safe until your return from Dunvegan."

With her hand still on the hilt of the Claymore, Maureen stared at this mysterious man. He was the same height as she, with long silver hair. He bore markings of entwined vines and leaves around the edge of his hairline that continued down his neck to his chest. But the most captivating thing about him were his eyes. They were like bright green emeralds, mesmerizing, and she found it difficult to look away. She was not sure why, but this man frightened her.

"It is alright Maureen," she heard Shalynn say. "They will keep it safe."

Reluctantly, she removed the sword and handed it over to Diancecht. He passed the sword off to the sentries who took it to the other end of the chamber, removed it from its scabbard and placed it in a mounting on the chamber wall.

"Shalynn, why do we tarry here?" Maureen whispered. "I must get to Dunvegan."

"And we will help you get there, but we need your help in return, and it cannot wait," Shalynn replied. "Come."

The Fey elders had begun to move into another room at the end of the chamber. They passed through a small ivy covered archway that lead into the circular room. In the center of the room was the base of a large tree that had been ornately carved into a ritual font and filled with the waters of the pools. It was dark with the only light coming from the doorway.

When Maureen passed through the archway and saw the font, she knew immediately what the Fey wanted from her.

"No, no Shalynn, I can nay look," she said as she backed away. "I can nay control the gift and I do nay understand what I see. Do nay make me, I beg ya."

Shalynn took her gently by the shoulders, "Do not be afraid child, I will help you. Come, we need you; your friends need you. If we are to help, we must see what is happening."

The walls of the room were covered with vines that had been intricately woven together to form seven arched niches around the font. The elders had taken their places inside each niche.

The air inside was heavy and still. It made Maureen's skin crawl and caused her to struggle for her breath. Reluctantly, she pushed her shirtsleeves up above her elbows and stepped up to the font. Shalynn had removed her own wrist guards and stood beside her.

"I will help you, just like before. I will see what you see." Shalynn reassured her. "Do not look away, child. Whatever you do, do not look away."

A faint light rose around each of the Fey elders and began to illuminate the room. Maureen drew a deep breath, trying to clear her mind and then slipped her hands into the font.

The water began to slowly spin, steadily gaining speed as the water whirled. A mist began to form across the top of the water and floated in unison, spinning to a peak in the center of the font. Shalynn gently slid her hand into the water taking Maureen's hand in hers.

Standing directly behind Shalynn was Diancecht. As the vision began to unfold, Shalynn reached back to him with her other hand. The Fey elders joined to him; now all would wait and see through the eyes of the young Watcher.

The mist lifted from the surface and the water became as glass. Shalynn felt Maureen's hand shaking beneath the water and knew the girl was frightened.

The first images were of a ship carrying warriors, many warriors, but it was not clear to Maureen which way they were going. She did not recognize the lands off the starboard side of the ship as it sailed. Now the ship began to fade and there before her eyes was Katie.

"Oh, Katie. Me sweet Katie. Where are ya girl?" Maureen whispered. She was sitting in a room that looked to have stone walls – Dunvegan, she is still at Dunvegan, Maureen thought.

Now Katie faded and the vision turned horrible. She saw cattle lying dead in a field, skinned and left to rot. Villages burned, women and children dead, livestock butchered. She saw the bodies of dead warriors toppled on each other on the ground.

She was beginning to tremble and tried to look away when she heard Shalynn whisper, "Do not look away child, be strong."

Through sheer will, Maureen pushed her hands farther into the font pressing them hard against the bottom. The water swirled once more and then suddenly stopped.

She saw the red haired man, the same man she had seen before. He was leading warriors toward Dunvegan castle. She saw the coastline and the Old Man of Stor. Just out to sea was another ship. A ship carrying MacDonald warriors.

She was tiring and having trouble keeping her thoughts. The vision was beginning to fade. In one last glimpse she saw the red haired man running from the castle, waiving a yellow cloth in his hand.

The water went dark; it was done. Maureen leaned forward on her elbows in the water, exhausted. Shalynn was leaning against the font as well. Diancecht and the others left the room immediately and as the Fey left the room their light went with them.

In the darkness of the chamber, Shalynn looked to the young Watcher, "You have done well, child. Come we must join the elders. There are plans to be made."

She started toward the chamber opening, but Maureen did not follow. She was still leaning forward, elbow deep in the water.

"Child, are you all right?" she asked.

"Shalynn, I do nay believe I can walk," Maureen whispered.

Shalynn went to the doorway and called for the sentries. They wrapped Maureen's dripping arms over their shoulders. Her steps were unstable and her knees did not want to hold her weight. They helped her out to the stone bench at the council table.

She slumped down, folded her arms on the table and rested her head. She was completely exhausted. The elders were already discussing what she saw in the font.

"The north, the attack is coming from the north," Diancecht said as he paced along the length of the room. "And at least two ships bring warriors into battle, one up the west coast and one sails around the peninsula."

When Maureen heard this she raised her head to listen. Katie, Katie was in the castle, she saw her there. She must get to her before it was too late.

"And what of the Braolauch shi My Lord?" Airmid asked. "It must not fall into the hands of Sorely Boy MacDonald, it must not."

"Sorely Boy MacDonald!" Maureen blurted out. So the red haired man was old Sorley Boy. Maureen had heard Maitiú's story of Sorely Boy and now she understood why he and Dónal were in peril.

It was then that the eyes of the elders turned to the young Watcher. Shalynn came to stand behind Maureen putting her hands on her shoulders as if to protect her. She knew what would be asked of the girl, but feared she would not be up to this quest. Maureen did not know enough yet and did not understand.

When the elder's eyes met hers, Maureen's skin began to crawl. She felt as if she was being hunted. Every instinct in her body told her to run. Their silent stare lasted for only a few moments but it felt as if time had stopped. She glanced back to Shalynn.

"What be wrong Shalynn, why do they watch me like that?" she quietly asked.

Shalynn did not reply. Maureen felt Shalynn's hands tighten on her shoulders. Shalynn's eyes were on her grandfather.

Finally, Diancecht broke the silence, "Séamus, bring their weapons, they leave as soon as the soft horses are ready. Shalynn, take her to the Braolauch shi." He then turned to Macha, "Ready your warriors My Lady, we leave the mound for Dunvegan at first light."

Everyone began to move at once. When Maureen tried to stand her legs would not hold her and she dropped back down on the bench. Shalynn went to Diancecht, "Grandfather, the youngling cannot leave now. The seeing has weakened her. She must rest first."

Diancecht looked across the room to see Maureen slumped on the council table.

"You are a healer Shalynn, see that she has what she needs to be ready," he said. "You have until first light." Then he turned and left the council chamber.

Airmid came to her daughter's side. "Take her to your quarters Shalynn, let her rest in the pools. The waters will help restore her strength. I will bring the herbs for the tonic."

Shalynn watched as Airmid seemed to float out of the room. Clothed in a light flowing gown threaded in silver, she walked with a grace and confidence that comes with the knowledge and wisdom of the ages. Shalynn smiled to herself as she looked down at her own garments. One would never see Airmid dressed in a leather jerkin and breaches – never.

Maureen was dozing when Shalynn came back around the end of the table.

"Come child, come," she said as she tapped Maureen's shoulder to wake her. "We must get you ready for Dunvegan."

The waters of the pool in Shalynn's quarters were rejuvenating indeed. A natural well in the stone fed by the waters from the Black Cullin Mountains. The bathing chamber walls were covered in live ferns and ivy. Candles placed around the chamber softly lit the room. The small pool was large enough for two, and the stone sides were polished smooth by the swirling waters. Strangely warm and aromatic, the water smelled of lavender. As she floated naked in the warm swirling water, Maureen's thoughts went to William. Soon this quest would be over. Katie was there at Dunvegan, she had seen her there, and Maitiú and Dónal as well. Soon they would be together again. And then, then she could return to William, for good.

"It is near time to go, child."

Maureen opened her eyes to see Shalynn and Airmid standing at the edge of the pool with a large drying cloth in their hands.

Maureen quickly crossed her arms across her breasts and turn her back to the women as she slipped out of the pool. She had entered the pool in private and had not expected them to just walk in on her.

Airmid and Shalynn exchanged a painful and troubled glance between them, as they both saw the marks across the youngling's back left by the sting of a master's whip. Neither women made mention of it, just simply wrapped the girl in the cloth to dry.

"This is my mother, Airmid." Shalynn said.

Maureen respectfully bowed her head, "Me thanks fer yer kindness M'lady."

"Drink this young one," Airmid said as she handed a chalice to Maureen. "It will give you strength."

The chalice was filled with a tea that was dark and warm, and tasted of mint and honey.

Airmid reached for Maureen and gently ran her fingers around her face to her chin, "You must dress quickly, time is short." She said and left the room.

Airmid's potion, whatever it was, had done its job. By the time she was dressed, Maureen was wide awake and had regained her strength. She met Shalynn at the door to the chamber and together they hurried through the hollow to the horses.

Fiann and Séamus waited next to the horses with new weapons for both of them. Shalynn quickly buckled her sword around her waist and tied the scabbard securely around her thigh.

When Séamus handed the Fey battle sword to Maureen, her mind went back to Heber and his words to her before she left him: *This be no little skirmish or cattle raid girl – this be clan war.*

The blatant reality of where she was going was suddenly very clear to her, and a cold chill ran through her body. She realized that she was scared, scared right down to the bone.

Shalynn had told her of the Flag of the Fey, the Braolauch shi, and the power that it held. Shalynn needed to get to the flag before any harm came to it. That was Shalynn's mission. All Maureen wanted to do was to get to the castle and find her friends. To find Katie, Philip, and the Irishmen and bring them to safety.

"My lady?" Séamus' voice brought her back. "Do you need assistance?" He asked. Maureen looked blankly at him and did not answer.

Shalynn noticed the hesitation and apprehension in the girl's eyes.

"She is fine Séamus," Shalynn snapped. "Come child. First light is near, we must hurry."

Maureen pulled her other belt and slid off the sheath for her doe-hoofed dagger, sliding it onto the new belt. She buckled the sword belt tightly around her waist and tied the scabbard to her leg.

They were ready. The horses knelt for their riders and they headed back out of the hollow. Diancecht and Macha met them on the stone platform in front of the door.

"We follow behind you, we will wait for the sign, Shalynn." Diancecht said. "You must not fail."

Chapter Twenty

The Siege of Dunvegan

The clan MacDonald final strategy evolved after months of vigorous debate. Some of the clan wanted a united force coming up from Sleat. Others pointed out how this had been tried numerous times in the past without success. The new strategy would be to split the forces and have one come up from Sleat and another come down from the Staffin side of the Isle. Dunvegan would be pinched between the two forces and popped like a puss-filled boil.

But there were critics of this plan who pointed out that coordinating such an attack would be nearly impossible to execute. There would be no element of surprise and the ultimate result would be a siege. Without siege guns, there would be no breech of the walls, and supplies of weapons and food could not be maintained for long in hostile territory.

Finally, a compromise was reached. From Sleat, would be a large force moving slowly and deliberately. The second force from the Staffin side would be a smaller, elite force comprised of battle-hardened warriors using stealth and surprise. And so it came to be that Sorley Boy MacDonald from the Glens of Antrim and his men would lead the Staffin force.

The slow approach from Sleat would draw attention away from the smaller Staffin force. Sorley Boy and his lads knew that success withstanding a siege depended on the defenders having sufficient food and drink to sustain them.

Being the reivers that they were, the MacDonalds of Antrim 'acquired' a small herd of twenty shagging cows that would be their key to unlocking the gates of Dunvegan.

They would claim to be MacNeils from Barra. Longtime friends and allies to Clan MacLeod, and frequent trading partners.

The herd arrived before the gates of Dunvegan in the pre-dawn hours, after the moon had set and before the sun rose. The hours of the morning when most people die and on this morning, many would die.

Among the shaggy beasts were six men walking in a stooped manner and draped with cowhides. They were not noticed in the dimness of the early morn. Rumbling hooves and the calls of the cattle muffled any sounds they made.

A single MacDonald walked alongside the herd and called to the watchman on the tower.

"Good marrow and peace be with ya good sir. A gift from the MacNeils of Barra to the MacLeods of Dunvegan."

The watchman gave him a friendly wave and signaled down to the gatekeeper. The castle gates opened. The one man herding the cattle walked up to the gatekeeper, put his hand across his mouth and promptly slit his throat.

Silently and quickly the other six men doffed the hides and slipped into the gatehouse making their way to the ramparts, quickly and quietly slitting the throats of unsuspecting guards on the stairways. Unattended, the rest of the herd of cattle turned and headed away from the castle gate.

Once key positions were neutralized a loud voice bellowed, "Air muir s'Air Tir!!" It was the war cry of Clan MacDonald. The gates were easily breeched on both the Staffin side and the Sleat side and a mad rush of usurpers surged into the castle slamming into the defenders.

In the melee and confusion that followed, MacDonalds from Sleat battled both MacLeods and MacDonalds from Staffin. As the sun rose and lifted away the dimness of dawn, the noise of cursing, screaming, grunting, and the clanging of steel lifted as well.

Sorely Boy battled his way across the courtyard and made his way to the keep where the MacLeods kept their sacred relics, including the Fairy Flag. Should he seize it and waive it for the honor of Clan MacDonald, he would become a living legend. The thought of such glory gave him an overwhelming sense of power.

Their surprise assault had been successful and very soon he would hold Dunvegan Castle for Clan MacDonald. Or so he thought.

As Olaf and Rhea set foot on the ground, the sounds of battle carried loudly across the meadow. Clan MacDonald had breached the gate of Castle Dunvegan— the battle had begun. Were they too late?

"Please God," Maureen prayed as the horses slowed their pace. "Please let me find Katie well and safe."

They jumped down from Olaf and Rhea, who quickly vanished into the trees surrounding the meadow. They ran as fast as they could toward the castle gate, holding close to the tree line until there was no more forest to protect them.

They moved along the gravel road toward the front gate. Up ahead they could see warriors fully engaged in battle, and many already lying dead upon the ground.

"Draw your sword child and take my hand!" Shalynn said as they came closer to the battle. "Stay quiet now, and do not let go."

Maureen did not question her. She pulled the Fey battle sword from its sheath and reached for Shalynn's hand. Shalynn pulled her sword as well and together they moved, one behind the other; Shalynn's sword in her left hand, Maureen's in her right and their hands joined in the middle.

But instead of running to the gate at full speed, Shalynn now slowed and move carefully and tactically through the mayhem. *They can nay see us,* Maureen thought. *She be hidin' us from them.*

The sight before their eyes was horrifying. Maureen wanted to move quickly through this brutal and sickening mêlée, but they must get to the Braolauch shi safely and not be seen.

They made their way through the gate and into the courtyard. They were trying to stay low and close, but the courtyard was overwhelmed with the battle cries of warriors, the clanging of steel and the screams of the dying.

The entrance to the lower level of the castle and the chamber of the relics was just across the courtyard. Shalynn began to pick up her pace, all that lay between them and the Braolauch shi were a few wounded on the ground. They jumped over the first man, but as they came down Maureen's boots slipped out from under her as she stepped down into a puddle of blood. She lost her grip with Shalynn's hand and fell right on top of a dead MacDonald warrior, her sword clattering to the ground.

Their link was broken and Maureen was now outside the sphere of Shalynn's protection. When she raised her head up, she was looking straight into the vacant eyes of an eviscerated man. All that blood on the ground and the putrid smell of him were more than she could bear. She began to retch and tried to get up to get away.

Shalynn was nowhere in sight and Maureen's sword was a good twenty feet away. As she struggled to regain herself, she looked across the courtyard, and there, coming up from the lower level of the castle was the red-haired man. And in his hand he held the Braolauch shi.

Still hidden from the eyes of men, Shalynn watched as Sorley Boy emerged from the keep. He was heading for the gatehouse and the stairs that led to the rampart. He must be stopped.

She was only a short distance from the young Watcher. She grabbed Maureen's sword and then moved directly into Sorley Boy's path. She crouched down in front of him, causing him to trip over her and fall to the ground.

He tumbled forward coming to rest right in front of Maureen. The Braolauch shi was within her reach.

Shalynn dropped her cover and shouted to the girl, "Take it child, take it!"

Maureen grabbed the end of the flag hanging from Sorley Boy's hand and tried to run, but he would not let go. He turned to her yelling, "Let go ya bloody little bitch!"

With her sword gone. She pulled the doe-hoofed dagger from her belt and slashed the big man across his forearm, just above his armguard. Her blade bit into bare skin and he yelled out in pain, releasing his grip.

"This be mine, not yers," Maureen said as she yanked the flag from his hand. As she turned to run away, she saw Shalynn reaching out to her.

"Take my hand!" Shalynn called as she reached for the young Watcher.

Sorley Boy scrambled to regain his footing, but as he turned to go after the girl, she vanished right before his eyes.

"Ya fookin' little witch! I'll kill ya! I swear I'll kill ya!" He shouted.

Maureen and Shalynn made for the sea gate and hurried up the stairs that led to the rampart. Below them the MacLeod warriors were being overrun, time was running out.

"Open the flag Maureen, open it for all to see," Shalynn said as they ran along the rampart.

Maureen stopped and climbed up on the battlement. She unfolded the flag and holding the corners in each hand, raised it above her head. The wind caught it and snapped it open.

"Warriors of Clan MacLeod!" She shouted. "Behold the Braolauch shi!" The small flag flapped in the wind and a deafening clap of thunder rang across the land. Clouds quickly gathered above them, and a bright flash of lightening cracked across the sky above the castle. Flashes of light, like shooting stars, began to fall from the clouds. Every warrior on the battleground turned to look, including Sorely Boy MacDonald.

From the edge of the forest Macha's warriors swarmed the castle. They seemed to come from everywhere. The MacDonalds were confused and could not recognize the Fey warriors from their own men. It did not take long for the Macleod forces to regain the interior of the castle and secure the gatehouse.

The battle continued on the castle grounds, but not for long. Retreat was sounded and what was left of the Clan MacDonald brigades began to scurry to their ships and curraghs; defeated once again.

Chapter Twenty-One

Return to Dunvegan

To Coleman's dismay, only a few of the MacDonalds disembarked at Armdale. The MacDonald guard remaining on board, seeing Coleman's confusion said, "We nay be done with ya yet paddy."

Shortly thereafter, a messenger from the MacDonald stronghold jogged back to the ship.

He rushed over to Coleman and the guard, "Yer ta take this wreck back up the coast and inform the lads from Staffin to attack in three days' time. If these curs," he said, pointing to the Irish crew, "do nay do what they be told, yer ta shoot them and we will send backup."

Coleman recoiled. Then, realizing his situation, regained his composure and replied, "If that's how ya be wantin' it." Their passengers were about two dozen or so MacDonald interlopers. Coleman turned the ship around and headed back up the coast of Skye toward Dunvegan.

They passed the inlet that held Dunvegan and dropped anchor. They watched and listened carefully for any sign of the Staffin MacDonalds.

Over the noise of the surf, could be heard the sounds of battle. Gunshots and blood curdling war cries were heard. Flashes of powder could be seen. The Staffin MacDonalds were fully engaged with the MacLeods.

These MacLeods advanced from Dunvegan and executed a surprise attack on their would-be attackers. Clan MacDonald was taking a beating. There would be no coordinated attack on Dunvegan. Rather, there would be only rescue and evacuation of the surviving Staffin MacDonalds.

They were retrieved in curraghs, five or six at a time. Coleman's crew pulled them on board one at a time. On one of the boats was Sorely Boy MacDonald. His plate and helm were dented. The cotúm under his plate was torn and blood stained. Was it blood from a MacDonald or a MacLeod? No one could tell. His flaming red hair was matted and dried, dark blood streaks trailed down the side of his face, dripping from his strong, squared jaw line and there was a deep wound across his left arm.

It was Dónal who pulled Sorely Boy on board, wounds and all. Dónal exclaimed with exaggerated courtesy, "Mo thiarna, how grand it be ta see ya on this fine day. And 'tis well ya are? Dónal MacMaitiú de Faoite at yer service."

MacDonald sneered and snarled through his blood stained teeth, "Go hifreann leat! Ta Hell with ya!"

"You first, yer honor." Dónal mocked.

"There be no lack of kin down there fer ya, O Lord of the Glenns," Maitiú added.

"Po mo thóin, ya wretched spawn of Munster!" Sorley Boy snapped.

Captain Coleman smirked when he heard 'spawn of Munster'.

"Who be this prick, Maitiú, that he should step on me ship and insult Munster. By the sound of him he brays like an Ulster jackass," Coleman taunted.

A MacDonald Lieutenant standing nearby shouted, "Dún bhur mbéal, shut yer mouths! Keep yer Irish politics ta yerselves and get this ship back to Sleat. Anois, now!"

With a nod from Coleman, Maitiú and Dónal quickly moved out of sight, as Sorley Boy was helped to his quarters by man servants, and followed by the ship's surgeon. The deck of the ship was utter chaos as wounded, bleeding MacDonald warriors were brought on board wailing in pain.

"Dónal, go below and gather our belongin's, we're gettin' off this ship," Maitiú instructed. Dónal departed immediately following his father's instructions.

Maitiú moved down the corridor toward Sorley Boy's quarters. As he listened, Sorley Boy began to yell and struggle with the ship's surgeon and the men who were doing their best to help him.

Maitiú knew that he and Dónal could not stay on this ship any longer. Sorley Boy now knew who he was and he would waste no time coming after him. After listening to the MacDonald Chieftain ranting at everyone in his cabin, Maitiú was ready to go in search of Coleman when the conversation coming from Sorley Boy's cabin caught his ear.

"This be a nasty wound on yer arm M'lord, please hold still so we can close it up. How did ya ever get cut above yer arm guards?" asked the ship surgeon.

"Some little MacLeod bitch with a doe-hoofed blade slashed me arm and took the flag of Dunvegan from me," Sorley Boy growled. "And as soon as I'm done stranglin' two Irishmen, I be goin' back after her. Now stitch up the arm man and get me on me way."

Maitiú quickly moved down the narrow corridor, making his way out on deck in search of Captain Craig. He and Dónal had to get off this ship now. Maureen was at Dunvegan Castle and that bastard was going back after her. They had to find her first.

He raced up on deck to find Captain Craig on the aft deck, flanked by MacDonald's cronies. They were getting ready to weigh anchor and leave as soon as the curraghs returned with the last of the wounded MacDonald warriors.

Maitiú waited until Craig caught his glance. With a nod of his head he signaled Craig to meet him below deck. He watched as Craig excused himself from the captivity of the MacDonald Lieutenants and headed down the stairs from the aft deck.

He followed Maitiú below deck and into the ships galley. As soon as Craig came through the door, Maitiú grabbed him by the coat collars and yanked him out of sight.

"Craig, I need yer help me friend," he said as he backed Craig up against the galley wall.

"Easy boyo, easy now," Craig cautioned. "Lower yer voice man."

Maitiú quickly checked the corridor for any other shipmates and then turned back to Craig.

"Me and me boy need ta get off this ship now. Sorely Boy knows who we are and its goin' ta be trouble"

Coleman knew Maitiú was right. The ship was already in complete mayhem with all of the wounded, the last thing he needed was an uprising between the MacDonalds and his Irish crewmen.

"Gather yer things, boyo," he instructed. "Ya can take the next curragh that comes in and head to the loch."

"Yer a good man Craig Coleman. Should ya find yerself in port at Dunbarton, come by the Wycked Aye Tavern and I'll buy ya a pint of me finest." Maitiú said. He patted him on the shoulders and then quickly ducked down the corridor after Dónal.

Coleman went straight back up on deck to check on the wounded and watch for the next curragh coming in.

Maitiú met Dónal in the corridor coming up from their berths. Dónal tossed his father's sword and brat to him, and they scurried up on deck as well.

It was now mid-afternoon. The tide was beginning to change and seas were getting rough. The deckhands were having trouble getting the last of the wounded on board as the curraghs bounced and swayed on the swells.

On the port side, one of the curraghs was waiting as the last man aboard reached for the rope ladder to climb to safety. Now was their chance. Maitiú and Dónal pulled the man onboard and hurried down the rope. The boatman, one of the Irish crew, was surprised to see the two men coming down.

"What's this now lads?" he asked. "This be the last run fer this boat."

"Aye mate, the last it be fer certain, we be goin' back to shore," Dónal shouted as he jumped down into the boat. "Come along if ya want, but this one will nay be comin' back."

Maitiú dropped into the boat behind his son. Dónal turned to the boatman, "Are ya comin' or goin'?"

"She be all yers lads, God speed ta ya both," he replied. He waited for the next swell, grabbed a ratline and climbed up the ropes.

Dónal let loose of the mooring rope and pushed off from the big ship. They were on their way. Maitiú was free from Sorely Boy MacDonald once more.

The last of the curraghs were empty and what remained of the MacDonald contingent were brought onboard, wounded and defeated. Coleman, still under the hold of the MacDonald Lieutenants, was readying his ship to weigh anchor and get underway when he heard Sorley Boy storming up on deck. The ship's surgeon had closed the wounds on his arm and head. And, although most of the blood had been washed clean from his face, he was still red with anger.

He yanked at crewmen, pushing and shoving them as he frantically searched for Maitiú and Dónal.

The crew stopped working and stood straight and still on the deck, the wounded MacDonalds left to lay helpless.

A smile crossed Coleman's face as he watched his loyal crewmen stand in defiance against this fooking amadan. Coleman was fed up with him as well. His keen eye noticed a hint of disgust on the faces of many of the MacDonalds, both the wounded and the able-bodied. It was time to end this and take back his ship and his crew.

"Where are they Coleman? Where are those filthy, Irish bilge rats?" Sorley Boy barked as he turned to Coleman.

"The only bilge rat I see stands before me, jock. As to me friends Dónal and Maitiú, well, they have taken their leave ya miserable, wee gobshite!" Coleman chuckled as he turned his gaze to port.

Seeing this and following Coleman's gaze, Sorley Boy stormed to the port rail and looking out across the water saw the curragh containing the de Faoites. Adding fuel to his blistering rage, he saw Dónal stop rowing and blow him a kiss off the end of his middle finger. Then it was back to the oars as they rowed across the loch to Dunvegan.

Blind with fury Sorley Boy charged toward the aft deck only to be blocked by two of his own men who happened to be Irishmen who had been forced into Sorley Boy's service against their will, and they too were finished with him.

"Control yerself sir, ya dishonor us!"

"Out of my way!" Sorley Boy brawled.

Two more MacDonald men stood. These two were MacQuillans from the Glens of Antrim, pressed into service by Sorley Boy. They were no longer in awe of their overlord; they were disgusted.

"Yer no longer our Captain or Commander ya blaggard. We stand with the Corkman," said one of the men. The other nodded his head in agreement.

Sorley Boy lunged at the MacQuillans only to be pushed back. In unison, the sailors pulled their blades to hold the wild-eyed MacDonald at bay.

From behind, Sorely Boy heard his men grumble and begin to call out, "Sin é, go direach," and "Tá sin ceart," *That's it exactly, that be right.*

Even the wounded MacDonalds, who would otherwise be loyal, were saying, "Remove this embarrassment. Take us to Cork paddy!"

Coleman strode down the steps of the aft deck and came to stand before Sorley Boy.

"We'll drop a Curragh fer ya MacDonald. Now gather yer belongin's and get yer sorry arse the hell off me ship. Consider it a mercy that I do nay just throw ya over the side!"

He turned to address the crew. "Weigh anchor lads and hoist the colors, this ship sails for Ireland!"

Cheers went up from every deck and the men hurried to get the ship underway. Sorley Boy was escorted to his cabin where he gathered his sword and bow. They led him to edge of the ship and dumped him in a waiting curragh.

The sailors raised canvas and the call came out from the foredeck, "She's aweigh Captain!" Coleman watched from the port rail as the ship sailed away, leaving Sorley Boy MacDonald alone on Loch Dunvegan.

Chapter Twenty-Two

Flight from Dunvegan

As each piece of ground was reclaimed for Clan MacLeod, the Fey warriors disappeared just as quickly as they had come.

Maureen jumped down from the battlement and carefully folded the flag. But before she could hand it off to Shalynn, they heard footsteps coming up the stairs to the rampart. Both women drew weapons and braced themselves against the battlement. When Shalynn saw the man, she placed her hand in front of Maureen signaling her to stand down. For standing before them was the Chieftain of Clan MacLeod, William MacLeod, the MacLeod of MacLeod.

There was no need to hide their presence from this man. He knew the Aes Sidhe well and without saying a word bent a knee to Shalynn. She turned to Maureen, who handed her the small saffron flag.

"I return the Braolauch shi to you and your people My Lord. Dunvegan is now safe," she said as she handed him the flag. Then turning to look at Maureen she added, "And your Watcher has come home."

"Many thanks ta you and yer people Lady Shalynn," he said as he accepted the flag. "I be at yer service 'til the end of me days."

He then turned his attention to Maureen. He raised up from his knee and bowed before her, then offered her his hand.

"I thank the Gods fer yer return Lady..." he turned to Shalynn.

"Maureen." She prompted.

"...Lady Maureen. Welcome home, whatever ya ask shall be yers," he pledged.

Maureen stared at this great man bowing before her. She did not understand what was going on and did not know how to properly respond to this man.

He was a big man and reminded her very much of her own William. A handsome man with long dark hair and blue eyes. He wore a full beard closely trimmed and showing a bit of grey. He was dressed in full battle arraignment and had taken a few small wounds as his shirt, breastplate and kilt were blood stained.

When he stood up straight, he was near six feet tall. To her, he was like a king to her people – royalty. When she finally composed herself she said, "'Tis good ta be home M'lord and there be something ya can do fer me. I search for me kinswoman, Katie MacLeod. Where might I find her?"

He turned and pointed to the opposite side of the courtyard.

"There," he said. "The women, children and the aged are safely guarded in the servant's quarters."

Maureen bowed her head to him and then started to head for the stairway down to the courtyard.

"Child!" Shalynn called back to her, "Find your kin and then go to the meadow. Rhea will take you to safety."

Maureen nodded and then continued on her way.

"She be young," MacLeod said as he watched Maureen hurry down the stairs to the courtyard.

"Yes, My Lord, she is. But she is powerful and she will serve us well." Shalynn replied.

"And the Keeper, what of the Keeper?" He asked.

"Dead, My Lord. The Keeper is dead."

MacLeod leaned on the stone wall of the battlement and looked out over the loch.

"So, she be the last."

Shalynn did not respond to him as she too turned her gaze out to the sea. There she spied a single curragh rowing back into the loch when all of the others had already fled for open sea.

A faint smile crossed her face as she recognized a familiar saffron léine and the black tunic of the Papal army. As the boat approached shore, Macleod warriors began to head toward them readying their weapons.

"My Lord, these men who approach, let them pass," she said. "They are friends to the young Watcher and friends of Clan MacLeod.

The Chieftain called down to his warriors and, to their surprise, the Irishmen were escorted through the sea gate and on to the castle courtyard.

As a seasoned soldier of the papal army, Dónal's hand went straight to the hilt of his sword when he saw the confusion and casualties of the castle courtyard.

He stepped protectively in front of his father, "Da, we can nay tarry long in place, we need to find Maureen and..."

As he scanned the courtyard he felt as if someone was watching him. It was then that he spied Shalynn standing on the rampart. Maitiú turned to see her as well.

She pointed across the courtyard.

Maureen crossed the courtyard as fast as she could. The anticipation of seeing Katie again was great and she could hardly contain herself. When she reached the servant's quarters, the women and children had started to wander out on to the courtyard. Maureen pushed her way between them frantically searching for Katie.

She went from chamber to chamber, hallway to hallway but could not find Katie anywhere. She turned around and headed back out toward the courtyard. Maybe she had missed Katie in the crowd of people. As she hurried through the passage ways she began to call out.

"Katie! Katie MacLeod! Katie!" *She has to be here*, Maureen thought to herself.

Dónal and Maitiú were cautiously making their way through the courtyard when Dónal turned to his father, "Da, Da do ya hear that?"

They stopped and listened, and heard Maureen's voice calling out to Katie. Dónal spied her first, "There Da look!" he shouted as they both began to run at full speed toward her.

"Maureen MacLeod!" Dónal shouted. "Maureen, over here girl!"

Maureen stopped, and looked around to see who was calling to her. When her eyes met Dónal's she whispered, "Búiochas do Dhia, thanks be to God." She crossed herself and headed straight for them. Her first few steps were nothing more than a hurried walk that quickly turned into a run. She met Dónal at a full run and throwing herself into his arms, she wrapped her arms around his neck as he swung her around in a full circle.

When he put her down, he gave her a look over saying, "Ya look quite fetchin' in leather and breeches, lass." Then he gave her a brotherly punch in the shoulder.

She then turned to Maitiú and, hugging him tightly, said, "Thank God Maitiú, thank God ya be alright," as tears welled her eyes.

Maitiú took her face in his hands and looked deep into her eyes. Maureen covered his hands with hers. She could see that his skin was weathered and his beard was scruffy and showing bits of grey. Both men were ragged and weary from their journey.

"It be a miracle we found ya lass," he said as he wrapped his arms tightly around her.

"I be thankful ya did," she whispered.

For although Maureen had felt protected by Shalynn and the Fey, now she was safe. This man had been her first friend at the Wycked Aye. They had laughed together, cried together, drank, danced and sang together. But most of all, they had prayed together. Their faith was something that had bound them together from the first moment they met. He watched out for her as if she were his own daughter. And Dónal had been like a brother to her. She was back in the arms of her family and she was safe.

"Da, we need to get out of here. Old Sorley Boy will nay be far behind us." Dónal warned.

"Sorley Boy?" Maureen asked. "The red-haired man?"

"Aye lass, he be lookin' fer all of us now, we need ta go," Maitiú said. He took Maureen's hand and started to move toward the gatehouse.

"Wait Maitiú, I can nay leave without Katie. Please help me find her," Maureen cried.

"She nay be here, lass," Dónal said.

Maureen looked at them stunned. Katie had to be here, she had seen her here.

"She be safe, lass," Maitiú said. "Safe with Philip at the castle in Armdale. Now come on girl, we'll tell ya 'bout it later. We have to go now." At that, Maitiú took her under one arm and Dónal under the other as they made for the gatehouse.

As they ran from the Castle, Maureen began to relive the vision that had been revealed to her in Badenoch. Panic began to take hold and she ran as fast as she could to try and catch up with Maitiú and Dónal. She had to stop this; she could not allow this nightmare to come true.

Keeping up with the two Irishmen was nearly impossible. Finally, they slowed down and turned to check on her. "Come on lass, hurry!" they called to her.

The edge of the forest was near and she knew what lay ahead. They must hurry or it would be too late. Just down the road she could see the stone bridge covered in moss, and just beyond that was the edge of the forest.

They waited for her to get close and then began to run again with Dónal in the lead. They passed under the stone bridge and headed toward the safety of the forest just up ahead.

Maureen looked back to see the tall man with flaming red hair standing on the stone bridge with a bow in hand just as she had seen him in her vision.

"Get down Maitiú, get down!" she yelled to him, but he did not hear her.

Sorely Boy MacDonald walked out on the bridge to see the three of them running from the castle.

"I knew ya were a bloody arse traitor de Faoite, and yer little MacLeod bitch is a damn thief. Now, I'm goin' to hurt ya where it'll hurt ya the most. Let's see if ya can out run this bogtrotter." He pulled an arrow from his quiver and primed his bow.

Maureen caught up with Maitiú just as Sorley Boy let lose the arrow from his bow. She threw herself on Maitiú's back hoping to knock him down and out of the path of the arrow. But she was not big enough to bring the Irishman down, and within a few seconds Sorley Boy's arrow found its target.

Their legs became tangled together and they tumbled to the ground. They were just off the edge of the forest. Maureen hit the ground hard and Maitiú tumbled forward rolling on the rock path.

"Da!" Dónal yelled as he ran back to his father. "Da, Da, are ya all right?" he said as he tried to help him up.

229

"Are ya wounded Da?" When Maitiú looked up at his son, his face was scrapped up from falling on the rock path, but he was otherwise unharmed.

Maitiú saw Maureen lying on the road behind them, face down with an arrow through her back. She was not moving.

"No, no, dear God in heaven, no!" Maitiú cried. The two men ran to her and gently rolled her over as far as the shaft of the arrow would allow. She was barely conscious. She raised her hand and pointed to edge of the tree line. With a voice choked with pain she whispered, "Get ta the forest, Maitiú."

As they picked her up between them, Dónal looked back to the bridge to see Sorely Boy knocking another arrow.

"Christ almighty! Run Da!" he exclaimed.

Maitiú looked back and saw Sorley Boy staring him down, "Ya bastard MacDonald! Ya'll never be forgiven for this, never!" He shouted.

"Come on Da!" Dónal urged. They turned and hurried into the forest just as Sorely Boy's arrow skipped across the ground behind them.

They ran through almost fifty yards of trees and brush before they broke into a small, secluded green meadow. They placed the young lass on the ground and laid her on her left side so as not to put any pressure on the arrow. It had gone all the way through her right shoulder.

"What are we goin' to do Da? She be badly wounded and we can nay help her out here," Dónal asked.

Maitiú knelt beside her, "I do nay know Dónal. I know not which way to go. But we must find her a healer quickly, she can nay survive much longer." Maitiú brushed her hair away from her face. She was shaking with pain.

"She took an arrow that was meant fer me. I will nay let her die out here." He stood up and looked around. He was unsure which way to go. There was nothing in the meadow; no paths, no streams to follow, nothing. He took a deep breath, closed his eyes and looked up to heaven, "If ya ever heard a prayer, Father, ya need to hear this one," he said.

He opened his eyes and looked around the meadow once more. To his surprise, from the opposite side of the meadow walked an old, white mare. Rhea was trotting directly toward them. They watched as she came right up to them and put her head down to where Maureen lay.

"I don't fookin' believe it," Maitiú said.

Dónal looked at his father and said, "Da, if there ever be a time to just believe, this be it."

Maitiú reached forward and patted the horse's matted mane, "I be not sure what ya are, but I thank God fer sendin' ya. Now old girl, can ya help us get this lass to a healer?"

The horse turned and gently laid herself down next to Maureen. Maitiú and Dónal lifted her onto the back of the horse with Maitiú sitting behind her, holding her up. As the horse raised herself from the ground, she changed from an old, tired mare to a strong and beautiful horse.

Dónal hopped up on her back behind Maitiú and she headed straight for the edge of the meadow from which she came.

Maureen began to cry out as the bouncing of the horse was painful. She leaned her head back against Maitiú's shoulder and whispered, "It hurts Maitiú, it hurts."

It tore at his heart to see her like this. He pushed back his tears as he said, "Ya stay with me now girl. It will nay be long. Stay with me."

As Rhea ran through the tree line the forest began to fill with mist. Suddenly, there was no more bouncing, there were no sounds of horse hooves hitting the ground. The soft horse of Skye had taken flight.

As they moved through the mist, Maitiú thought to himself, *I'm sorry I doubted ya Philip, please forgive me.*

Shalynn looked out over the wall of the castle, the bodies of dead MacDonalds and MacLeods lay side-by-side upon the battle field. The assault upon Dunvegan had been thwarted, but at such a high cost. The young Watcher had come to the aide of Clan MacLeod as Watchers and Keepers have done for all time. Now she went to the aid of her friends to see them safely out of danger.

Shalynn drew a deep clearing breath, the Fey could now stand down and return to their place as guardians, not warriors. She would begin the task of teaching the girl-child of the ancient ways of the Fey and the depth of her own gifts.

But as she turned to leave the castle, an intense pain suddenly shot through her body causing her to stagger against the castle wall.

By the greater powers, this cannot be, she thought. She struggled to regain herself, then ran as fast as she could to the nearest cluster of trees where Olaf waited for her, and then disappeared into the forest.

Within moments of Rhea touching ground, Shalynn came running out from the trees toward them.

"This way," she directed.

They ran through a canopy of trees and up a long path of stone stairs. Huge, moss covered rocks surrounded the path as it wound up the hill. Waiting for them at the end of the pathway was Morríghan Macaulay. "Bring her, quickly," she said.

They carried Maureen into Morríghan's house and laid her on a straw cot. They quickly cut her clothes away from the wound and the arrow.

Dónal and Maitiú were pacing back and forth as the two women worked frantically to pull the arrow from Maureen's chest. They had managed to cut the shaft but neither of them were strong enough to pull it out. Each short pull was causing more damage and the pain was becoming too much for Maureen to bear.

"Come Maitiú, help me!" Shalynn shouted.

Maitiú came to Maureen's side. He could see that she was slipping away, the sight shocked him and he hesitated. Shalynn reached over and put her hand on his arm, "We cannot save her without you, it is time for you to be the healer Maitiú."

He looked at Shalynn and then to his son, "Come Dónal, hold her shoulders." Maitiú placed one hand around the base of the arrow and against her chest, and grabbed the remaining shaft with the other hand.

"Please God, let me pull straight and true," he prayed. And then, with one great motion, he yanked the arrow from her body.

Maureen screamed out in pain and then lost consciousness. With the arrow removed, blood began to pour from the openings on both sides of her shoulder.

"Quickly now, hand me the Carraban," Shalynn ordered.

Now it was Morríghan who hesitated, "But Shalynn, humankind can nay take Fey blood."

"We have no time to argue, bring me the Carraban!" Shalynn snapped.

Reluctantly, Morríghan turned to an apothecary jar

233

on her table. Inside the jar was a sea moss called Carraban. A standard medicinal for most, but when put in the hands of the Fey it became something very different.

Morríghan handed two bundles of the wet moss to Shalynn who gently rolled them in her hands and then laid them over the wounds. The moss seemed to come alive on Maureen's skin. As it worked its way into her wounds, the bleeding began to slow. Shalynn pulled a blade from her belt and sliced open the palms of both of her hands. She began to reach for Maureen when Morríghan stopped her.

"It will kill her Great One," Morríghan whispered.

"No my old friend, it will not. Now, help me to hold her up." Morríghan sat behind Maureen and lifted her body upright. As Shalynn placed her hands against the Carraban it began to work its way into her wounds as well. The joining of blood caused Maureen to take a great gasp of air and then she slumped back against Morríghan.

Shalynn began to quietly speak the ancient words of healing:

My blood is your blood,
and your blood is mine.
As our blood flows together
this wound we shall bind.
Two separate hearts
that now beat as one,
Together they beat as
the healing is done.
Blood of my blood,
heart of my heart,
What is now joined together
shall never part.

Shalynn's heart would keep Maureen's heart beating, and her blood would help to heal the wounds.

As Morríghan held Maureen propped up against her, she began to realize who the young woman was. She pushed Maureen's hair aside to reveal the mark of the black rose on the back of her neck.

It can nay be, she said to herself. *After all these years, it can nay be.*

It had been well over two hours and Shalynn still sat with her hands joined to Maureen's wounds. Shalynn's Fey blood had caused the girl no apparent harm.

Dónal came to Morríghan and asked, "How long?" She looked at him and he asked again, "How long will they stay like this?"

"Until the Carraban releases them, it could take hours," she quietly replied.

The healing was taking its toll on Shalynn, as well. She was tiring and having trouble holding herself up.

"Irishman," Morríghan whispered to Dónal. "Pull a chair and let Shalynn rest against ya. She tires."

Dónal pulled a chair from the table and sat up next to Shalynn. He gently touched her shoulders and she leaned back against him. She did not speak as her concentration was focused on the healing. Dónal looked down at the small woman he now held in his arms and then to Morríghan.

"Fey blood, ya said Fey blood. Would she truly be Fey?"

Morríghan looked in the young man's eyes. She could clearly see the confusion and conflict his mind was trying sort out.

"'Twould it be that hard fer ya to believe?" she

whispered.

"Ya called her Great One, why did ya call her that?" Dónal pressed.

"Ah, that would nay be me place to say." Morríghan looked over to the table where Maitiú was sitting, listening to the exchange.

"Maitiú be it?" she asked. "Come good sir, I need a rest as well. Come and hold the girl-child and I'll fix us some food."

Maitiú slid behind Maureen, taking the old woman's place. As he let her lean back against him, he saw the whip scars across her bare back. He knew she had suffered at the hands of the Armstrongs, but he did not realize the extent of that suffering until now.

Morríghan went to the cupboard and pulled a jug and three cups from the shelf. She poured a cup of mead for each of them. They took their cups in silence and waited.

It was well after dark when Shalynn's hands finally slid away from Maureen's wounds. The Carraban dropped to the floor, stained black with their blood. Morríghan came to her immediately. Shalynn's hands were healed but she was completely exhausted.

"Take her, Dónal, to the back of the house to me bed and let her rest."

Dónal laid Shalynn back into his arms and carried her to the old woman's bed. As he walked to the bed chamber he watched as markings began to appear on Shalynn's face and arms. It was clear she had been hiding her true appearance from them. He laid her gently on the bed, placing her on her side. He brushed her hair back away from her face, softly running his finger along the markings.

She reached her hand up to his and whispered, "Do not be afraid of what you see, Dónal."

"I nay be," he replied. "I think yer beautiful." Then she fell fast asleep. He pulled a quilt to cover her and then returned to his father and Morríghan.

Morríghan began to tend to Maureen's wounds. They were healing, but still needed attention and bandaging.

"Lay her down now, Maitiú," Morríghan instructed. "The danger be past, she will live."

Maitiú slipped out from behind the girl and laid her gently on the straw cot.

"What now?" Maitiú asked of the old woman.

"Now they will sleep, as we will. There be a place for ya both to rest this night. Ya be safe here, no one has followed ya to this place." She turned and began to walk to the back of her cottage.

"Good woman," Maitiú called back to her. "Ya have taken us inta yer home, helped to heal our friend, fed us and now ya offer us shelter. Yet, we do nay know yer name."

Morríghan turned back to them and with an old woman's crooked smile said, "I be Morríghan MacLeod Macaulay. They call me the witch of the moors, rest well, lads."

The next morning when the two men woke, Morríghan was not in the house. Dónal rolled over in his bed to see Maitiú sitting up by the fire looking around.

This was no peasant's hovel. It was a large, two level, stone manor with two hearths and fine glass windows. It resembled the home of a wealthy merchant.

Maitiú got up and began to move through the house. The walls of the kitchen pantry were lined with cupboards filled with apothecary jars. From the ceiling bundles of herbs and flowers hung upside-down, drying. Small handmade talismans had been placed about the house and the framing around the door had been carved with ancient symbols.

But the one thing that Maitiú noticed more than anything else was the wooden cross that hung above the entry door. He knew then that the old woman was no witch. She was a skilled healer, and a MacLeod woman with gifts just like Maureen, nothing more.

Morríghan had left food for them on the pantry table: fresh berries, biscuits and cheese.

Maitiú walked over to Maureen, she was asleep but restless with pain. He watched her as her eyes shifted back and forth beneath her eyelids. In the back of the house, Shalynn was sleeping peacefully in Morríghan's bed.

Dónal watched in silence as his father moved through the house, running his fingers along the cupboards and reaching up to touch the bundles that hung from above.

"Da?" Dónal asked. "Ya alright?"

Maitiú turned to him slowly, "Ah, good marrow to ya mo chroí. Peace be with ya."

"And with ya as well Da," Dónal returned. "How be our girl?"

Maitiú glanced back in Maureen's direction, "I do nay know lad, she seems restless. Morríghan has left us breakfast if ya be hungry at all, and there be a kettle on the pantry fire."

Dónal got up and went to the pantry. He cut some cheese for himself and his father, and poured two mugs of tea. Handing the mug to Maitiú he said, "So what do we do now Da? How long do we wait here?"

"I do nay know fer certain," Maitiú pondered. "I can nay say where we are. 'Twould be best to wait for the old woman and ask her counsel. She will know…"

Before Maitiú could finish, Morríghan entered the house.

She carried a basket full of plants, berries and nuts from the forest. When she was done emptying her basket, she took one of the plants and crushed it on a stone mortar. She then put it in a cup with hot water to steep. She looked to Maitiú. "How be the girl-child?" she asked as she went to Maureen's bed.

"Restless," he replied. "She be in pain I think. Why do her eyes move like that?"

Morríghan looked down at her and could see her eyes moving beneath her eyelids.

"It be not the pain," Morríghan replied. "She sees. It be the Fey blood." She touched the girl's forehead and gently ran her fingers around her face.

"She will sleep for many days; we will see ta the youngling now. Ya must make yer way home Maitiú, for ya have yer own wounds to heal." She got up and went back to the pantry for the steeping cup.

Maitiú looked at her with astonishment. "What do ya mean?"

"A bond has been broken, it needs to be mended," she said as she strained the leaves from the cup.

"How do ya know that woman?" Maitiú asked.

"I know many things Irishman, does nay matter how."

She sat down next to Maureen with the cup. She dipped a cloth in it and slowly dripped the potion on to her lips.

"What be that yer givin' her?" Dónal asked as he moved toward the bed in a protective, brotherly manner.

"It be alright lad; it be only a tonic of Valerian. "Twill help her to sleep and ease her pain."

Dónal looked to his father, "We need to get word to Heber, Da. He needs to know...."

"We will send word to the MacPherson." Morríghan

offered. "It be time for you two to return to yer home."

Maitiú looked at his son, "I believe she be right, Dónal. Home to Ireland it be."

"Nay Maitiú, nay to Ireland." Morríghan warned. "To Dumbartonshire, that be where ya'll find what ya need."

Maitiú looked at the old woman with wonder. He did not respond to her, there was no need. He knew full well that the words of this old sage were sound. He would heed her counsel; it would be foolish not to.

The men gathered their belongings and began to prepare for their journey.

"Morríghan, which way do we go?" Maitiú asked.

She gestured for the two men to follow her outside. They walked down the moss covered stone path and out to the meadow. She whistled twice, and out from the tree line trotted two, huge horses. Maitiú looked at her. "There be two of them?" he asked.

"Nay." Morríghan replied. "There be many of 'em, one for each of the great ones, and a few more. They'll take ya where ya need to go—trust them now."

There were no saddles or bridles on these horses for they were not meant to be led by men. As Dónal and Maitiú approached the two magnificent creatures, Dónal turned to his father and asked, "Da, be that Olaf?

Maitiú recognized him as well and called out, "Hello, old friend."

Olaf's ears perked up and he trotted over to Maitiú and nuzzled him as Maitiú rubbed his neck with his whiskered face. Olaf leaned into Maitiú and nearly knocked him over.

When Olaf saw Dónal he neighed and shuffled his feet.

"Happy feet, Olaf!" I be glad to see you too!"

The two great horses knelt on their front legs so the men could mount them easily.

When they were ready to ride, Dónal looked back to

Morríghan, "Many thanks for yer kindness good woman."

Morríghan bowed her head to them, "This place will always welcome ya both. Good journey to ya lads."

Maitiú looked back to the house. He was uncomfortable leaving Maureen behind. How would he explain to Heber what had happened here?

Morríghan sensed his uneasiness, "Do nay worry for her Maitiú, ya will see her again."

With the old woman's final words, the horses began to move together toward the edge of the trees, and as the mist formed around them the horses took flight, leaving Maureen, Shalynn and the witch of the moors behind.

Chapter Twenty-Three

An Uncomfortable Reunion

Philip and Katie walked slowly on the road out of Armdale. Philip's explanations to her had reaped a harvest of cold, tense silence. The more he tried to explain the more withdrawn she became. Finally, he resolved himself to the fact that he must simply wait for time or some future event to ease the situation.

She was angry to near rage at the way he behaved toward the Irishmen. To his deep regret, Philip knew he was likely never to see the two of them again. It would be a burden he would probably carry with him the length of his remaining days.

It was mid-afternoon and they were just on the outskirts of Armdale when Philip notice two clouds moving quickly across the sky; one grey and one white. He watched as the two clouds floated down into the trees and disappeared.

Katie saw them first. "Well I'll be damned!" she exclaimed. "Philip look!"

Out from the trees, just up ahead, came two men on horseback; one wearing the black tunic of the Papal Army and the other a familiar saffron léine.

Olaf and Rhea pranced right up to them with their heads held high and their beautiful, full manes blowing in the wind. Katie and Philip were gobsmacked.

Maitiú looked right into Katie's eyes, he was smiling from ear-to-ear.

"Never have I received such service. One could grow very fond of these Skye horses. They are very light on their feet, would ya nay agree Philip?" Maitiú said as he turned to make eye contact with him.

Olaf and Rhea knelt gracefully for Maitiú and Dónal to dismount. The men then turned to their mounts, hugging them around their necks in gratitude for their service. Olaf turned to Dónal and tapped his front hooves on the ground.

Dónal laughed and said, "Happy feet again, Olaf."

Maitiú then whispered in Olaf's ear, "Go to her now, and we be seein' ya again old friend." Everyone stood silent as the two horses rode off, returning back into the forest.

"I be so glad to see ya lads," Katie said as she walked up to greet them. She turned back to Philip to see why he had not come forward. When she saw his face, she could tell that he was positively livid.

Katie turned back to the Irishmen and suddenly a troubled look crossed her brow. She stepped close to Maitiú and asked, "Maitiú, if Olaf be here, where be me cousin, Maureen?"

Maitiú and Dónal exchanged a worried glance. The afternoon light was beginning to fade and they needed to find shelter for the night.

"Come Katie, Philip. We need to find a place for the night," Maitiú warned. "We have much to talk about."

As they walked, they told Katie and Philip about their journey with Captain Coleman and Sorely Boy, but they had not said anything yet about Maureen.

About a mile down the road they found an abandoned cabin where they could take shelter. A bit of the thatched roof had collapsed, but other than that it would provide a warm place for the night and offered enough privacy for everyone. It sat slightly above and just off the edge of the road. It must have been the home of a prominent person or strong tenant, as it had a stone floor and a hearth.

Katie and Philip went to the back of the shelter and made their place behind a partial wall. Philip's temperament was worsening by the minute. All of

243

Philip's previous regrets for his two Irish friends were now overshadowed by a vicious resentment. He pushed past Maitiú and Dónal as they entered the shelter, grumbling about the place they had chosen, and that they should have kept moving.

When they were alone, Katie came to him and asked, "What be wrong Philip, why do ya harbor such anger fer these two men? They've done ya no wrong. They brought me to safety, ya should be grateful."

He tried to turn away from her but she would not let him, "Philip, please?" she urged.

"This be our land, Katie," he said slowly as he turned back to her. "The magic of this place be for us, not them. How could these foreigners receive such an honor?"

He was rambling and Katie had no idea what he was getting at.

Maitiú and Dónal, though they did not mean to listen, could hear them from the front of the shelter.

"And Olaf, a soft horse," Philip continued. "Why had Maureen not told me of him and her visions. She should 'a trusted me, she should 'a...."

"She should 'a what?" Dónal had heard enough. He stepped into the opening in the wall, confronting Philip.

"Easy boyo," Maitiú warned.

"Do nay worry Da, I will nay dishonor ya," Dónal assured him.

He turned back to Philip and took a step forward, "I asked ya sir, what should she 'a done? She came here alone. She came here because of her love fer Katie and you, and fer me Da and me. And now, she lies in a bed in Portree with an arrow wound to her chest. So I ask ya once more, sir, what should she 'a done?"

Philip fell silent as the anger drained from him, replaced by worry and sorrow. Katie was in shock and walked around Dónal to the front of the shelter.

"Maitiú, be this true?" she asked as she held back

tears.

"Aye Katie, it be true. Come, let's get a fire goin' and we'll tell ya that we know."

When they were warm around the fire, Maitiú brought forth a small satchel of food. Morríghan had not sent them off empty handed. There were nuts, berries, some brown bread and a few oat cakes. It was not much, but it would fill them for the night.

Philip accepted the food and sat quietly by himself just back from the fire. Finally, Katie could stand the wait no longer.

"Maitiú please, tell me of me cousin. Where is she?" she pleaded.

Maitiú and Dónal told Katie all they knew to be true of what had happened to them all after leaving Coleman's ship. They spoke only to Katie and answered her questions as best they could.

"She has the gift, Katie," Maitiú whispered. "She saw that ya were in danger; all she wanted was to get to ya and bring ya home."

At last, with night having grown late and the dawn coming sooner than what would be comfortable, they readied their beds for sleep.

Maitiú and Dónal went to their side of the hovel, and Philip and Katie to theirs. Philip had nothing to say. His thoughts and emotions stewed in the cauldron of his heart and mind.

Katie whispered to him, "Philip, have ya nothin' to say?"

Philip just shook his head, wrapped up in his plaidie and laid down. He turned away from Katie as if to go to sleep, but he did not.

Katie quickly fell into a troubled sleep. Philip listened

carefully to the slow and steady rhythm of her breathing. He turned his ear to the far side of the hovel. He heard snoring, but no movement. Assuming the Irishmen were fast asleep, he got up slowly and quietly peaked around the wall to look in on them.

The fire was raked and the only light came from the stars and the waning crescent moon hanging low in the night sky. It was an unusually clear night for late autumn in the Highlands.

As his eyes adjusted to the night, he saw Dónal's blonde hair at the top of a bundle of black blankets. Dónal was the source of the snoring he had heard. His gaze scanned left and right looking for the other Irishman. With a bit of a startle, he spied Maitiú sitting up against the wall, staring right back at him.

"Cad é, what?" That was all Maitiú said.

Philip signaled with his hand that they should step out and away from the shelter. After a long and unresponsive pause, Maitiú rose and followed Philip out into the darkness. They walked near fifty paces away to a small, open meadow fully illuminated by the moon and stars.

"Maitiú, a chara..." Philip began.

"A chara, be it?" Maitiú interrupted. "Ya use that word rather loosely. As I see it, you and I be friends no longer."

Philip turned away from him and took a few steps. Maitiú was ready to leave and go back into the shelter when Philip turned back to him.

"I am sorry me friend," Philip said softly.

Not hearing him, Maitiú prompted, "Dear God Philip, ya have yer head so far up yer arse that…. Say that again?"

Philip drew a deep breath and took the two steps back to him, "I said I be sorry, truly sorry a chara," he repeated.

Maitiú said nothing at first. He stared blankly at the man before him. In his mind, he played back all that had happened between the two of them: the good and the bad. He cast his eyes to the vast darkness of the night sky. Drawing a deep breath, he looked to Philip, "Ya be forgiven. God help me, I forgive ya."

"If me Da forgives ya, Master Philip, so shall I." Dónal said as he walked toward the two men. They were surprised to see him.

"Did ya truly think ya could sneak past a soldier of the Papal army and not be heard?" Dónal mocked.

The three men shook hands and embraced each other as men do.

"What has happened to us?" Dónal said as they turned to walk back to the hovel. "What I mean is, since we left Dumbartonshire, what the hell has happened to us?"

Maitiú grabbed Philip by the arm, "I rode the soft horse of Skye—Olaf! And did ya know Philip, boyo, there be more than one of them!"

Philip looked down, shaking his head at Maitiú's childlike amazement. "So what say you now, Christian, about the magic of Skye?" He asked of the Irishman.

"That God almighty can manifest Himself in any way he chooses to achieve His will," Dónal replied as if reciting his catechism.

It was then that Philip grabbed both men by their sleeves and said, "Ya know, both of ya must know, that ya can nay speak of them. Not to anyone." Maitiú and Dónal did not respond, but simply nodded in acceptance.

"Surely, Christian, ya understand," Philip counseled. "There be things in this world that should remain a mystery."

All three paused for a moment and then continued their walk back to the hovel, laughing and talking. As they entered the shelter a voice came from the back room.

"Go to sleep ya bloody eejits. There be plenty of time to talk on the road tomorrow." Katie grumbled.

The men made their way to their beds and quickly fell asleep, leaving Katie wide awake and listening to the sound of three snoring eejits.

Morning broke, but the travelers were late in rising. Katie was the last to wake. When she opened her eyes, she found all three men just sitting there staring at her.

"What the hell are you gobshites starin' at?" she snapped.

Dónal looked over at his Da and with an impish grim said, "Da, I do believe I've seen happier faces eatin' grass in a pasture."

At that, Katie reached for her shoe and flung it at Dónal's head.

Ducking out of the way, Dónal said, "Yer woman has quite an arm on her Philip."

"Aye, that she does," Philip replied.

"Husband, I believe I will leave you and Maitiú here to discuss the mysteries of our world, and I be taken' this wee Irish smartass with me into the forest to find us some berries and greens fer breakfast."

With that she retrieved her shoe, took Dónal by the ear and led him out of the shelter.

"I could use a pint right about now." Maitiú fancied.

"At last, Christian, somethin' we can agree on." Philip replied.

The four travelers had a long journey ahead of them. Katie and Dónal returned with enough berries and greens to feed them all as they continued on to Badenoch.

They took the ferry from Kylerhea to Glenelg. Just out of Glenelg, a kind old crofter let them ride on the back of his hay cart all the way to Glenghiel.

They were unsure of just how far it was to Heber's manor. Philip had some recollection of this country from his earlier days as a traveling poet.

When they could, they found natural shelter off the roadside. Katie was astute at gathering what could be eaten from the land, while Dónal and Maitiú managed to snare rabbits and knock down fowl. Nevertheless, it was not enough and they were perpetually hungry, cold and tired.

On the third night they rieved a wee lamb and roasted it. While they ate, Maitiú and Philip debated how stealing was a sin, but rieving was not.

Philip could see how this journey was wearing down his friends and his wife, so he made a proposal.

"I believe we be very near Newtonmore," he said. "There be an inn there, or at least there was the last time I was there. Maybe the innkeeper would feed us for our stories and poems." All agreed it was worth a try.

When they arrived, they were surprised to see that this was no ragged, riverside pub. It was much like the Wycked Aye, with a fine dining hall and full rooms for lodging. A warm fire burned in a large stone hearth. The patrons were talking and laughing with each other as they ate and drank. It felt like home to the four weary travelers.

The innkeeper had them perform for his wife and family. Philip recited his finest poems. Maitiú recited traditional tales of Finn MacCool and Cu Chulann with an Irish twist, and Dónal told tales of his adventures in Morocco fighting the Moors. Katie offered her services to the kitchen.

So delighted was the innkeeper, he begged the

entertainers to stay for the night, eat their fill and sleep in warm beds.

The news of the new entertainment spread across the surrounding shire and the inn was full that night. It did not take much persuasion to get the trio to stay for an additional night.

Katie was more than pleased to stay two nights, alone with her husband in a private room with a feather bed away from two snoring, farting Irishmen.

The next day, while Philip was discussing staying a third night with the innkeeper, a young messenger came running into the inn. A party of horsemen and a single carriage had arrived in town.

When the boy left, the innkeeper turned to Philip, "Master MacAlasdair, a Chattan Lord has arrived and he be askin' to speak with ya. His name be Heber MacPherson."

Philip could not believe his ears. He rose immediately and rushed outside to meet Heber.

The sky had begun to cloud over and it looked very much like rain was on the way, maybe a bit of snow. The days were getting short and winter would soon be upon the Highlands.

Maitiú and Dónal had gone out behind the inn for the afternoon to practice sword drills and do a bit of father-and-son sparing. With steel clanking they did not hear the horses or Heber's carriage approach.

Philip met Heber at the edge of the road as he and Fionnula were stepping out of the carriage. Katie came behind Philip and hurried to greet their old and dear friends.

"Fionnula!" Katie called out. The two women embraced each other laughing and giggling like young lasses.

Heber offered his hand to Philip, "Good ta have ya home safe Master MacAlasdair."

"'Tis good ta be back in the Highlands My Lord."

"And where be our two Irishmen?" Heber asked as he glanced around.

Philip pointed to his ear and then to the back of the inn. Heber could hear the sound of steel on steel and began to walk down the side of the inn.

When they reached the end of the building, Heber smiled at Fionnula and put a finger to his lips so she would not give him away. Then he stepped around the back corner of the inn and shouted, "Féach, de Faoite!"

Dónal snapped to attention for a brief moment and then shouted back, "Mo Chaptaen!"

He dropped his sword and ran to meet Heber. Heber opened his arms to the lad and buried him in his embrace.

When Maitiú saw the big man, a wave of relief washed over him. He lowered his sword tip to the ground and leaned on the hilt. Their struggles were over, but now he must explain to Heber about Maureen.

It was then that Fionnula stepped out from behind Heber. When Maitiú saw her he dropped his head covering his eyes to hide his tears of joy. Fionnula rushed to embrace him, "Oh cousin, how I've missed ya."

When they released each other from a tearful embrace, they all walked back to the front of the inn.

"Come, let's go in by the fire and share an ale to celebrate," Philip said.

Maitiú and Heber locked eyes and without a spoken word the two stepped away from the company of the others and walked over to a stone slab that served as an outdoor table. Before Maitiú could speak, Fionnula caught sight of what was happening and went straight to Heber's side.

"I was about to have a quiet word with ya M'lord, but it appears we have an audience," he said as Katie and Philip walked up to join them.

"What news of me daughter, Maitiú?" Heber asked. "Maureen, man, what of Maureen?"

Dónal stepped up, "A Chaptaen, she be hurt bad, but she be with two healers and..."

"Dún do bhéal, de Faoite! Mind yerself lad!" Heber snapped. "Let yer father speak."

Maitiú cast his son a comforting glance. "The boy be right, Heber, our girl be badly wounded but she be in good hands. She be in Portree at the home of woman-healer, Morríghan Macaulay, and another woman who goes by the name of Shalynn. They be taking good care of the girl. They have ways of healin' Heber, things I have nay seen before. They saved the girl, that be fer certain. Shalynn has gifts, Heber, she be blessed in some way."

"How was she wounded?" Heber asked as he pulled Fionnula close to him.

"As we ran from the battle at Dunvegan, she took an arrow in the back from Sorley Boy," Maitiú said softly.

Fionnula put her hand to her mouth in concern and moved closer to Heber for comfort.

"She be alive and she be safe, M'lord," Maitiú continued. "I be not worried about Maureen somehow. I've been prayin' for her."

"We all have," added Dónal.

After a few moments of awkward silence, the reunited family of the Wycked Aye agreed to stay the night at the inn and then return with Heber and Fionnula to the MacPherson manor house on the marrow. As they walked back around to the front of the inn, Heber looked to Philip.

"Ya've become quite famous here and about, Philip. Fionnula and I came down when we heard news of a wonderful poet reciting at the inn in Newtonmore. We knew it had to be you."

The inn was a full house for their last night. The innkeeper was delighted, for just in time a wagon came down from Kingussie with two kegs of local ale courtesy of Heber MacPherson.

Calling Dónal over, Heber warned, "Keep these away from yer Da." Then shaking his head, he laughed, "And you keep away from 'em too."

The next morning, Maitiú and Fionnula found some time to walk together through the countryside. A storm had come during the night and a light dusting of snow covered the ground.

Maitiú wanted to know of their family and of her time in Ireland. They talked of politics and especially of Desmond. Then it came down to what had happened in Skye.

"Dónal and I have seen things that would get us both burned at the stake should I recite them in Rome," Maitiú confided.

"Then we shall nay make mention of such things...in Rome," Fionnula said. "Dónal be right to say God manifests himself in any way he sees fit. You and I Maitiú, we were raised ta believe this, it be our way, the Irish way. For ya see me dear cousin, I see the people of the Forest. I have always seen them, and they be God's creatures too. But Maitiú, we must nay speak of them."

"Well then, we be keepin' it ta ourselves, Fionnula, a ghrá," he said. "The Calvinists may burn us at the stake, but I'd hate ta think the curate would fan the flames."

It was mid-day when Heber and Fionnula, Maitiú and Dónal, Philip and Katie, along with the host of the MacPherson retinue made for Heber's manor house in Badenoch on Spey. There the company of travelers would rest before their trip home to Dumbartonshire and the Wycked Aye Tavern.

Chapter Twenty-Four

The Awakening

Shalynn sat on the edge of the bed watching the youngling as she slept. She watched Maureen's eyes shift beneath her eyelids. Her body would twitch occasionally and she would utter slight moans or try to speak.

"We must wake her soon," Morríghan said as she walked up behind Shalynn and moved around to the head of the bed to face her.

"We must not force her awakening," Shalynn whispered. "I fear breaking the vision."

Morríghan bent down and carefully pulled back the bed covers to check the wounds on Maureen's shoulder.

"Ya see Great One," she said exposing the wounds. "Her healin' slows. 'Thas been three days since the Irishmen left. She has taken no food and little water. The child was frail to begin with but now she weakens and withers," Morríghan said as she reached for Shalynn's hand. "She must take food and water or she will nay heal, ya know this."

Morríghan was right. But what Shalynn had done for the youngling had never been done before. She had no idea if or how her Fey blood would change the girl. Her grandfather, Diancecht, the greatest of healers, had once tried to save the life of a MacLeod Chieftain by blood sharing. The man's body did not accept Fey blood and he died quickly. The Fey had used the method many times on their own people, and they recovered and awakened within a few hours.

Three days had now passed and the girl-child did not wake. Shalynn did not understand what was happening, and feared waking Maureen from her visions. But mostly, she feared losing the youngling completely. Maureen had been gone from Skye for so long; now she was home, where she was meant to be. Shalynn could not bear to lose her now.

What she had done was strictly against the laws of the Tuatha. She knew that when Diancecht found out he would be furious with her. She had shared blood with a human. But not just any human, a MacLeod woman and the Watcher of the Aes Sidhe. Even so, she needed help. Regardless of his anger, she needed Diancecht.

"Morríghan, have the sentries arrived?" she asked as she rose from the bed.

"Aye, My Lady, they wait at the end of the stone path." Morríghan replied.

"Good," she said as she left the cottage to send the sentries for her grandfather.

Over the next few hours, Morríghan did her best to drip small amounts of water on Maureen's lips. If she could not eat, she must at least take water.

It was nearing sunset when the women heard the sound of hoofs coming up the stone path and then a knock came on Morríghan's door. Shalynn hurried to the door to greet her grandfather. But instead, standing before her was William Macaulay.

"Good marrow M'lady. Me gran, be she here?" he asked of Shalynn.

When Morríghan heard his voice she came quickly from the back room, "William, what are ya doin' here son?" she asked. It had been so long since she had seen her grandson.

William stepped through the door and reached to embrace his gran; Shalynn quickly slipped away to the back room closing the door behind her.

"'Tis good to see ya, Gran, ya look well. I've missed ya," he said.

As Morríghan embraced him, she could feel the urgency in his manner, and immediately sensed why he was there.

She held her grandson at arm's length and looked up in his eyes. It was clear to see that the man had traveled long and hard to reach her. His eyes were weary and his shoulders slumped from exhaustion.

"Come William," she said as she led him to the pantry. "Sit yerself down lad, let me get ya some food and drink."

William dropped into a chair. Leaning forward and bracing himself on his knees. His long dark hair fell forward as he dropped his head, drawing a deep breath.

Morríghan turned to look at him. The last time she had seen him, he was but a youth. Now she saw a man before her, and a fine man he had grown to be.

"What brings ya to the Isle, William? Yer father finally let ya come back, did he?" she asked.

He looked up to her, and although her hair was greying, her face showed little sign of aging. He could see that beneath her simple kirtle and skirts, she was still trim and strong.

"He does nay know I be here, Gran. He thinks I be in Badenoch. I be sorry ta arrive without notice, but I be in great need of yer help."

Shalynn listened from the back room as William began the story of his journey. A story she did not need to hear. She knew that what he searched for was already here.

She had little time, Diancecht would be here at any moment. If he was to be angry with her, he might as well be angry about everything at once. She rose from Maureen's bedside and walked to the pantry.

Morríghan saw her, but did not speak. William turned to face the her as she entered the room.

"William, I am Shalynn." She said. "You need not look any further, Maureen is here."

He slowly rose from his chair and looked to the back

of the cottage. When he started to head in that direction, Shalynn tried to stop him.

"Wait," she said as she reached for his hand to pull him back. "Before you see her, there are things you must know."

William did not care to hear anything she had to say and yanked his hand away.

"Stop William, please!" Shalynn pleaded. "She has been wounded," she said as she followed him to Maureen's bed.

When William saw Maureen he stopped dead in his tracks. She was pale, very pale. The bed covers were still pulled back and the bandages on her wounds were stained with blood. The bed quilt just covered her bare chest, as the women had removed her clothes to bathe her and change her bandages. Her long auburn hair was braided and tied back with strips of cloth. When he turned back to Shalynn she could tell that he was truly frightened.

"Will, will she live?" He humbly asked of her.

"We have done all we can and we have sent for another healer to help us," she replied.

Morríghan began to light candles in the room as the sun had passed behind the mountains and darkness began to fill the cottage.

"Why can we nay just wake her up?" William asked as he sat down next to her on the edge of the bed.

"We cannot break her vision," Shalynn replied. "I am afraid to...."

"Yes, we can," came a voice from the front of the cottage.

Standing in the doorway was Diancecht flanked on both sides by Maureen's sentries. When he saw the youngling, he came immediately to the opposite side of the bed from where William was sitting. He leaned on the bed, looking down on her, watching her closely for

257

several minutes. He raised her bandages and saw the remaining pieces of Carraban still inside her wounds. He then turned to Shalynn.

"How did this happen? How long has she been drifting?" He snapped.

Shalynn hesitated, "She was wounded at Dunvegan, it has been near three days, My Lord."

Diancecht looked at her with an expression she had never seen from him before. He was angry, but he was also bewildered.

William watched the silent exchange between them and sensed their uncertainty on how to proceed. He looked at this man who was clearly of great importance, but at that moment in time he did not give a damn who he was.

"What the bloody hell be the problem?" he said as he leaned toward Diancecht. "Ya said ya could wake her, so do it man."

He met Williams eyes and then said, "Leave us."

Morríghan came to William, putting her hands on his shoulders and turning him away from Diancecht.

"Come William, come with me now," she urged. "Let them work son, they will nay harm her." Morríghan led him out and into the pantry.

The moment the door closed behind them Diancecht came around to the end of the bed and put his hands on Shalynn's shoulders. He looked sternly into her eyes and in a harsh whisper asked, "Did you blood this child Shalynn? Did you blood her?"

Shalynn turned her face away from him and did not answer. He tightened his grip.

"Shalynn?" he asked again.

As tears welled in her eyes, she turned to face him, placing her hands on his forearms and gripping him firmly. She pulled him forward and looking him straight in the eyes said, "How could you think for one moment,

Grandfather, that I would let my daughter die?"

She released her grip and fell against him as he wrapped his arms around her. He understood that she had done what she had to do. She was much like he was, strong on the outside, but beneath a lover of all life, and a healer. He reached down and took her chin so that he might bring her eyes to meet his.

"Come, we have work to do. Let us bring your child out of her darkness. I believe, together, we can wake her."

From the front room of the cottage, William stood staring at the closed chamber door, saying nothing. Morríghan came to him and placed a cup of mead in his hand.

Fiann and Séamus began to start fires in the hearths, as they knew they would be awake long into the night.

"Who be these people Gran? Why they be marked like that?" he asked.

"Come, William, and sit. They be an ancient people William. They be the Aes Sidhe, the Tuatha de Danann. They be the guardians and allies of Clan MacLeod," Morríghan said. "There be things you must know, William. It be clear to me that ya love this girl with all yer heart. I feel it in ya. But lovin' this woman will nay be easy."

She took a chair as well and sat right in front of him. "I probably know more about Maureen MacLeod than she knows of herself," Morríghan began.

William downed the mead she had given him in one tip of the cup.

"I be listenin' Gran," he prompted, unsure if he truly wanted to hear what she had to say.

She filled his cup again, and poured one for herself.

"Ya see William, the girl's father, Robert MacLeod, was heir to the seat of Chieftain of Clan MacLeod. He was matched to a young lass named Maire MacCrimmon in what was to be an advantageous marriage for both clans. Not long after they were joined, Robert was approached by an elder of Clan MacLeod and the man who now stands behind that door," she said as she pointed to the bed chamber.

"Since times long past, William, once in every hundred years of men, a girl-child be born between the Aes Sidhe and Clan MacLeod. Because of his bloodline, Robert was chosen to sire that child with a Fey woman, who also be of special blood."

William looked at his gran in amazement and asked, "A changeling? Me girl be a changeling?"

"Aye William, a changeling and a powerful seer," she said.

Fiann and Séamus both stood now and faced her, shaking their heads and cautioning her not to say anything further.

"Watcher, you must not say..." Fiann began.

Morríghan raised her hand to him, assuring him she understood her boundary and then she continued.

"Maureen was born two days before Maire began to labor with her own child. Maire struggled terribly and the woman faded from wakefulness, unable to deliver the child on her own. I was her mid-wife, and I was forced to take a lifeless infant from her womb. When Maire regained herself and opened her eyes, I laid a healthy baby girl in her arms – she never knew the difference and never would."

Morríghan sighed. "I be the one who brought Maureen into this world, William, and I be the one who exchanged her for Maire MacCrimmon's stillborn son."

Morríghan raised from her chair and went to the pantry counter. William was watching every move she

260

made, waiting for her to finish. He could tell she was holding something back. Finally, she turned back to him.

"Ya see, William," she continued, "Robert was sworn to silence by the Clan elders and the Fey Council. But the man be beyond himself with grief and anger over the loss of his son, and his heir to the seat of Dunvegan. He resented poor, young Maire. He blamed her for the death of a boy-child she knew nothin' about, and he wanted nothin' to do with his infant daughter. 'Twas just six months or so when Robert up and left the Isle. Why he took Maire and Maureen with him I can nay say. But I can tell ya, that girl-child was never meant to leave the Isle of Skye. She belongs to the Fey."

William raised from his chair and began to pace around the room trying to take in all that Morríghan had told him. He paced back and forth in front of the hearth, then turn to her and asked, "Gran, if Maire MacCrimmon be not her mother, who would be?"

"I am," came the answer from the chamber doorway. Shalynn stood there and Diancecht stood behind her with his hands on her shoulders. She slowly walked up to William, raising her left hand and revealing the mark of the black rose on her palm.

He looked at her hand and then to the open door of the bed chamber.

"The vision is broken," Shalynn said. "Her mind is at rest, but she is weak. Go to her."

He pushed past them and went straight to Maureen, closing the chamber door behind him.

William sat down slowly on the edge of the bed and reached for her, gently lifting her to him, wrapping the bed covers around her and cradling her head in his hand. Her breath was shallow and he could barely feel the beat of her heart. He put his cheek to hers and whispered, "Come back to me lass, ya can nay leave me now. Please I beg ya girl, come back."

He held her, talked to her and rocked her in his arms, but she did not wake. Finally, he laid her back down and curled up around her on the bed.

Deep into the night, he woke to the sound of her voice. He raised himself on his elbow and looked down at her, touching his fingers to her cheek. She was awake. When she saw him she softly whispered, "William."

When William emerged from the bed chamber it was just before dawn and Diancecht was gone. Morríghan and Shalynn were both still asleep, as was Maureen. He looked out the pantry windows to see the Sentries standing watch along the path, and out in the meadow grazed Olaf, his own horse and five other magnificent white horses.

He remembered coming to his gran's as a boy and seeing the white horses. His father had always spoken bitterly about living on the outskirts of Portree and raising horses. He never liked bringing William and Patrick to Skye to see their gran. His father had tried to bring her back with them to Dumbartonshire but she had always refused to leave Skye.

Things were now beginning to make sense to William. He realized now that his father never knew about the Fey, or the horses, or his own mother.

He started a fire in the hearth and put a kettle on. The fire began to crackle and warmth soon filled the pantry. It was not long until Morríghan came in to join him, her long graying hair flowing freely over the shoulders of her chamber robe.

"Good marrow, William," she said softly. "How are ya son? How be our girl?"

Leaning on his elbows on the pantry washboard, he turned to her as she came to stand beside him.

"I be well Gran; Maureen still be sleepin'. She barely opened her eyes, but she did speak ta me. She knows I be here."

They both looked out the window in silence watching the horses meander around the meadow, the morning mist hovering low over the ground.

Morríghan began to busy herself preparing cups for tea and food for their breakfast. William watched her move about the pantry with ease. She was surprisingly spry for her age. Her skin was soft and smooth with very few wrinkles. Her hands were still nimble as she chopped leaves for tea. William turned around and leaned back against the counter crossing his arms over his chest.

"How old are ya, Gran?" he asked.

William's question brought Morríghan to a standstill. She did not answer. She did not turn around to face him. She knew now she had told him too much the night before.

"Now, William, what kind of question be that ta ask of a lady?" she said evasively.

He pulled away from the counter and stepped slowly toward her.

"Yer just like Maureen, are ya not, Gran?" he asked softly. "Ya be a changeling, just like her. Ya be the one they call the old Watcher."

He gently reached over and pushed Morríghan's long hair away from the back of her neck. She did not flinch or pull away from him. She let him see what he already knew was there. Just below her hairline was the mark of the black rose.

"I can say no more, William, they be tellin' ya the rest. Ya be part of it now." Morríghan said as she handed William a cup of Valerian tea. "Take this ta the youngling and wake her, she must eat or she will nay heal."

263

William bent down and placed a kiss on his grandmother's cheek. He took the cup and began to leave the pantry when he turned back to her.

"Gran, Da never knew did he?" he asked.

"No, William, he did not."

Maureen was just waking when he came back into the room. He put the tea down on the table next to the bed and took her around her waist to help her sit up.

When she raised her head and opened her eyes, William could not believe what he was seeing. He was so startled that he scooted back away from her for a moment.

"Gran. Gran! Gran!!" he called out.

"William, what be wrong?" Morríghan asked as she entered the room.

Shalynn, awakened by the commotion, came in right behind her.

"William, what be wrong, son?" Morríghan asked again.

"Her eyes, Gran, look at her eyes," he exclaimed.

Maureen looked at them as they stared at her unable to speak.

"William, yer frightenin' me," Maureen, still weak, said. "What be wrong? Why do ya gawk at me like that?"

She looked down at the half healed wounds on her shoulder and the deep bruising across her chest. Shalynn handed her a small looking glass from the dressing table and sat down next to her on the bed.

When she saw her own reflection she gasped, "His eyes, I have his eyes. Dear God in heaven, what happened ta me?"

Chapter Twenty-Five

A Message

Katie, Philip and the Irishmen had been at Heber's manor for nearly a week. Their days were filled with rides along the River Spey, sword play and entertaining the local Clansmen of Badenoch.

Maitiú was happy to be reunited with his Connemara ponies, Hope and Grace. He and Dónal took them out every day to ride. But on this cold, late autumn morn, Maitiú rode out alone, for troubled had been his heart of late.

Morríghan had told them they would send word to Heber, but no word had come. He walked Hope over to a quiet place along the bank of the river and let her graze while he stood on the rocks at the edge of the water consumed in his own thoughts.

He reached around his neck and pulled the silver cross from beneath his léine. The silver cross that Maureen had placed around his neck that night in her cottage so long ago. Maitiú could still hear her whisper, "May God keep ya safe me friend."

He turned the cross in his fingers wondering if she was alright or if they had lost her. Then he brought it to his lips and placed kiss upon it. "May God keep ya safe too, lass," he said.

He closed his eyes and drew a deep breath. The cold autumn air bit at his lungs and he felt a chill run through his body. He prayed for God to watch over Maureen and for William to find her and bring her home.

His thoughts went to his own daughters and his beloved wife. It seemed so long since they had been together. Seeing Fionnula had stirred something within him and he now longed to return to his family and Ireland. His final prayers were for them, that they would soon be together again and find their way home to Waterford.

When he opened his eyes, he sensed a strange quietness around him. There were no sounds of birds in the trees or the small creatures that scurry through the meadow grass. Even the river seemed to flow silently.

He felt uneasy, as if he were being watched. His first thought went to Sorley Boy and a sickening feeling shot through him. He looked back across the meadow but all he saw was Hope meandering around, eating what was left of the grass.

"Over here, Maitiú, I am over here good sir."

Maitiú snapped around, following the voice upstream to a small cluster of trees. Out from behind the trunks stepped a small man with light hair.

"Do I know ya, sir?" Maitiú asked cautiously.

"I mean you no harm. My name is Fiann. Lady Shalynn sends word to the MacPherson and to you," he said, as the two men began to walk toward each other. Fiann could see the concern and uncertainty on Maitiú's face.

"You need not worry, sir," Fiann continued. "The youngling is well and healing. The Gael, Macaulay, is with her."

"William?" Maitiú asked.

"Yes, they will return soon. Lady Shalynn wishes a meeting with the MacPherson. You will deliver this message?" Fiann said.

"Aye, sir, I will. Me thanks to ya and…yer people," Maitiú offered. He watched as Fiann walked back to the cluster of trees and seemed to disappear.

Maitiú delivered the message to Heber as Fiann requested. That night the men gathered to discuss what had happened.

"Who be this Shalynn? Heber asked.

"She be the healer that saved Maureen," Maitiú replied. "She has an interest in the girl, Heber, I can nay say why."

Dónal listened anxiously to the conversation. Shalynn was coming to them. An excitement filled him and he felt a kind of anticipation he had not known before. He knew Shalynn to be Fey. He had seen her without disguise, he had held her, touched her, and she had touched him as well. He wanted desperately to see her again.

"And when and where be this meeting, Maitiú?" Heber continued.

"The small man did nay say when. Mayhaps they ride together now." Maitiú said.

"They will find ya when the time be right," Philip added.

"They?" Heber questioned.

"The forest people, M'lord," Philip replied. "They will find you."

Chapter Twenty-Six

The Watcher's Chamber

"Where are we William? I do nay recall comin' ta this place. Maitiú and Dónal, be they here? I do nay remember..."

Maureen was frustrated and confused. She did not remember anything after running from Dunvegan. And now that she was awake, the pain in her body was agonizing.

"Ssshhh, lass. It be alright. Ya be at me gran's house in Portree. Maitiú and Dónal brought ya here." William said as he tried to calm her.

"Ya were hurt girl, do ya remember?" he asked.

She shook her head, "I recall runnin' with Maitiú and Dónal, seein' the red-haired man and..."

"The blood, the Fey blood," Morríghan said as she looked to Shalynn. "Could it have turned her?"

William shot a fearful look to his Gran. *Turned her?* he thought.

Shalynn scooted up close to Maureen, "How do you feel, child? What else to you remember?"

"Feel?" Maureen snapped. "I feel like shite and I be bloody arse starvin'!"

A faint smile crossed William's face for he knew at that moment his lass would be just fine. For those were the words and temperament of the woman he knew and loved so much. He moved up next to her and pulled her close.

Shalynn gave her a moment and then asked again. "Try and think child, what did you see, what did you hear?"

"While I be sleepin' Shalynn, the old ones took me ta a castle, a castle in the clouds," Maureen began. "I saw there a woman, a most beautiful woman with golden hair. I saw many things, Shalynn, many places. I heard so many voices, I...." She closed her eyes and rested her head against William. Her eyes began to fill with tears, "I...I thought it be heaven. I thought I be dead."

"It is alright child, rest now. We will talk later," Shalynn said as she watched Maureen begin to drift off. She turned to William and said, "Do not let her sleep." Shalynn got up to leave the room and gestured for Morríghan to follow.

When the two women had left the room Maureen opened her eyes and looked up at William, "When I be in the clouds, I thought I would never see ya again. 'Twas yer voice that called me back, William, not them, you. I love ya, William Macaulay, with all me heart, and I never want to be parted from ya ever again."

He leaned forward and gently kissed her, wiping her tears from her cheeks. "Ya never will, lass. I promise ya that."

"We have much ta talk of William," she continued. "They think I do nay remember, but I do."

William knew he had to tell her the truth about Shalynn. He would not hide it from her, it would not be right.

"Aye, me girl, ya be right. We have much to talk about," he said and he began to tell Maureen what Morríghan had told him.

"How could this have happened?" Shalynn said as she paced around the pantry table. "Diancecht is the only one who bears the emerald eyes of the ancients."

She continued pacing, trying to understand. Before Maureen was brought back from the clouds, Shalynn could sense her thoughts drifting aimlessly. They too heard the voices Maureen was hearing but had no idea where they were coming from or who they belonged to.

When the vision was broken, Diancecht left immediately for the hollow and the High Council. Did he know something she did not?

"Mayhaps it 'twas the blooding, Shalynn?" Morríghan pondered. "She saw the old ones. They came to her."

It was then they heard the bedchamber door open and Maureen walked slowly toward them with William right behind her.

Shalynn turned to her, "Child, you should not be up, you are too weak."

Maureen walked silently up to her, Shalynn could feel that something was very wrong.

"Ya lied to me Shalynn. That day on the moors, ya lied to me." Maureen was hurt and angry. Shalynn was caught completely off guard.

"Why did ya nay tell me the truth? Why did ya leave me to go through all of this?" She said as she narrowed her eyes and cast a hardened glance at Shalynn.

"That day on the moors, child, you had fallen from your horse, you were wounded." Shalynn began. "I had been searching for you for many years. When Olaf found you and led you to the Wycked Aye, you were finally within my reach. You needed help that day, and what I told you were not all lies."

Shalynn moved next to Maureen and place her hand on her shoulder trying to calm and comfort her. But Maureen would not have it and moved away, stepping back against William.

"That night in the circle of Rowan, the woman I saw was nay me mother was it Shalynn? It be you."

Shalynn took a step closer, "Yes, child, it was."

"Stop callin' me child!" Maureen shouted. "Ya may have been the one who bore me Shalynn, but ya nay be me mother. Maire MacCrimmon raised me, cared fer me and loved me. She be mother, nay you!"

"I cannot change the past." Shalynn lamented. "Had your father not taken you from the Isle, you would have learned about your gift."

Maureen had heard enough. She could no longer hold her anger and pushed Shalynn out of her way. The sudden movement caused her pain and she cringed, reaching to her shoulder.

"Gift! This be no gift! 'Tis nothin' but a bloody arse curse," she shouted as she turned back to Shalynn. "This gift put me dear friends in grave danger and damn near got me killed!"

She could no longer look at Shalynn and had no desire to speak with her any longer. She just wanted to be alone. She began to walk to the door to leave.

"Lass wait," William called to her.

"Let her go, son," Morríghan said as she stepped in front of him. "Let her go."

Clothed only in a dressing gown and chamber robe, Maureen walked barefoot down the stone path from Morríghan's house to the meadow where the soft horses grazed.

It was cold and the stone steps made her feet ache. When she stepped out into the meadow, Olaf and Rhea came to meet her.

"So me beauty," she said to Olaf, "Ya were part of all of this too, eh?"

She buried her face in his mane and held him tight around his neck.

"Ya've watched out fer me more than anyone could. But ya be home now, where ya belong."

Never had she imagined that she would ever be separated from Olaf. He had been her friend and companion for over ten years. Leaving him behind would be the hardest thing she would ever do.

"Olaf, me beauty, take me fer one last ride, take me ta the sea," she said.

They watched from the window as Maureen and the king of the soft horses rose into the mist and disappeared.

Olaf came to rest on a small beach not far from Morríghan's manor. He trotted down the beach to a narrow path that led up to the edge of a cliff and knelt down for Maureen to get off. At the top of the path she could just make out a small stone building.

"What be this place, Olaf?" she asked.

He lowered his head and gave her a push toward the stone path.

Large, square, stone steps were set in the path. It was covered with dried, fallen leaves and the small trees that lined the pathway stood barren, waiting for the coming of winter. The only sound was that of a few patches of beach grass rustling in the sea breeze.

She slowly started up the path. The building looked more like the stone houses the nobles built for their dead. She could tell that this place had stood on this shoreline for a very long time. An intricate iron gate covered the arched doorway, there was no solid door. The other three walls all had window openings that were covered only by vines and plants that had grown into the building itself.

As she peeked through the gate she could see that the building held nothing but a stone font sitting directly in the center of the floor. Vines had grown along the walls and moss hung from the bare branches that covered the ceiling.

She lifted the latch and the hinges creaked as she slowly opened the iron gate. There was a heaviness to the air inside, just like the seer's chamber in the great hollow. The air smelled musty and damp, and the ground felt warm beneath her bare feet.

She took cautious steps around the room, being careful not to touch the font or the water. *This be the Watcher's chamber,* she thought to herself, *and the house, it be the Watcher's house.*

"William's gran be the old Watcher," she said out loud.

She walked around the perimeter of the small chamber, running her hands along the vines and touching the stone walls. Though she knew she had never been here before, this place seemed strangely familiar to her. Somehow, she understood its purpose and she knew she belonged here.

She needed time to try and understand all that had happened. Before, all she wanted was to return to the Isle of Skye. Even before she knew Katie, she had been drawn to this Isle. Now all she wanted was to go with William back to Dumbartonshire and back to the Wycked Aye Tavern.

She knew in her heart this Isle would be where she would spend her days. The old ones in the clouds had told her. She was part of a cycle that had been turning on this Isle since the days of old. But for now, she longed for her family at the Wycked Aye.

The sound of horse's hooves on the beach caught her ear. She looked out the window over the edge of the small cliff and saw Rhea standing with Olaf. When she turned to the door, Shalynn was standing before her. Maureen turned her back to Shalynn and moved to the back of the chamber. She did not want to face her.

Shalynn took a few steps into the chamber and stood near the font.

"It is a great honor among our people to be chosen to bear the changeling," Shalynn began. "After you were born, I was only given two days to be with you before you were taken from me. After that, I would come to you in the night and watch you sleep. I would sing to you and cover you in my light as Fey women have done since the first changeling was born. I was always there my child; you just never saw me."

Maureen's anger began to wane as she listened. She walked back up to the font on the opposite side of Shalynn placing her hands on the edge of the pool and leaned across.

"Ya used me. Ya used me love for me friends to bring me here to do yer bidding," Maureen challenged.

"I brought you back to your home so that you could save your people and your friends from harm. You were the only one left who could raise the Braolauch shi," Shalynn said sternly. "It is your calling for Clan MacLeod and the Fey."

"Me calling?" Maureen shouted as she slapped her hand through the water in the font."

Shalynn waited as the youngling paced along the walls of the chamber. Regardless of how Maureen felt, she was destined to serve the Fey as their Watcher, and she must come to terms with that. She knew the girl wanted nothing more than to return to the Highlands with young Macaulay and lead a simple and peaceful life.

But she was, in truth, highborn; highborn in two realms. She was of noble blood to MacLeod of MacLeod, and a changeling of an elder of the Fey High Council. She must come to terms with that as well.

Shalynn could feel the tension between them and it weighed heavy on her heart. She had waited so long for Maureen to return to the Isle and wanted to be close to her daughter. She deeply regretted the way things had come to pass, but she hoped that in time those wounds would heal. And they would have plenty of time.

Maureen walked to the corner of the room and stood facing the wall, holding on to the vines that grew along the walls – she was weeping. Partly from having to face the truth of her past and partly from the pain in her body.

Shalynn came to her, but did not touch her.

"Let it go now child. Worry not over your gift or your calling. Go back to your tavern with William and take him as your mate. But you must return Maureen. For your own safety, you must return to the Isle."

As Maureen turned, Shalynn opened her arms to her. Maureen hesitated for a moment, then surrendered herself to Shalynn's arms. She laid her head on Shalynn's shoulder and began to cry uncontrollably.

"I do nay want this Shalynn. I do nay want this fer me life," she uttered in between her sobbing.

"I know, child, I know," Shalynn softly replied as she held her youngling close. "I'm...I'm truly sorry."

They sat quietly by the hearth watching the flames flicker in the dim light of the cottage.

"I want to go home, William, back to Badenoch. Can we leave on the morrow?" Maureen asked.

William looked at her with concern, "Ya be in no condition to make such a journey, lass. It be a ten-day ride at best."

Maureen looked to Shalynn. She knew that the soft horses could have them to the mound at Glenelg in little more than an hour and they could be back to Badenoch in one day's ride.

Shalynn sensed what Maureen was thinking, and if William was going to take her as his own the care of the soft horses would be his charge. To guard the Braolauch shi and see to the soft horses was the duty of the Keeper. It was time he came to understand the world of the Fey, Maureen's world, and the calling that would be placed before him.

"If you are asking for the soft horses, they can certainly take you," Shalynn said. "But your man is right. You are not in any condition to be traveling, not even a short distance."

Maureen did not want to wait. The weather was changing. Snow was beginning to fall on the Isle and all across the Highlands. If they were to return, they must go soon.

However, she also knew Shalynn and William were right, she was not fit to travel. The pain in her body was great and the arrow wounds had not yet closed. The arrow had broken one of her ribs; she was bruised and found it difficult to breathe. She would stay a few more days to rest and then return to Badenoch.

She leaned against William as they sat together before the fire. She was exhausted and uncomfortable.

"Take her to bed William," Shalynn said as she came over to check Maureen's wounds. "I will bring a tonic for her pain."

William lifted Maureen up in his arms and began to carry her back to the bed chamber when Shalynn touched his arm, "Get her settled and them come back to us, William. We will tell you what you need to know."

Maureen was insistent upon leaving Portree for Badenoch as soon as she was able. She needed to be back with normal people where she could think. All that she had come to learn and had been forced to accept had been almost too much for her to comprehend.

When William put her down on the bed, she got up on her knees and leaned against his chest.

"Please, William, I want ta go back ta Badenoch and then back ta the Wycked Aye. Will ya take me?"

He laid his hand against the back of her neck and worked his fingers into her hair, softly kissing her.

"And if I take ya back ta the Wycked Aye, me love, would ya do me the honor of acceptin' me hand?" He asked.

"Oh, William, I would take yer hand fer certain and never let it go."

When Morríghan entered the room they were sitting together on the bed, quietly holding each other. She cleared her throat to announce her presence.

"Do nay be getting' her all excited now lad, she needs ta rest."

They smiled at each other and slowly released their embrace.

"Go now, William, Shalynn waits fer ya. I be watchin' over the youngling. Now go," and she shooed him out of the room.

She helped Maureen get settled in bed and then handed her the Valerian tea. Maureen made a face when she took the first sip.

"Aye, 'tis nay too tasty, but it will ease yer pain, child." Morríghan said.

They sat together in awkward silence. Maureen and Morríghan had not actually been introduced yet.

"He loves ya," Morríghan said. "Me handsome grandson, he loves ya somethin' fierce."

Maureen raised her eyes from her cup and smiled, "He asked fer me hand. I gave it."

"Did he now?" Morríghan said with a smile. "Well, ya best be callin' me Gran from now on."

When she finished the tea, Morríghan took the cup and turned to leave when Maureen reached for her hand.

"We be the same, Morríghan...Gran. You and I, we be the same?" she asked.

"Aye, child, we are."

Maureen lowered her eyes for a moment. The tea was taking effect and she was becoming drowsy. She rested her head back on her pillow and grimaced a bit. Morríghan put the cup down and took a last look at her wounds.

As Morríghan pulled the quilt up around her, Maureen said, "I be frightened, Gran. The seein', it frightens me. Will ya teach me?"

With a sympathetic smile Morríghan replied, "Aye, me little Watcher, I'll teach ya."

"Please sit, William," Shalynn said. "It is difficult to speak with you when you are standing up."

He took a chair by the fire and poured himself a cup of mead from the pitcher on the table. He was weary as well, and Shalynn's directness irritated him.

"Should you take Maureen as your own..." she began. But William cut her off in mid-sentence.

"I asked fer her hand, M'lady. She has given it. We be leavin' in a few days fer Badenoch."

A smile crossed Shalynn's face and William knew that this news had pleased her. She gave him a slight bow of her head.

"Fiann and Séamus will accompany you. Humans cannot pass through the mounds without escort, and Maureen is not well enough for a long journey."

Assuming that was the end of their discussion, William began to get up when Shalynn continued.

"Please, William, there is something I need to ask of you." He sat back down and waited for her to continue.

"You see, when a changeling is born William, the MacLeod who sires that changeling becomes what is called the Keeper..."

William sighed and slouched back against the chair. He was in no mood to listen to more stories, with their traditions and responsibilities.

"Please, William, I will not keep you long. I know you want to go to her, but you must listen now," Shalynn cautioned. "Maureen's father, Robert, was sworn as the Keeper before she was even conceived, but he abandoned his duty and now he is gone."

William knew immediately where she was going with this discussion and he sat himself up straight in his chair.

"The Keeper serves both the Fey and Clan MacLeod as the guardian of the Watcher, the Braolauch shi, and the soft horses of Skye." She paused momentarily then said, "It is a great honor William. I wish to offer you to the Fey Counsel and to the MacLeod of MacLeod as Keeper."

William's first reaction was to shake his head in denial as he sat forward in the chair.

"M'lady, I'll always protect Maureen, to me death if need be, and carin' for horses has been me work all me life, but I be no warrior. 'Tis not me way. I thank ya, but no." With that he got up to leave.

"Take the time in Badenoch and the Wycked Aye to consider this William." Shalynn said as he walked away. "Should you accept the calling of the Keeper, you would be pledged in service to the Aes Sidhe and the MacLeod of MacLeod."

William walked away without speaking and closed the bed chamber door behind him.

Three days later, William and Maureen left early in the morning on a cold and cloudy day. Winter had come to the Isle of Skye and snow was beginning to cover most of the land.

Both Morríghan and Shalynn were against their

leaving so soon. Maureen was in no condition to be traveling, but she insisted on going now. Morríghan had prepared the herbs to help with her pain and healing.

Rhea would carry them to the mounds at Glenelg, and then on to Badenoch. Fiann and Seamus would ride as their escorts to see them safely through the mounds.

"Good journey to you, child," Shalynn said as they prepared to leave. "We shall see you at the tavern soon. Your sentries will be nearby should you need them." Shalynn then placed the Fey medallion she had given Maureen at the Sacred Circle of Rowan back around her neck.

"Be safe my youngling," she said. Turning to William she added, "Care for her William, she is now your charge. Consider what I asked of you."

Shalynn and Morríghan watched as they left the meadow. As soon as they were out of sight, the two women looked at each other with great concern.

"It be dangerous fer her to travel so close ta the lowlands Great One. What happened at Dunvegan has most certainly reached Ireland by now. The Éire Fey will be lookin' fer her," Morríghan warned.

"Yes, I know," Shalynn replied.

"At least William will watch out fer them," Morríghan said. "Ya did tell him? Ya told him about the Éire Fey, did ya not?

Shalynn looked back to her slowly, "No my old friend, I did not."

Chapter Twenty-Seven

A Proposal

It was late afternoon when Maureen and William reached the boundary of MacPherson land. The sky had clouded over and rain would soon begin to fall. They should just make the manor house in time.

Everyone was gathered in the main room of the house preparing for their evening meal. Heber and the men were standing near the hearth with tankards of ale discussing politics and what would happen on Skye now that Clan MacDonald had been defeated.

The women sat together around a small table working on their stitchery and discussing what the ladies of Clan Lachlan had worn to their last gathering, when Collin came bursting in.

"M'lord!" he called to Heber.

Heber turned to him, perturbed by his interruption.

"What be the meaning of this lack of propriety, Collin?" he asked.

"Forgive me M'lord, but the Skye boy returns and the young mistress be with him."

Heber and Maitiú moved immediately, sliding their ale cups onto the table and bolting past Collin to the front door. Philip and Dónal were right behind them.

The women tossed their sewing aside and followed the men out of the house as fast as they could.

When Heber first saw them his heart sank. They rode bareback atop a huge white horse, no bridle or reins. Maureen rode sidesaddle as William held her across his lab, his arms wrapped around her.

Rhea walked slowly up to the four men standing in the road. Heber stepped forward to meet them. He looked to William, but before he could speak William said, "'Tis alright M'lord, she be alright, just weary from the journey."

Maureen pushed back the hood from her cloak. "Father," she said as she reached for him, sliding from Rhea's back right into Heber's arms. "M'lord, I be so glad to be back. I missed ya so much."

Heber kissed her on her forehead, "Ah girl, I've worried for ya lass. Thank God yer home." He tightened his arms around her causing her to grimace.

"What be wrong girl?" he asked as he released his embrace.

"Her wounds have not yet healed M'lord," William said. "But she would nay stay in Portree any longer. Ya know how it be when herself makes up her mind."

Heber chuckled, "Aye lad, that I do." It was then that he noticed her eyes.

"Yer eyes lass, what's happened to them?" he asked as he put his strong hands around her face.

"I do nay know how it happened, M'lord." She replied as she lowered her eyes.

Rhea then knelt down for William to dismount. Dónal and Maitiú met him with a handshake.

"Well met William, many thanks fer bringin' our girl home." Maitiú said.

Dónal gave Rhea a pat on the neck as she stood back up and whispered, "Good to see ya again, Great One."

It was then that Maureen spied Philip, standing back from the others. She went to him, reaching for him. He took her in his arms, "Oh God, Philip, I be so sorry. So sorry for being the cause of all of this. I beg ya to forgive me, I..."

"Sssshhh lass, there now. There be no need. 'Tis alright," he said as he held her. He released his embraced and looked in her eyes. "They have touched ya," he whispered to her.

She nodded to him and then laid her head back on his

shoulder, "Aye Philip, they have."

When they heard the footsteps of the women coming down the road, Philip turned Maureen to see Meg, Fionnula and Katie coming toward them.

Philip released her and, though it pained her to do so, Maureen lifted her skirts off the ground and began to run. "Katie!!" She cried.

"Katie, me Katie," Maureen whispered to her as the two women embraced. "I've prayed fer this fer so long." They held each other close, to take in the warmth and essence of each other.

"Why did ya go runnin' off ta Skye alone, girl?" Katie asked.

"Ya were in trouble Katie. I saw it, I had ta try." Maureen replied. "And Andrew? What of Andrew?"

Katie slowly shook her head.

"Oh, God, Katie, I be so sorry."

The first few drops of rain began to fall and the women began to walk back to the house.

"Collin," Heber called. "Get that horse out of the rain, see that she be fed and watered."

"Collin, wait," Maureen interrupted. "Rhea will nay be stayin', she must go back ta Skye." She walked over to the soft horse and petted her gently on her neck.

"Farewell Rhea, we be seein' ya soon. Take care of Olaf now won't ya?" Rhea bounced her head and then turned and trotted back down the road. Maureen went back to Katie and the two of them walked arm-in-arm back to the house.

When the men began to head back, William hurried up next to Heber. His heart was in his throat as he spoke to the big man.

"M'lord" he began. "M'lord, I...I wish to ask fer the hand of yer daughter, sir."

Heber stopped and turned toward William. Philip, Maitiú and Dónal all stopped as well. All eyes were on

Heber.

"Well, well," Heber began. "Ya wish ta wed that little green-eyed wildcat do ya?"

Heber paused for a moment, making William wait just a bit longer for his answer.

"I have no objection lad. I can nay think of a finer match fer me girl. Ya most certainly have me consent," he said.

Dónal came up to William and put his arm around his neck giving him a brotherly punch in the chest, "Well met boyo, well met!"

"Have ya asked her yet?" Heber asked.

"Aye sir, I have," William replied.

"And what of yer father, William? He does nay approve of the match, ya know this?" Heber cautioned.

"Aye sir, I know," William replied. "I do nay care. We'll only be stayin' in Dumbartonshire fer a short time. We must return to Skye, sir."

It was clear to Heber that William had much more to tell him. But now was not the time or the place.

"We'll speak to yer Da fer ya William," Maitiú said as he stepped forward. "Do nay worry son, we'll bring old Séan around."

"Well then," Heber continued. "We'll be doin' a bit of celebratin' this night, won't we lads?"

When Heber announced the match at their evening meal, everyone was filled with joy. The women immediately began to make plans, while the men drank more ale. But the celebration was short lived for Maureen. She was still weak and the journey had taken its toll.

William watched her as she occasionally reached to her shoulder and the pain would show on her face. She was standing next to Dónal near the fire when her weakness overtook her and she stumbled against him. He caught her before she fell and scooped her up in his arms.

"I think the party be over for this one," he said as he smiled at her. "Come on little Sis, yer goin' to bed girl."

Maitiú smiled when he heard Dónal's words. His son cared for Maureen as he did his own sisters. She had filled a place for Dónal he had missed for a long time.

Dónal headed up the stairs to the bed chambers. When he reached Maureen's chamber she said, "Put down me down now brother, I can stand on me own now."

William and Katie had followed them up the stairs. William took her in his arms saying, "get some sleep now girl, I be up later to kiss ya goodnight."

"I'll see to her now William," Katie said. She took Maureen by the arm and led her into her chamber, closing the door behind them.

William and Dónal went back down the stairs to meet with Heber.

"Tell me about the healin' Dónal," William asked. "Maureen does nay remember a thing about it. I need ta know what happened."

Dónal stopped and leaned up against the handrail. William stopped a few steps below him.

"The arrow she took was big enough to bring down a deer. It went clean through her. She was dyin', Will. When me Da yanked that arrow from her chest she be bleedin' bad. Shalynn gave the girl her own blood. I never seen anythin' like it. She cut open her hands and put them to Maureen's wounds. I can nay say how she did it, but it saved the girl fer certain, that I know."

William now understood what had happened. Now he knew what Morríghan had meant when she said it had turned her.

"And the one who shot her, Dónal, she called him the red-haired man."

"Aye, old Sorley Boy," Dónal replied.

Upon hearing the name William let his weight fall back against the handrail.

"Me Da's been carryin' the blame fer it. He be certain that arrow be meant fer him," Dónal said as he lowered his eyes, shaking his head.

"Ya do nay think it was?" William prompted.

Dónal looked up at William and folded his arms across his chest. "Old Sorley Boy hit her square in the back. I be thinkin' that arrow be meant fer her. She had a go with him at Dunvegan, cut him with her doe-hoof pretty good and took somethin' from him. That evil bastard finds out she be alive, he be comin fer her and me Da as well."

The concern on William's face was clear. He stood silent for a moment and then asked, "Where be this Sorley Boy now?"

"Can nay say," Dónal replied. "We left him standin' on the old bridge at Dunvegan."

Dónal took a step down and put his hand on William's shoulder. "Do nay worry over it, Will. He does nay know where she be."

William thanked him and they headed back down the steps to speak with Heber. They were almost to the bottom of the staircase when Dónal said, "Can I give ya a bit of advise me bother-ta-be? If that girl be mine, I'd take that blade away from her first chance I got."

William chuckled. "Aye, I think ya be right about that one, Dónal."

The meeting with Heber was short. It was decided they would leave as soon as possible for the Wycked Aye. Maitiú and Dónal would take Hope and Grace back with them. Katie and Maureen would travel in the big

286

carriage with Heber and Fionnula, and Philip and William would ride on two of Heber's finest Clydesdales.

As the meeting ended and everyone began to retire to their chambers, William held back a moment to speak with Heber.

The others had left the room and Heber looked to the young man with concern.

"What be wrong William?" he asked. "Somethin' be weighin' heavy on yer mind lad. I see it in ya."

"Aye sir, it be Maureen. She be different now, I believe ya already know that. She can nay stay in Dumbartsonshire or Badenoch. I must take her back ta Skye. Me Da, he be none to happy about her ta begin with, and when he hears we be goin' back ta Skye...."

Heber came to him and put a comforting hand on his shoulder, "Do nay worry over it William, ya love the girl, that be all that matters. Now go and rest yerself, we have a busy day on the morrow."

William turned to leave when Heber called back to him, "And William, well met lad. I thank ya fer bringin' her back."

When William reached the top of the stairs, Maitiú was waiting for him, leaning against the railing in front of Maureen's chamber. As William approached he stood up to meet him.

"William, do nay worry over yer Da," he began. "He'll come around. When we get back ta the shire, let me speak with Séan before ya see him. Yer Da and I, well...we go back a bit."

William looked at him with a curious glance, but was far too tired to question him. He gave Maitiú a nod and opened the chamber door.

On the morning of their departure, Fionnula and Maitiú met for a quiet walk before breakfast. The time they had been able to spend together had been rejuvenating for them both but now it was coming to an end. The last part of the journey was at hand. Maitiú had no idea what he would find when he returned to the shire. He had left his brewery in the hands of Hamish, but that was almost two months ago.

They ended their walk on the house courtyard.

"What happens now, Maitiú? What will ya do?" Fionnula asked. "If Argyll has taken yer brewery, how will ya live?"

"Dónal be talkin' about goin' to the Knights of St. John to fight the Turks. Mayhaps I be joinin' him as a brewer," he jested. "All armies need a brewer and I hear the Caliph drinks like a fish."

Fionnula gave him a loving smile and then a momentary silence fell between them. It was peaceful out on the courtyard of the manor house. A light blanket of snow covered the ground and only a few little birds chirped as they flitted through the trees looking for their morning meal.

"Mayhaps it be time fer ya to go home to Ireland," Fionnula said. "Ireland needs people like you and Dónal. One day, we be a nation again...one day. Ireland needs ya cousin."

Maitiú looked at his sweet cousin. She always had a way of knowing what was truly in his heart.

"Ya know Fionnula, the old woman in Portree told me I would find what I needed in Dumbartonshire. So I think I be goin' there first ta see our girl happily wed to young Macaulay, and then home ta Ireland it be. Now if I may ask ya cousin, if ya could leave me ta me thoughts, I would be most grateful."

Fionnula kissed him on the cheek and then took her leave. As long as she had known Maitiú, it had been his custom to spend quiet time alone in the morning with his thoughts and his prayers. Fionnula smiled to herself as she walked away, for although he was indeed a devout Catholic, Maitiú was more like the people of the forest than he knew. For he was Irish, and the magic of Ireland ran through his veins just as the magic of Skye ran through Maureen's.

Chapter Twenty-Eight

Coming Home

The journey from Badenoch to the Wycked Aye was leisurely and without incident. Maureen was beginning to regain herself while everyone else, especially Maitiú and Dónal, took this time to turn over in their minds all that had happened.

As Maureen was still weak, William tended to her every need, while Maitiú and Dónal tended to William.

Once outside of Stirling, Heber pulled William aside. "We need to be talkin' to yer father immediately upon our arrival," he said.

"Aye M'lord, but let Maitiú talk to Da first." William replied.

"Maitiú?" Heber questioned.

"Aye, he spoke to me about this before we left Badenoch, 'twas his suggestion. It appears he knows me Da from time past. He just asked to give him some time," William explained.

Heber gave William a quizzical look, "Did he say how he knew yer Da?"

William shrugged, "Nay M'lord, he did not. Must have somethin' ta do with horses or beer wagons. He just asked to give him some time."

As they entered the shire, Maitiú and Dónal took their leave of the group. "We have a meetin' with an old friend and then with our priest." Maitiú said.

"And in that order to be sure," Dónal added.

"We be seein' ya all at the tavern," Maitiú said. He gave a nod to his son and they kicked the ponies into a trot, heading toward the courier's office.

The rest turned up the road toward the tavern stables. The men unhitched the carriage and William stayed behind to unsaddle the horses and get them into their stalls for the evening.

When the Badenoch travelers approached the tavern, it was agreed to have Maureen enter quietly and surprise the staff. With her hood up and her cloak pulled tightly around her, she slipped through the door unnoticed. She looked around trying to see where everyone was. She saw the bar, the Chieftain's table, and the back pantry door to the kitchen. She saw the patron's tables, about half-full as it was just about mid-day.

Seeing a new patron, Fiona hustled over to ask the lone, cloaked woman if she could be of service. The woman seemed cold and alone, and Fiona, being the kind, sweet thing that she was, led the hooded woman to a place near the fire. It was then that Maureen pulled back her hood and looked straight into Fiona's eyes.

Fiona's mouth dropped open and, after a momentary pause, she let out a scream of joy that turned every head in the tavern.

Once enwrapped in Fiona's arms, more shouts of joy were heard as Detta and Maggie, and Isabella and Sara came to realize Maureen was home. She was nearly crushed with love. Her wounds did not hurt, not one bit.

When the rest of the company heard the ruckus they came inside one-by-one. When Fionnula entered another chorus of hoots and hollers went up and she too was swarmed by the family of the Wycked Aye, as were Katie and Philip.

The men of the shire offered Philip congratulations for a successful quest to Skye and for bringing Katie home safe. Heber must have shaken every hand in the tavern.

Maureen was looking on when Master Thomas came up beside her and softly kissed her hand. "My Lady, welcome home," he said.

"Oh, Thomas," she whispered, and jumped straight into his warm embrace.

"I missed ya me little green-eyed wildcat," Thomas jested. He set her down and looked at her. "Well," he said when he noticed her eyes. He took her chin between his thumb and forefinger and shifted her face from side-to-side.

"Ya've changed lass, I see it in ya," he said.

"Aye Thomas, I have, but only a little." She teased.

Maureen could not have hoped for a finer homecoming, but little did she know that the greatest surprise was yet to come. Thomas took her by the hand and led her up to the bar. He walked around the back and brought out two small glasses and the good whisky. The one thing she and Thomas had always shared was a glass of good whisky. He poured them both a wee dram. They tapped their cups and tossed back the whisky. Now, she was home.

But before Maureen could say a word, an apron landed on the bar next to her and she heard a voice say, "And just what do ya think ya be doin' lass, we have a tavern ta run ya know."

Maureen knew that voice, without turning around she shouted, "Morna, Morna!"

Morna MacGregor had returned to the Wycked Aye as well. "Dear God, Morna, what ya be doin' here?" Maureen asked. "I thought ya be at court and..."

Morna put her hands on Maureen shoulders. "Now girl," she said. "We both know that you and I belong at the Wycked Aye."

Sara pulled Master Thomas aside, "Get the musicians, Thomas. We be havin' a wee ce'ili this night to celebrate the return of our friends."

When William came into the tavern, the first person he saw was Braden, sitting with his wife Akira. He had a walking stick leaning against the table.

"Braden, me man," William said. "'Tis good ta see ya well, sir. How be yer leg, man?"

"It be comin' along William. Father Brain and I seem ta have the same limp," Braden jested.

Connor walked up to the table with three tankards of ale. He offered William his hand saying, "A successful quest William, well met lad. I be proud of ya."

"Thank ya Connor, have ya seen me girl?" William asked.

Connor pointed to the bar, William bowed out and went straight to Maureen. He took her face in his hands and gave her a long, deep kiss.

"Well, now that be more like it!" Thomas exclaimed. He reached across the bar and offered his hand to William. "Well met lad, well met indeed."

"I need ta see me Da, lass," he whispered to Maureen. "Where be Heber?"

She turned and pointed to the Chieftain's table. "Do nay worry, William," she said comfortingly. "'Twill be alright."

William came over to Heber just as he was sitting down with Fionnula and Sara.

"M'lord, We need ta go speak with me father."

"Do ya know if our Irish peacemakers have had a chance to speak with him yet?" Heber asked.

"I do nay know, sir, but I can wait no longer. I must go ta him now."

Heber could see the urgency in his future son-in-law and did not wish to make him wait any longer.

"I beg yer leave me ladies, but young Mr. Macaulay and I have a meeting to attend, and I fear it may be a difficult one." Heber gave Fionnula a kiss and bowed his head to Sarah.

293

As they were heading for the door, Hamish and two stout lads from the brewery came in with three kegs of Munster red ale. He went to Sara saying, "The boss has been by and said ya would be needin' these," nodding toward the kegs.

Heber and William now knew that Maitiú and Dónal had at least been by the brewery.

"Lad, have ya seen yer boss then?" Heber asked.

"Aye sir indeed, and now he be off ta Macaulay's to call on the old man," Hamish blurted out. Seeing William, he backtracked, "Oh, pray pardon lad. He be off to see yer Da. That be near half hour ago, in case ya be askin'."

When Maitiú and Dónal got to the courier's office they found old Séan in the stables with William's brother, Patrick.

"Good day to ya Séan Macaulay," Maitiú called out as he and Dónal approached.

"Good day ta ya Irish," Séan replied. "What brings ya ta me stable, de Faoite. Been a long time, eh?"

Maitiú shook hands with Séan but did not release his grip.

"Oh, a wee errand fer someone very dear ta us. Ya know Séan, I nay be the kind of a man to call in a favor too very often. But, ya remember those days in Cork City don't ya now, Séan?" Maitiú began.

Séan nodded his head slowly, still holding on to the Irishman's hand. Suddenly, he felt uneasy and was unsure where this conversation was going.

"Well, I be here ta tell that yer boy be home from Skye and he has our girl with him."

Séan's eyes lit up when he heard William was home, and Maitiú could tell by the pull on his hand that Séan

294

wanted to break away and go to his son. But Maitiú would not release his grip.

Patrick, seeing what was happening, stopped working and stood up from the horse he was shoeing to listen.

"Hold on now old friend," Maitiú cautioned. "Before ya go runnin' off, me boy and I need just a wee bit of yer time. All I be askin' of ya Séan be that ya hear me out about our girl, Maureen."

Séan nodded in agreement and the four men went into the courier's office to talk.

Heber and William left the tavern and were headed down the lane toward the livery when they saw Séan and Patrick walking briskly toward them.

"Da!" William called out.

Sean looked up and, upon seeing his son, both he and Patrick broke into a full run. Séan greeted William with a tackle that was really a warm, fatherly embrace. Patrick wrapped his arms around his brother as well.

"Oh, son, me boy, ya be so dear ta me. It be so good ta see ya home and safe. I be so very proud of ya, William!" Séan exclaimed. He then turned to recognize Heber.

"Me humble thanks to ya MacPherson fer seein' be boy home," he said as he shook Heber's hand.

"Da," William interrupted. "Da, I need ta speak with ya...about Maureen. It be important Da."

Sean waived William off, "There be no need of that now, boy. Let's go the pub fer a pint of the Irish and ya can tell me there."

William was frustrated. He had prepared himself for a conversation much different than this. He wanted it settled and settled now. He had no intention of waiting for he and Maureen to be wed and he needed to know where his father stood.

"But Da, I said it be about Maureen," William pressed.

"I know, I know, I heard ya boy. She be a fine lass indeed and she'll make me a fine daughter fer certain."

William could not believe what he was hearing. He stood staring blankly at his father. He was at a complete loss for words.

Heber raised his eyebrows in surprise. The last time he and Séan had spoken, the old man was dead set against the match. Séan had called the girl a worthless wench and a broken woman.

"I must say Séan, based on our last meetin' I be just a bit gobsmacked," Heber began, "Why all of a sudden such a change of heart? What changed yer mind about the girl?"

All Sean said was, "Maitiú de Faoite."

Patrick put his arm around William's neck and whispered, "Do nay worry brother, the Irishman worked it out fer ya."

"And where might our bogtrotter be now?" Heber asked.

"Off ta see his Priest," Patrick replied. "He said he and his boy would be along but," he paused, "it might be a while."

With that, Séan put his arms around his two sons and they walked toward the tavern. As Heber walked along behind them, he thought to himself, *What the hell has that Irishman done now?*

It was just a short distance from Macaulay's office to the shire Chapel. Maitiú and Dónal leisurely walked Hope and Grace down the dirt road. Both men were looking forward to being back in the old Chapel once more and giving their confessions before Mass on the Sabbath.

"Ya remember what Philip said Da? We can nay speak of them, even in confession," Dónal warned. Though he had never held anything back from his priests in confession before, Dónal knew Philip was right – some things must remain a mystery. Shalynn and her people must remain a myth.

Maitiú looked curiously at his son, "Me confession be me own son, ya must do as yer own heart tells ya."

But Maitiú's concern was not for the Fey. It was for a part of his past that had put his son and himself in danger, and nearly killed an innocent young woman. Sorley Boy.

He had carried this anger and anxiety toward Sorley Boy MacDonald for too long. For years it had slowly eaten away at him, but no more.

As he and Dónal walked their horses to chapel it was clear in his mind and in his heart that forgiveness was the only way to rid himself of this burden.

The actions and contempt Sorley Boy had taken against Maitiú had been cruel and unwarranted. And although he could not meet Sorley Boy face-to-face, he would ask Father Bryan to help him forgive the warrior of the Glens of Antrim once and for all.

Dónal sensed his father's anxiousness, "'Twas nay yer fault, Da," Dónal said. "What happened on Skye 'twas nay yer fault."

Maitiú and Dónal had much to say to Father Bryan. They gave their confessions consecutively and it nearly took up Father Bryan's entire afternoon.

Afterwards both Dónal and Maitiú felt as light as clouds, released from their burdens. In that spirit, they asked Father Bryan if he would accompany them to the Wycked Aye for dinner and a pint...or more.

As they entered the tavern the ce'ili was in full swing. Before they could reach the bar, Maggie came by with a pint of the Munster Red for each of them.

When everyone was gathered, Heber banged his tankard on the Chieftain's table and then stood up on the bench to speak. William stood behind Maureen and wrapped his arms around her.

"Pray heed good gentles one and all," he began. "I be honored this night ta announce that a match has been made between House MacPherson and House Macaulay."

Maureen gasped as she looked up at William. "He agreed?" she asked. William just smiled at her.

"But how?" she pressed. William pointed across the room to Maitiú and Dónal. When Maureen met their eyes, they both just smiled and raised their tankards.

"Well, I'll be damned," she whispered. "God, I bloody love those Irishmen."

The sun had long set and the celebration continued. Dónal stepped out the back of the tavern to take some air and clear his head a bit from the many tankards of ale. As he sat resting on the fence rail he spied a flash of light in the trees just down the road. He watched, and within a few moments he saw a figure walking toward him. He knew the size and stride of this person very well. Excitement and anticipation filled him, clearing his head immediately.

"Lady Shalynn, it be good ta see ya again," he said as they met in the dim light surrounding the tavern.

"Greetings Dónal, it is good to see you as well," she replied. She was dressed in her jerkin, breeches and boots; and wrapped in a deep green cloak. Her face showed no signs of the markings of her people.

He ran his fingers down the side of her face, "Ya look a bit different from the last time I saw ya," he said.

She just smiled and said, "I have come to see the MacPherson, Dónal. Will you bring him to me?"

"Aye, I will. Would ya like me Da and me to come along? Be this about Maureen?" he asked.

She was touched with his concern for her youngling, but she needed to see the MacPherson and his woman alone. Diancecht and the sentries were waiting at Maureen's cottage to speak with them.

"No Dónal, not this time. Just MacPherson and his ginger woman. Send them to Maureen's cottage. We will meet them there."

As she turned to leave, Dónal reached for her hand. "Wait...will I see ya again?"

"Maureen and young Macaulay are to be joined, yes?" she asked.

"Aye, they are indeed."

"Then," she said taking his other hand, "you will see me again."

Dónal went first to his father and then to Heber's table.

"Pray pardon mo Chaptaen," Dónal said. He bent down and whispered into Heber's ear, "The Fey have come. They wait at Maureen's cottage fer you and Lady MacPherson."

Heber quickly gathered Fionnula and left the tavern. As they approached Maureen's cottage, they could see smoke from her chimney. The door was open and the candles were lit.

Shalynn met them at the door, "Welcome, My Lord MacPherson. Please, come in. We have much to talk about."

Heber and Fionnula cautiously entered the cottage and Shalynn shut the door behind them.

Chapter Twenty-Nine

A Joining of Houses

It was three days until the Sabbath and Father Bryan agreed to join William and Maureen following Mass. To William's disappointment, Katie insisted that Maureen stay with her and Philip so that Katie could care for her.

When Mass was ended, the men led William away, while Katie, Maureen and Isabella remained in a small room at the chapel.

Maureen felt badly that she did not have a fine dress to wear for her wedding, but there had not been time to prepare a proper one. Her Sabbath skirts and bodice would have to do. They were getting Maureen ready when there was a knock at the door.

Maureen opened it to see Shalynn standing before her. She was dressed in a beautiful deep green dress that seemed to float around her and she was holding two boxes in her hands. Maureen stood staring, speechless.

"May I come in? I bring a gift," she said.

Maureen turned to Katie and Isabella, "M'ladies, could ya leave us for just a bit?"

When they were alone, Shalynn opened the box and pulled out a gown, much like the one Maureen had seen Airmid wearing in the great hollow. Soft, white, flowing fabric woven with silver threads. When Maureen put it on the full bell sleeves trimmed in silver lace dropped from her wrists to the floor. A belt of finely woven silver wrapped tightly around her waist. There was no corset or rigid bodice, only a chemise. The gown was simple and beautiful; it was the gown of a Fey woman.

Shalynn opened the second smaller box which held a silver headband with an emerald that dropped from the center, just like Shalynn's, and a matching veil. She braided Maureen's hair and wove it around the headband with green and silver ribbons. Then placed the veil in her hair.

When Maureen was dressed, she looked down at her gown and said, "It be beautiful. Thank you...Mother."

A knock came to the door, it was Katie.

"He be waitin' fer ya lass," she said. "Ya look like an angel."

Heber was waiting to walk her to William. Dónal offered a hand to Shalynn, which she graciously accepted. When they entered the chapel and William saw her, his jaw dropped and his knees weakened.

"Easy boyo," Patrick said as he braced up his brother.

Katie stood by Maureen, and Patrick stood by William. As Maitiú listened to William and Maureen pledge themselves to each other, his thoughts went to his wife, Séaron. At that moment, his mind was made up, he just wanted to go home.

All would be gathered at the Wycked Aye for the celebration, but only a few of William and Maureen's loved ones were present in the chapel. For although they cared very much for William and Maureen, to be seen in a Catholic Church could cause questions to be asked of them, and place them in danger. But the tavern was a place where all were welcome. It had always been that way and always would be.

The new couple arrived to cheers of congratulations. Thomas and Isabelle had laid a feast upon the tables fit for nobility. Maitiú had sent over another barrel of Irish red and a full barrel of Desmond ale from the brewery. It would be a fine celebration indeed.

As Maitiú entered the tavern his heart was heavy. Fionnula came to him with a tankard of ale.

"I have a bit of surprise for ya cousin," she teased. She put her arm around his waist and pointed to the other side of the room. There, to his surprise, was his other dear cousin Gwen and Lord Cullen Elliot. Gwen gave him an excited wave and gestured for him to come over.

Maitiú tapped Dónal on the shoulder and together they worked their way across the room. Gwen and Cullen were standing side-by-side, and Lady Gwen had a smile on her face that Maitiú recognized from his childhood. Something was afoot.

When he and Dónal were within a few feet from them, the two of them stepped aside and there standing between them, was Séaron.

Maitiú's breath left him and he nearly went to the ground. He could not believe what he was seeing. He began to move slowly toward her, when Gwen and Cullen stepped even farther apart, and standing next to Séaron were his two daughters, Maire and Bridget.

Dónal went immediate to his mother holding her tightly. Then put his arms around his sisters and pulled them to him.

Within an instant Maitiú realized what Morríghan's words had meant; this was the bond that had been broken. He took Séaron in his arms and kissed her, then extended his arms to his daughters.

He turned to Gwen, "How Gwen? How did ya know?"

"We heard the news of Dunvegan," she said as she embraced him. "Fionnula sent word ya were comin' back and to send fer Séaron and the girls."

He looked back across the room to Fionnula who just smiled and blew him a kiss.

The sun had set and the celebration was still going strong. William stood across the room, his foot up on a chair, watching Maureen as she moved across the floor. He wanted to take her away. He wanted her alone, all to himself.

Master Thomas saw him from across the room. He went to the bar and pulled a bottle of the good whisky. He walked up to William, took a swig off the bottle and handed it over.

"Yer eyes look like the eyes of a wolf, boyo," Thomas said. "She be yers now. If ya want her, why do ya nay just take her?"

William looked at him, took a hit off the bottle and handed it back.

Thomas put hand around the back of Williams neck and said, "What ya waitin' fer man, go get yer woman."

They both took another swig of whisky and then William walked out on the floor, scooped Maureen up in his arms and left the tavern.

Candles burned along the cottage path. The front shutters were open and they could see that a fire had already been laid and was burning bright. The door opened to a room set with candles and flowers everywhere. The table was laden with mead, ale, oat cakes and dried fruit, and on her bed was a beautiful new quilt.

Now William understood why Master Thomas prompted him to bring her home.

While she stood, taking in the kindness and warmth that surrounded her, William moved to close the front shutters. He looked out to see Master Thomas and Isabella standing on the path with their cups raised to him. He gave them a grateful nod and closed the shutters.

William turned back to Maureen as she said, "Look at what they've done William. Would ya like...."

"Leave it lass," He said as he took her hand and pulled her to him. He wanted no more food, no more ale. He knew what he wanted and would not wait for it any longer.

He took her face in his hands and placed a long, soft kiss upon her lips. She stepped back and unlaced her dress letting it drop to the floor, presenting herself to him in just her chemise.

William pulled his shirt over his head, removed his belt and let his kilt fall. He moved slowly watching every move on her face. She was no longer afraid.

Pulling the ribbon on her chemise, he slipped it off her shoulders letting if fall to the ground.

He ran his fingertips across the bones of her neck and across her chest, gently following the curve of her breasts.

She stepped free of the chemise, and pressed herself up against him. She placed her lips to his chest and kissed him, causing him to pull a quick breath through clenched teeth.

He ran his hand down her back to her thigh, raising her leg and wrapping it around him. He pulled her up into his lap and eased them on to the bed.

Grabbing her hips, he slid her forward. Her body was anxious and ready for him. She reached down caressing him, gently guiding him to her. There was no hesitation, no fear. She gave herself to him completely.

Her strong legs gripped tightly to his hips as they moved together in perfect rhythm. With his hands on her waist, he guided her as she rose the full length of him again and again.

As he felt her body tighten around him, he pulled her to him, rolled her on to her back and buried himself deep inside her as her body trembled beneath him.

He slipped his arm beneath her and she wrapped her legs around him as he lifted her up to meet him. He felt her fingers dig into his back and her breath leave her as he moved faster and faster, bringing himself to his peak and leaving her with all he had to offer.

He took her twice more during the night. With pleasured hands he held her close as they lay together in the wee hours of the morning. She was now his to guard and care for. He understood the calling placed before her, and he would protect her always.

Atop the hill behind the tavern, Diancecht and Shalynn watched as the light began to fade in Maureen's cottage.

"They have joined." Diancecht said.

"Yes, Grandfather, they have."

"You have done well Shalynn, everything is now as it should be."

Shalynn gave him a slight bow of her head and then turned her attention back to the cottage. She worried for her youngling. The blooding had indeed changed her, but she did not know to what extent and neither did Diancecht. He would be watching her carefully.

"And her mate, he understands his place?" he asked coldly.

"Yes My Lord he does, and he is willing." Shalynn replied.

"Good, now all we have to do is wait."

Shalynn turned to him a bit confused, "Wait, My Lord? For what?"

"For their first born," he said as he turned and walked away.

Shalynn watched as he walked back down the hill to the trees and then vanished. An uneasiness filled her as she turned back to the cottage. It had never crossed her mind until that moment.

"By the Gods," she said out loud. "Their bloodlines."

Epilogue

Kathryn Maire Macaulay was born on the Isle of Skye just before the Fall Equinox following William and Maureen's joining.

It had been nearly three years since they returned to Skye. Maureen had learned much from Morríghan in the few years they had been together. She was coming to understand her gift and had been called many times to the service of the Fey Counsel, and the MacLeod of MacLeod.

Shalynn spent a great deal of time at the Watcher's house, to be with her granddaughter and to share her knowledge of healing and medicinals with Maureen.

William had taken up the guardianship of the Watchers and the care of the soft horses, but had not yet taken the oath of the Keeper. He spent much of his time learning from Eochaid, the horseman, and one of the Fey elders.

He and his Gran had grown very close. He had not realized how much he had missed her. All in all, their lives were peaceful and happy.

It was nearing late-afternoon when William came through the door with little Katie on his shoulders.

Maureen and Morríghan were preparing their meal at the pantry counter while a rabbit roasted on a spit in the hearth.

William sat little Katie down on the counter. He kissed his wife and Gran, and then filled a basin with water to wash up before dinner. He had taken little Katie riding and they both smelled of horses.

He placed the basin on the counter next to Katie while he rolled up his shirtsleeves. They were not watching when little Katie plunged her hands into the basin. When they heard her giggling to herself they all turned to look.

"Look, Mum, look!" she said laughing.

She was up to her elbows in the basin, laughing as the water whirled around and around her little hands.

They all just stopped and stared. Morríghan stepped in between William and Maureen. When she turned to them, her face was filled with apprehension and fear.

"They must never know; they can never know." She said as she grasped both William and Maureen's arms. "Do ya understand me? They must never know."

The Characters

The MacLeods:
Maureen MacLeod
Katie MacLeod
Maire MacCrimmon MacLeod
Robert MacLeod
Andrew James MacLeod

The Irish:
Maitiú MacRobaird de Faoite
Dónal MacMaitiú de Faoite
Maire MacMaitiú de Faoite
Bridget MacMaitiú de Faoite
Séaron de Faoite

The MacPhersons:
Heber MacPherson
Fionnula de Faoite MacPherson
Meg MacPherson

The Macaulays:
Séan Macaulay
William Macaulay
Patrick Macaulay
Morríghan MacLeod Macaulay

The MacBrides:
Chieftain Sara MacBride

The Elliots:
Lord Cullen Elliot
Lady Gwendolyn de Faoite Elliot
Akira Elliot
Braden Elliot

The Ellis's:
Conner Ellis
Elena MacPherson Ellis

The Campbells:
Thomas Campbell
Isabella MacDonald Campbell
Archibald Campbell – 4th Earl of Argyle

Gallowglass:
Bain and Cavan Moffett

The Aes Sidhe:
Shalynn
Airmid
Diancecht
Fiann and Séamus – The Sentries

The Girls of the Tavern:
Fiona
Maggie
Detta

www.ingramcontent.com/pod-product-compliance
Lightning Source LLC
Chambersburg PA
CBHW061515020726
47502CB00006B/2088